DEVILS GLEN

A BETTENDORF TALE BOOK 1

MATTHEW SPEAK

Shadow Woods Publishing

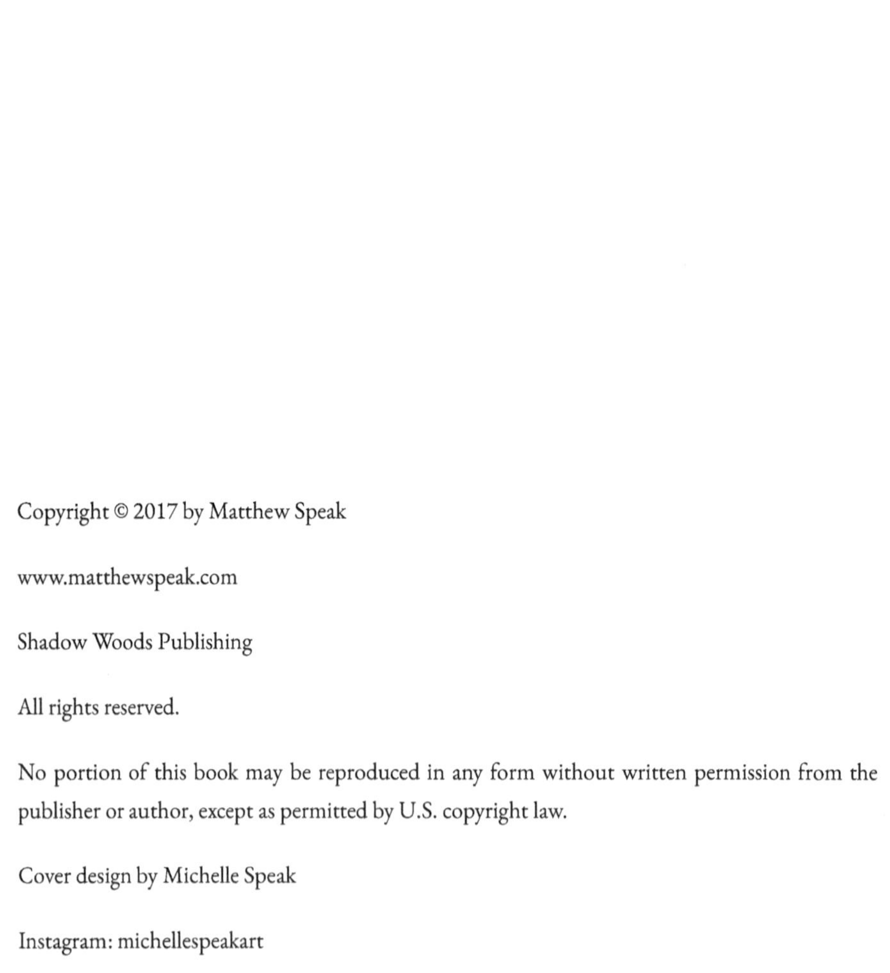

Contents

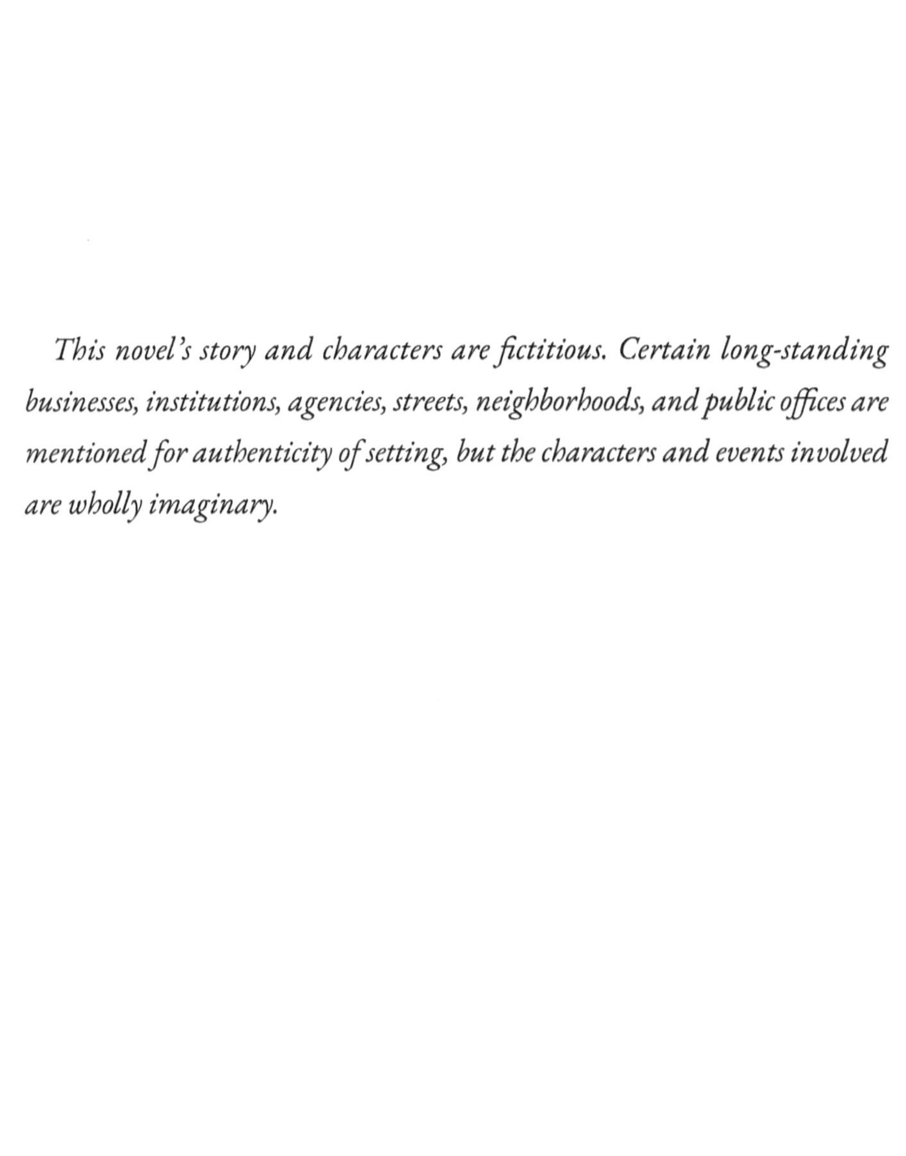

This novel's story and characters are fictitious. Certain long-standing businesses, institutions, agencies, streets, neighborhoods, and public offices are mentioned for authenticity of setting, but the characters and events involved are wholly imaginary.

For Ann Margaret Speak

Prologue: Autumn Branches

1.

Three knocks at the church door.

Brother Willy Clay hesitated, squeezing his eyes shut in prayer, his hand resting on the door handle. He'd hoped this preacher would be a no-show. *Don't let him in!*

He pushed the dark thoughts from his mind. The little church had so few prospects, Willy knew he didn't have a choice. *He'll be fine. I'm sure of it. You're too old, Willy. Too old and too worried.* Even his own mind couldn't decide. With a sigh, he opened the door, offering as wide a smile as he could fake.

A tall man sauntered into the chapel of the Valley Baptist Church. It was an odd hour for a tour, and Willy didn't like it one bit.

There was something familiar about the visitor, something that seemed at once comforting yet unsettling, both country-affable and city slick. He wore a cheap suit and too much grease in his combed-over hair. Above his lip was a sliver of a mustache. The oddest part was the black leather glove he wore on his right hand. The man's left hand was bare.

Willy disguised his suspicion and played the part of an old country preacher. "Now, Brother—uh, what was the name again?" Willy asked.

"Jones, sir. Brother Billy Jones," the stranger said.

"Ah yes, Brother Jones. You must excuse me, sir. My mind doesn't hold information with quite the strength it did merely a few years ago. But you'd expect as much when a man comes to the ripe old age of fourscore and thirteen."

"You do not say! I refuse to believe it. I can hardly believe you are a year older than sixty!"

The man seemed sincere in his delivery, but through it Willy sensed something else—a snake oil salesman behind a curtain, feeding lines to the showman like a Southern Cyrano.

"I thank you kindly. However, I am indeed ninety-three. My painful joints and hoarse voice confirm it. Where did you say you're from?" Willy asked.

"I don't think I did, sir. I am from Missouri. Liberty, Missouri."

"Is that right? Liberty, Missouri! I have a cousin down that way. Isn't it a small world?"

"It sure is," Jones said.

"I only ask because your accent sounded more Kentucky. That's where I spent part of my youth, ya see?"

"No, sir, I am from Missouri, though my Aunt Ophelia lived down in Tennessee. I spent a good many summers down there as a youth."

"Ah, you don't say? What part?"

"Sir?" Jones asked.

"Where in Tennessee did your aunt live?"

"Oh. It was out in the country—just a hint of a town, really. But I think I recall a place called Paris not far away. Paris, Tennessee."

"Paris, you say? Why, that's off Lake Kentucky! My daddy and I used to frequent a little camp down that way. Went fishing a few times if I remember. You ever fish?"

"Why yes, sir, here and there. My old man wasn't much interested in fishing—or spending time with his family to be honest. But I caught some sunfish on my own."

This account only partially satisfied Willy. There was a deeper story to the man; one he didn't care to learn. He resolved to finish the tour and send Jones on his way. He refused to leave his life's work in the care of some glad-handing hustler from who knows where.

"As you can see, this old place ain't much, just a tiny little chapel in sticks. Back in the day, we used to fill her up, but even full it only fits a hundred and fifty—and that's with extra chairs carried up from the basement. We still have our regulars, but most Sundays we're lucky to bring in fifty."

"Oh, that is fine by me! I happen to be looking to take a little church and help it grow into something extraordinary. I suppose you might say it is my calling. How much you think, sir?"

Jones stepped to the front of the church and stared at the pulpit. Brother Willy guessed he was envisioning himself at that podium, presenting a thundering sermon.

"How much?" Willy asked. "Why, that's up to the deacons and the church board. Though I don't imagine it'll pay too much—a congregation this size doesn't provide much in tithings."

"Is there a parsonage attached?" Brother Jones asked.

"Yes, sir. Around back is the house, along with a pair of ancient buses to pick up children for Sunday school. One bus, the purple one, might need a little TLC, as they say. We have had little reason for two buses in some time, but the one painted red, white, and blue runs just fine if you know how to work her."

"Ah, that's no trouble at all. I've got me a fellow as handy with a box of tools as anyone you've ever met. Old Carl will get that bus running lickity-split. Brother Clay, you sure have a fine little chapel here. I'll take it!" Brother Jones exclaimed as he sauntered behind the pulpit, slapping his gloved hand upon it like an auctioneer.

Willy stared at him, mouth agape. "Well, it's not as straightforward as that. I mentioned the board would have to give you an interview. You'd need to deliver a sermon or two—like an audition, I suppose. I'm sure they have one or two others who are interested, so they must give them a go too. Why don't I give you my number and we can set something up once I talk to the deacons?"

"No, sir, you got it all wrong. I'm not looking for a job; I'm offering to purchase." Brother Jones stood there behind the podium with a wide grin that looked too much like Jack Nicholson's Joker in Batman, a film Brother Willy had seen just recently and didn't much care for.

You should never have let him in!

Willy cleared his throat. "Purchase, sir?"

"Yes, sir, that's right. I wish to buy this here old church. How much you want for it? Name your price."

"Oh well, I don't think the board is looking to sell, Brother Jones. They're just looking for a new preacher is all. I'm sorry if someone gave you the wrong idea."

Brother Jones leaned over the pulpit, and it seemed to Willy as if the lights had dimmed 10 percent. He looked up at the lights and then back at Jones. Jones's twinkle-eyed smile had turned into a twisted smirk, and Willy got the feeling he had made a mistake in opening his door to the man.

Jones straightened his sports coat. "Now, Brother Clay, I ain't used to calling any man a liar, least of all one I don't rightly know. But I find your words downright hard to believe. You are standing there, in the house of the Lord, telling me that the board of this here shitty little church will deny a name-thy-price offer from a bona fide man of faith? You will surely excuse me if I question your candor on that point."

"Brother Jones!" Willy exclaimed, stunned by the language. "Need I remind you—you are standing in a house of God? Watch your tongue, sir!"

"Oh, forgive me, sir. I occasionally let my language slip into a less flowery speech when I am disappointed. Thankfully, the good lord has seen that disappointment is a sentiment I seldom experience." He took a step around the pulpit toward the edge of the stage. "I already spoke to a few of your deacons earlier today, and they all seemed just overjoyed to be finally rid of this old place. I dare say I could have knocked them over with a feather, as they say. It seems none of your deacons relish trying to rebuild what you've let slip away."

Brother Willy gasped. "What I let—now, you look here, sir!"

"No! You look here, old fool. Take the cash and drift off into a peaceful retirement with what limited time you have left on this earth. It's the wise thing, I assure you. I would have wrapped this up with your board and sent you packing myself, but evidently there's one slight impediment in this situation. It seems you are the majority owner of this establishment—a fact you did not mention, sir. So I need you to tell me your price. This is your sole chance to do so. I suggest you accept it. My terms—well, they won't satisfy you at all."

The man strode to the main floor and stopped between two large altars on either side of the pulpit. All at once, a vision appeared to Willy of shadowy wings spreading out behind Brother Jones and long vines growing up the walls and reaching across the sanctuary like a black rot devouring the interior of the sanctuary. The old preacher had always professed to seeing visions, though it had been many years since he had had one as striking as this. The air had become warm and moist, and great beads of sweat prickled Willy's forehead. He took out his handkerchief and dabbed it dry as he backed away from Brother Jones.

"Foul creature!" Willy said. "I say you are as wicked as the Beast himself."

Too late...

Jones took an aggressive step toward him. "You see much, old as you are, so you must accept you have no choice in this matter."

"Vile thing! Get behind me! I say, get thee behind me! I will never agree to your wishes. Though the heavens may fall, I will stay true."

"If I am, as you say, in league with the Beast, do you not fear me?"

"I have met the Beast and his minions before. You are not the first to gain entry, nor will you be the last, I am sure. I sent them away many long years ago, and I will send them away again, standing as tall through the strength of my Lord. Tonight will be no different. Though my strength fades, I will die true to my word."

For a moment, Jones stared at the withered preacher as a lion might look upon a mouse standing on its hind feet in defiance. His smirk faded.

"Old man, you give me no choice but to relieve you of your obligations. Sad. I so wanted to let you see just what I did with your precious church."

Jones lifted his hand and advanced upon the tired preacher, removing his leather glove one finger at a time.

2.

Jack Davies lay in bed, covers pulled to his chin. The closet door was once again creaking open and closed with the rhythm of the old house's many drafts. Through that crack, he could just barely see a pale arm and one milky eye staring out at him.

This was Jack's life. *Night visitors. The dead kind.*

When he was eleven, Jack made the mistake of telling his parents about the visitors, but all it got him were uncomfortable meetings with a frumpy school psychologist and Sunday "rap sessions" with his church youth pastor. Neither of which helped his situation, though they seemed to make his parents feel better.

But lately, they'd gotten worse. *Anne! Where are you?*

Most nights his sister sat at the foot of his bed, reassuring him as he pretended not to acknowledge the skeletal face glaring at him through his bedroom window or the little girl floating near the ceiling in the corner of his room. Tonight was like any other night, except Anne was not responding.

Night visitors. The dead kind.

Jack shuddered. "Anne," he whispered at the bedroom door, but still no response. A huge part of him wanted to run downstairs to his mom and dad, but that would lead to more trouble than it was worth.

Ride it out. They're only ghosts.

Then, just as his closet door opened a full six inches, and a decaying arm reached out to him, a soft melody floated into the bedroom from another part of the house. The sound washed over him like a warm bath.

Anne!

As his eyelids grew heavy, Anne glided into the room singing a soft lullaby with words of another language, a foreign tongue Jack never understood.

His sister stopped before him with a doting smile, turned, and lifted a hand to the closet. She whispered something Jack couldn't quite hear. The closet door sealed shut, the latch clicking as it fell home. And as the last flickers of consciousness melted and Jack's eyelids finally closed for the night, his sister lightly kissed his forehead.

3.

Officer Mark Warren ducked under the rafters of the old attic in the home of Mrs. Magherius, an elderly Armenian widow who seemed to have a new intruder break into her home every other week. She'd had a stroke eight months earlier and suffered from recurrent bouts of dementia ever since. Her family looked in on her daily, but even they couldn't convince her to stop calling the police so often, reporting sightings of strange men in her cellar, a little girl in the pantry—or a woman in a sweet old lady's attic.

"She was up there, Officer! Right past the dress form!" the old woman shouted up to him from the bottom of the steps.

"OK, Mrs. Magherius. You stay down there, and I'll handle it."

A migraine had been creeping into his vision all night. He'd left his medication down in the cruiser, so there would be no relief until he cleared the attic. Mark rubbed his right temple with his thumb and squinted to get a better look around. The dress form stood in the back corner, surrounded by various dusty and forgotten items collected throughout the woman's long life. The attic's vaulted ceiling allowed just enough room for a man his size to walk upright, and he guessed the light from the lone incandescent bulb in the center of the ceiling must have been sixty watts, if that. It provided enough light to see half the room.

Mark pulled out a long black flashlight and turned it on. It blinked on and off for a moment, then went out. Mark froze where he stood, smacking the bottom of the light with the heel of his hand. His nerves raced—he had just changed the batteries two days ago, so there was no way it should be dead now. As he returned the light to its place on his belt, he heard a soft voice call to him from the back of the attic.

"Mark."

Hearing his name called out from the shadows, Mark froze where he stood. Beads of sweat rose on his forehead and his pulse quickened. Peering into the shadows and pulling out his service revolver, Mark saw what looked like a woman's shoulder with long brown hair cascading down the front, parted just enough to expose pale skin. He wiped his eyes and peered once again at the back corner. The mysterious woman was still there, her face half-hidden behind an empty bookshelf, one eye staring out at him through strands of dirty hair and twinkling in the dim light. Though he could see only a part of her, the familiarity was unmistakable.

"Jennifer?" He couldn't believe he said the name and speaking it brought tears to his eyes.

In response, the woman reached out toward him with one pleading hand and whispered in a weary voice, "Please!"

Just as Mark took a step toward her, his heart drumming heavily in his chest, the woman shot behind a shelving unit as if some unseen force had snatched her away. Mark immediately ran across the rickety wooden floor to the spot where he'd seen her and peered behind the bookshelf, praying she would still be there. All he found were packing crates and three old baskets full of discarded men's clothing.

Despite crossing back and forth throughout the attic, going through every box and under every piece of furniture, pulling on the walls and rafters searching for any sign of a secret passage, he could not find her. Eventually, he lumbered down the narrow stairs to the second-floor hallway, defeated and visibly shaken. Mrs. Magherius stood there at the foot of the steps, stroking a worn-out stuffed cat with one arthritic hand.

"Did you find her, Officer? She was over there behind the dress form looking out at me and crying. Did you see her?"

Mark considered the question for a moment. His head ached worse than before, and his hands trembled. "Yes, ma'am. I found her. I sent her home. She'll be fine."

"Oh, that's wonderful, Officer Warren! What a wonderful fellow you are. That poor woman has cried for help almost every night. You found her at last!"

Mark shivered as he continued out the front door, tears running down his face.

4.

Bettie Stone was obsessively drawing obscure, abstract symbols—ones she'd never seen before. She didn't know why she drew them. The images simply entered her mind as she sat in her bedroom. Whenever the images hit, she'd impulsively grab a sketch pad and copy them down, often for hours at a time. The images didn't always wait for her to be home in her room. Sometimes, the impulse would strike while she was at school or out for dinner with her parents. In those moments, she was powerless to restrain herself from the desire to draw whatever entered her mind. Her parents referred to them as "episodes," making her feel like some OCD freak and distancing her further from the already ambivalent kids at her stuck-up private school.

Tonight's was a rather potent episode. She was sketching the face and form of a girl, a girl who looked like she was at least a few years older than Bettie, perhaps sixteen or seventeen. The girl's features came into focus as Bettie's hand flew across the sketch pad. She lightly held the charcoal pencil to the paper, but with a firm grip at her fingertips. The girl she drew was gorgeous—long black hair with crystal-blue eyes; skin as pale as virgin snow; full lips turned up at the corners; and a hint of a cleft in her chin. When she finished, Bettie sprayed a fixative over the sketch and rolled it up, taking care not to leave a crease.

She made her way upstairs and through the living room. She passed her parents, who were sitting on the couch as always, frozen like two mannequins from an atomic test site. "I'll be right back," she called over her shoulder as the front door closed behind her, muffling the sound of her mother urging her not to be out late.

"No, it's a school night," Bettie replied into the night air.

5.

Lara Fanning stared at her toes, frustrated that she could never find time to get a proper pedicure. Once again, the Dawsons were not home when they said they'd be. The kids had been quiet, so she had finished her homework earlier than usual. Still, it was Thursday—a school night—and bedtime was calling. A twenty-minute drive lay ahead of her and a full day of classes in the morning. If these late nights kept happening, her mom would make her quit babysitting during the week. However, what was on her mind wasn't the late parents, or the possibility of lost revenue, or even the embarrassing state of her toenails. A man was outside in the darkness, watching the Dawson home.

This week she'd been watching way too much of AMC's Fear Fest, including the annual airing of When a Stranger Calls, so Lara's imagination was running wild. Fabricated spiderwebs and orange lights decorated yards all over the neighborhood, which would have made her excited for the upcoming night of parties and costumes, but tonight only gave her the chills.

Who in the hell is that?

Just then, a motorcycle hummed around the corner, and Lara recognized the driver as Leo Lourogen. Leo was four hundred pounds if he was an ounce, so it was hard to miss him. He drove up the street, looking off into the yard where Lara had seen the man standing. Leo stopped the engine and sat there for a time, looking up and down the lane. After a few moments, he started his Honda and rumbled around the block again.

What are you doing, Leo? Lara thought as she watched him ride out of sight.

When she returned her gaze to where the Peeping Tom had been standing, she found no one there. She hoped Leo had frightened him away.

As if on cue, the Dawsons' car pulled around the corner, belching dark smoke as it jostled up the road and into the driveway. Lara grabbed her things and shot out the front door, meeting them on the sidewalk.

"Hey, Lara!" Mr. Dawson yelled, drunk and stumbling around the car. "How's the best little babysitter in the state of Iowa?"

Lara grimaced, knowing she would have to put up with a lingering hug and an inappropriate comment or two from one or both of them. "Oh, just fine, thanks. I fed the kids and put them to bed. They've been asleep for a few hours."

"Oh yes, sorry, darlin'! We lost track of time." Mrs. Dawson gave her a sweaty hug that stank of cigarettes and cheap vodka.

"Yeah, Lara, we were having too much fun. Here's a little something extra for ya, OK?" Mr. Dawson broke in and gave her a long hug that ended with the palm of his hand grazing her backside.

Lara took off to her car, not bothering to count the money. The amount could be too much or too little when Mr. Dawson was drinking. From the feel of the wad of cash, it appeared this time he had erred on the side of too much. "That's what you get for touching my ass, you old perv," she mumbled as she started the car.

Glancing at her rearview mirror, her heart lurched a beat. In the middle of the street, a shadowy figure of a man watched her speed home.

6.

Stephanie Caine brushed her long red hair away from her face and kissed the boy, pulling his head back with a fistful of hair between her fingers. She swung her leg over the stick shift of the Toyota Corolla, sliding herself onto his lap and pushing her butt against the steering wheel for leverage.

Like most boys his age, this one did not understand how to kiss a girl, so Stephanie took control of the situation, directing his head from one side to the other and pushing him back when he got sloppy and overeager. She'd been kissing boys since the fifth grade, so she could work with a boy who needed guidance if he had a willingness to learn. Right then, his whole tongue shot straight into her mouth, making her gag and back away. Once again, she pulled his head to the side and returned to lip kissing.

"Jesus, stop yanking my head!" The boy pushed her off his lap and back into the passenger seat. "You don't have to be so in control."

"Oh, yeah?" Stephanie asked. "I'm trying to help you!"

"Help me? Who says I need help?"

"Look, Brad, it's OK. You need more practice, that's all. Come on, don't be like that." She was losing interest already.

"How would you like it if I called you a bad kisser?"

Stephanie straightened her skirt, buttoned her blouse, and grabbed her purse off the floor of the car. "I'd laugh in your face. I'm a great kisser!"

"Yeah, just ask anyone, right?"

Stephanie shot him a look of death. "What's that supposed to mean?"

"You know what I'm saying. You've done it with half the guys in school."

Moments later, Stephanie stormed down the road as Brad peeled away in his car, yelling through the passenger window, "Bitch!"

Devils Glen was dark, lit only by dim street lamps—making the park a perfect place to make out with random boys. However, that same seclusion made it a horrible place to be alone at night. The late-October wind made matters worse, given that Stephanie was wearing only a short skirt and a cardigan to protect against the weather. She struggled to hold her cardigan closed with one hand while she kept her skirt from flying up with the other.

As she walked, she caught a slight movement out of the corner of her eye somewhere deeper into the trees beyond the picnic areas. When she turned to look, she saw nothing but heard footsteps crackling through the dead leaves. Not being one to run from danger, Stephanie stopped to face whoever was moving beyond her vision.

"Hello!" she called into the shadows. "Who's out there? Whoever it is, I'm not some scared little girl. You better not try any shit!"

The footsteps stopped, but the darkness between the trees offered no reply. The wind whistled through the woods, and she got the feeling she'd better get out of the park as soon as she could. She quickened her pace almost to the point of jogging as she made her way down a steep hill toward the main road out of the park. She heard the footsteps behind her, closer now than before. When she glanced over her shoulder, she saw a large dark shadow of a man barreling toward her, moving with such speed she knew he would overtake her.

As her world went black, Stephanie thought she saw motorcycle lights in the distance, but before she could cry out for help, she felt icy hands cover her mouth and an inescapable force pulling her to the ground.

The Misadventures of Jack's Lap

There she was, sitting right next to him, inches away from his nervous body. Sarah Kristy, the goddess of the Bettendorf High School senior class, was seventeen and in the prime of her youthful looks. Her long blondish hair flowed down her shoulders, and her lilting laugh rang out above the marching band's din, accompanied by a natural flirtatiousness that drove the boys crazy—boys like Jack Davies.

Jack was a good looking, if somewhat awkward, teenager. Most of the girls thought he was "cute," though he would never have known it. He always felt more than a little awkward with girls.

His best friend, Randy, had an easier time talking to girls. Actually, Randy Wall had an easier time talking to just about everyone. Randy was blond with light hazel eyes. He was a little taller than Jack and more athletically built. Still, good looking or not, Jack and Randy were only sophomores, and Sarah Kristy was a senior. They had no chance in hell with her.

Sarah's attendance at a high school football game was a rarity. Such events usually bored her. She was more accustomed to attending college parties on Friday nights. But here she was sitting right next to Jack, though she wasn't paying attention to him or the game. She and her friends were mocking the cheerleaders below, feeling superior in their awkward adolescent way.

"Dude, look at her," Randy whispered into Jack's ear.

"Shh, I know," Jack replied, trying to keep his best friend from embarrassing him. Subtlety was not one of Randy's better traits.

"She's sitting right next to you, man!" Randy's voice had risen a full octave but luckily, the marching band drowned it out with a rousing rendition of Wang Chung's only hit.

"No shit! I can see that!"

"Dude, she likes you."

"Shut up!"

"Seriously."

"Don't embarrass me, Randy."

"But Jack!"

"I know!"

"Say something."

"I will. When I get a chance," Jack whispered back.

"Now is your chance!"

"She's talking to her friends. I'm not gonna interrupt!"

Unable to continue whispering, Randy groaned, "Oh my God, you're killing me here."

"Here, let's switch seats and you talk to her!" Jack said.

Randy flashed a brief deer-in-the-headlights look at Jack but recovered with, "Oh no. She sat next to you, not me."

"Seriously, shut up and watch the game, dickhead."

Ignoring his buddy, Randy hummed a love song, tightly pressing his lips together to produce a trumpet sound. Just as Sarah turned to see where the sound was coming from, Jack elbowed Randy in the ribs.

"Geez!" Randy whispered after Sarah turned back to her friends.

"Well, knock it off."

"OK, OK, Jesus. But seriously, I think she wants it."

"Shut up!"

Just then, a cheerleader threw a plastic souvenir football into the stands only a few feet from where they were sitting. A throng of teenagers launched over to them, and Sarah leaped backward to avoid the rush of arms and hands reaching for the ball. The momentum sent her into Jack's lap. Her round rump, legendary among the Bettendorf High School boy population, was now sitting directly on top of him as she giggled hysterically. Sarah looked down at Jack, raising an eyebrow as if waiting for the usual smarmy pickup line. When it didn't come, she smiled sympathetically at the poor boy below her, gracefully removed herself, and got back in her seat.

"Awkward," one of her friends said.

Jack froze, unable to speak or move. He didn't flinch when a second plastic football sailed over his head, and he barely noticed the mob of kids who subsequently dived behind him to snatch it up, one of them showering him with buttered popcorn. Eventually, he glanced over at Randy, who stared at him with his mouth hanging open. Jack stood and shuffled down the aisle, retreating to the concession stand. Within minutes, he was carefully carrying two magma-hot cups back to the bleachers. When he finally returned, Randy was alone.

"They left?" Jack asked.

"No shit they left. Actually, they're down by the fence talking to a bunch of guys who graduated last year. Do you believe that? If you've graduated, why the hell would you come back to a high school football game?"

"Sarah Kristy, Julie Melton, Lara Fanning—"

"Oh yeah. College guys! They've got all these hot chicks up in Iowa City to choose from, and they still come down here every Friday night to steal from us! Isn't college supposed to be fun? The University of Iowa is like this huge party school—frats and sororities on every corner. Who leaves that to come back to Bettendorf? Fucking losers!"

"Well, it is homecoming," Jack said.

"Bah! When I'm in college, you think I'm gonna give a shit about homecoming? Friday nights, I'm gonna be partying with the Tri-Delts."

"Yeah, I'm sure." Jack rolled his eyes.

"I fully intend to find a nice girl at some point. You know, connect on a more mature level, maybe sophomore year—junior year, maybe—once I've sown my oats, as they say. Find a nice English major. Study together in Starbucks. Go to poetry readings or whatnot—the whole thing. But freshman year? I'm gonna be a madman."

Randy's college dreams usually sounded like the plot of a dumb movie from the 80s, but anyone who knew him also knew he was all talk. In fact, Jack had a feeling Randy would fall in love with the first girl he dated and marry her right after graduation.

Jack's attention returned to the game as Kyle Turlington, Bettendorf's star quarterback and homecoming king, tossed a ten-yard-out pass that turned into a sixty-three-yard touchdown, thanks mostly to running back Trey Washington's surprising speed. The crowd erupted at once, and the BHS marching band launched into a raucous rendition of "Hail to the Victors."

As they returned to their seats, Randy asked, "Anyway, what took you so long with the cocoa?"

Right then, as if on cue, a yellow plastic football arched up above the stands in a perfect spiral, thrown by an unusually skilled, or lucky, senior cheerleader. Like a homing missile, the football sailed through the air and straight toward Jack, falling just short of his face but hitting his cup of hot cocoa instead. The force of it popped the Styrofoam cup out of his hands, sending it straight down onto his lap.

A rush of scalding pain washed across the tops of Jack's thighs, and for a moment Jack just sat frozen unable to make a sound. The best he could do was shoot a shocked look at Randy, who could muster no better response than a helpful "Holy shit," broken by the faintest hint of a laugh. Eventually, the pain was too much, and Jack let out a howling cry, drowned out by the roaring crowd.

Two hours later, the boys were walking home on Central Avenue basking in another Bulldogs victory. As they made their turn from Central onto Twenty-First Street, Randy picked up where he had left off earlier. "How could you? She's sitting there, just waiting for you to say something." He was talking loud enough for the entire neighborhood to hear.

"Not true."

"Come on, Jack. Are you kidding me? I mean, here she is." Randy positioned himself next to Jack. "She's just sitting there, almost on top of you! Dying for you to say something to her."

"No, she wasn't."

"It's Sarah Kristy!"

"I know."

"Sarah Kristy!"

"I know, Randy."

"On your lap!"

"That was a total accident. And just because Sarah sat *next* to me doesn't mean she was interested, ya know."

Randy stopped and grabbed him by the shoulders. "She was waiting! Just waiting for you to say something, anything! And what did you say?"

"Nothing," Jack replied.

"Exactly! Couldn't you have at least tried?"

"Next time, I promise."

"OK, fine, I'm done with you. So, what are we doing tomorrow?" Randy asked, rubbing his forehead.

"Aren't we playing two-hand touch at Devils Glen?" Jack was happy for the change of subject.

"Oh yeah, that's right."

"We're playing against those PV kids. Mike, Joe, Brian, and that goofy-looking kid."

Two-hand touch had been a neighborhood tradition in Bettendorf for as long as any of them could remember. Half the time they didn't play by the rules, and barely kept score. But this weekend would be different. A few guys from Pleasant Valley were coming over for some cross-town rivalry, which was a first.

"What time are we supposed to be there?"

"I don't know. Probably like one or something. Why? Do you have something else going on?"

"Nah," Randy said.

"You sure?" Jack asked.

Randy paused for a moment. "Yeah, Devils Glen is fine, I guess. That place just creeps me out. Plus, that whole Stephanie Caine thing, you know?"

"The cops are saying she took off with some guy."

"What? I thought someone had kidnapped her."

Jack stopped as he glimpsed something out of the corner of his eye. Actually, it was a glimpse of someone standing across the street near the line of fences that separated Twenty-First Street from the neighborhood known as Sunset Circle. As he turned to get a better look, the person disappeared behind the many bushes and vines covering the fence.

"What?"

"Hmm, I guess nothing," Jack said as he continued to scan the bushes. "I thought I saw someone over there across the street."

"Who?"

"I don't know," Jack replied. "It looked like a girl. I don't know. Maybe my eyes are playing tricks on me."

"Ooh, what if it's Sarah Kristy stalking you?" Randy called toward the bushes, "Hey, Sarah! Come on out and talk to us. Jack here has a lot of nothing to say to you!"

Jack punched him hard in the upper arm. "Shut up, dude!"

"Seriously, Sarah! Jack is kinda clumsy around girls and he spills things a lot, but he's a great guy."

This time, Jack punched him in the chest so hard that Randy doubled over.

"Jesus. Calm down!"

"Are you finished?" Jack asked, holding his fist back again.

"Yeah, yeah. Sarah, he wants to go home now," Randy called, narrowly avoiding another blow.

The boys reached the top of the hill overlooking downtown Bettendorf, the Mississippi River, and beyond it, Moline, Illinois. Randy lived about a block west of Jack on Nineteenth Street, across from TNT Hardware, in an old home that was once a farmhouse before they had developed the area. As they made their way down the hill, they passed the western edge of Sunnycrest Park, their oasis and escape during their childhoods. A modest place, the park comprised two swing sets, a rickety merry-go-round, a makeshift baseball diamond, a basketball court, and a small picnic gazebo that the neighborhood kids called "the shelter." However, the part of Sunnycrest that they loved most was the wooded area at the northern end. "The woods," as they called it, seemed endless to the kids who played there, although the area was only two acres at most. Jack's favorite childhood memories originated from the endless summer days exploring those woods.

When they reached the bottom of the hill, the boys exchanged a "later" before Randy took off down Mississippi Avenue toward his home. Jack stood there for a moment, enjoying the chilly October air infused with the smell of burning leaves. Someone was probably enjoying a bonfire; Jack could almost taste the roasted marshmallows.

As he made his way up to his front walk, something caught Jack's eye again. He looked up the street and saw the figure of a girl standing at the top of the hill, her slim form silhouetted by the streetlights. Jack couldn't tell much about her appearance, except that it was a girl probably around his age or younger. He stared at her, knowing she was looking right back at him. Usually, a girl staring at him would have excited him, but Jack felt a sharp chill race up his spine. Just as he moved to wave at her, she turned and disappeared.

Sunset Circle

Friday night, just as the Bettendorf Bulldogs were scoring the winning touchdown in their rivalry match against Pleasant Valley, Bettie Stone sat in her basement bedroom drawing symbols and figures on a pad of notepaper. She didn't know what the symbols represented; as far as she knew, she was creating them on the spot. She had been engaged in drawing them for many years and had accumulated an extensive library of sketch pads full of these strange drawings and symbols and complete journal entries written in some language she didn't understand. Once an image or text invaded her mind, she couldn't relax until she'd put it down on paper.

Dr. Walter Stone's daughter was an enigma to everyone in Bettendorf, even within her family. Dr. Stone was the head psychiatrist in the One North Unit at Davenport West Hospital. He was rarely home and paid little attention to his daughter's idiosyncrasies. She had been a mystery to him as far back as she could remember, and he had no time for puzzles. Not in his own home.

Dr. Stone, who was a renowned authority in psychiatry, was also an avid collector and connoisseur of vintage mid-century art, furniture, clothing, and memorabilia. It was an obsession. He routinely flew into rages if he found his wife looking like anything other than the perfect fifties housewife. He was ecstatic when the couple found out that their first child would be a daughter, and he immediately demanded that her name should be Bettie, after his favorite pinup model of the era, Bettie Page.

Unfortunately for Dr. Stone, Bettie did not live up to any of his expectations. First, she was blonde, and Bettie Page had black hair. This lack of conformity to the doctor's design was unacceptable, and so he ignored her as a mistake. Occasionally, he would even tell people they adopted her. The imperfection in her design gnawed at him.

Bettie felt her father's disappointment, so she dyed her hair jet-black and cutting her bangs straight across her forehead, hoping to appease him. It sometimes worked, if Dr. Stone wanted to pretend, but only for a while. He'd sit in his reading chair, cringing as he could see the truth growing out of her head inch by inch. He could show no love to Bettie, only looks of disappointment occasionally interrupted by pretending.

She was an attractive girl. In fact, most people described her as being striking. Bettie had little idea what that word meant, and she assumed it was insincere—something people said when they were polite. In time, she grew to despise it.

However, "striking" was a word that perfectly described her looks. She was a thirteen-year-old with dyed black hair and an ever-present serene expression on her round little face. She would have almost seemed cherubic if not for the darkness of her presence. Dogs instinctively backed far away from her when she looked at them, and virtually no one was comfortable when she was in the room. Schoolteachers fought to keep her out of their classes in elementary school, and one teacher's assistant even requested a transfer to another school after she noticed the headaches she would get whenever Bettie entered the room. Fortunately for the Bettendorf School District, Dr. Stone hated his daughter being in a public school, and he withdrew her halfway through second grade to enroll her in Saint Mark's School, a private facility only a block away from the Stones' home on Sunset Circle.

Bettie spent most Friday nights drawing or painting. Sometimes she would write in her journal, and when she did, she used a strange language. As with the drawings, she assumed she was making up the words as she went along. Journal after journal, diary after diary, she would write sentences, paragraphs, and entire novels in this undecipherable language, not knowing what any of it meant, nor why she felt compelled to do it. Her parents rarely entered her room, and if they saw her work, they made disinterested comments like, "Oh, beautiful, honey, so creative. Keep up the wonderful work, dear!"

From an early age she was happy drawing pictures most people found bizarre. She had taken on a minion, though she didn't remember how it had happened. One day, Richard just showed up offering his service and she found it only right he would do so. She loved having him do her bidding.

This Friday night started no differently from any other Friday night until a ringing started in Bettie's ears. She stood and searched her large room, under the bed, and in her closet, but could not locate the source. She went upstairs and found her father and mother. Dr. Stone was sitting on the living room sofa in his fifties casual home attire, posing with a newspaper he wasn't reading, with Mrs. Stone posed on the arm of the chair.

"Mom, Dad..."

"One moment, dear," Mrs. Stone said. "Your father is just finishing a most interesting article."

Bettie rolled her eyes but waited a few seconds until her father let out a fake laugh and set down the paper. "Ah, that Putin is something else! Yes, honey, what was it you wanted? Is everything OK?"

Bettie ignored the strained term of endearment and asked, "Do you guys hear a ringing sound?"

"Ringing sound, sweetie?" Mrs. Stone asked. "I don't hear a thing. Do you, dear?"

Dr. Stone shook his head and raised his right eyebrow. "No, dear, I don't hear a thing. It's been a quiet evening—until you came in, that is."

"OK, hmm, that's odd. Maybe I'm just hearing things. I think I'll go out and get some fresh air." Bettie walked to the front door and opened it.

"OK then, pumpkin. Don't be out late," Dr. Stone called out behind her.

"Yes, sweetie, don't be out late," Mrs. Stone echoed. "And perhaps you should put on a sweater! It might be chilly tonight!"

Bettie closed the door and walked out into the fall night. Sunset Circle was a large cul-de-sac between Eighteenth and Twenty-First Street, just south of Central Avenue, developed on land sold off from the Bennett estate. It was an old gated community. Most of the families had lived there for years, with homes passed from father to son for generations. The Stones, in fact, were relatively new residents, and were an anomaly. As Bettie scanned the houses of her neighborhood, she knew there had been other reasons the HOA had accepted the Stones. Every family in this community had some strange story or dark secret, and likewise, every family in the community also enrolled their children in Saint Mark's School. In fact, Bettie knew all the other kids on the block. Most of them were strange, though none of them were like her. Even in a school full of privileged weirdos, Bettie stood out. The other children avoided or ignored Bettie, which was fine.

However, one boy noticed Bettie, and he noticed her a lot. Justin Mackenzie seemed unable to keep his eyes off her whenever she was around. He was two years younger and spent almost as much time by himself as she did. As Bettie looked at the Mackenzie house, which was across the street and two houses down from her own, she spotted the boy's face in one upstairs window looking down at her, his thick glasses reflecting the streetlights below, giving him the appearance of a nerdy robot boy. Bettie smiled to herself and gave a little wave before returning her attention to the source of the ringing.

As she walked down the sidewalk, she thought she could hear the voices of two boys emerging from the ringing in her head. She couldn't hear the voices—not with her ears, at any rate. They were in her head, and the voices seemed to come from Twenty-First Street on the other side of the fence behind her house. She made her way around through her backyard and to a vine-covered opening in the fence.

By the time Bettie squeezed through, she could hear the boys with her ears. The ringing sound halted as she peered through the vines and spotted two teen boys walking down the street. She focused all her attention on one. As she stood there trying to remember his name, the boy stopped and looked right at her. Instinctively, she stepped back behind the vines.

She heard the shy boy say something about seeing a girl behind a bush. Then she heard the other one yell, "Hey, Sarah! Come on out and talk to us. Jack here has a lot of nothing to say to you!"

Jack Davies! Yes, that's his name, Bettie thought.

"Seriously, Sarah! Jack is kinda clumsy around girls and he spills things a lot, but he's a great guy!" the loud boy yelled.

Eventually, after much boyish punching and cursing, they continued down the street laughing and chatting at full volume without a care in the world. Bettie followed them to the top of the hill and watched as they continued on their way until they eventually split up—the loud one taking off somewhere to the west and Jack stopping at the front of his house. She knew he was looking up at her, and she didn't care.

THE CORNER OF THE DARK

1.

WHEN JACK WOKE UP on Saturday morning and made his way downstairs for a bowl of cereal, the entire embarrassing evening ran through his mind. However, the memory that lingered wasn't the football game or his awkward silence as he sat inches from Sarah Kristy, or even suffering through Randy's subsequent ridicule. The thought occupying his mind was the mysterious girl he'd seen on the way home.

"Don't trouble your mind about her," a soft voice above him said.

Jack looked up to see his twin sister, Anne. She had once again appeared out of nowhere.

"Who?"

"That girl. Do not worry about her."

"Which girl?"

"Whichever girl you're thinking about," Anne replied with a small laugh.

"Eh, I'm not worried," Jack lied.

Anne smiled and then glided out of the dining room, disappearing down the hall. As always, he immediately felt better. That was so very *Anne*. She always turned up when he needed her. If he was sad, Anne was there to soothe him. When a girl he had a crush on broke his heart, Anne would mend it with a funny song or a fantastic tale of some far-away world.

His friends always complained about their sisters. Randy often said his sister was annoying as hell, but Jack didn't identify with that—Anne was never like that. She was caring, funny, polite, and it always seemed to Jack like she came from a different era. If there was such a thing as a perfect sister, Anne was it. But there was one problem.

Anne wasn't real.

When Jack was young, he created two imaginary friends. The first was a boy named Johnny Raynis—a playmate of sorts who entertained and protected Jack during his early years. The second, his twin sister, came three years later. She had been a real person for a short time; an undetected heart condition took her life exactly one hour and seventeen minutes after she was born.

Her death shook the family to their core, severely testing their bonds. Their mother, Diane, slipped into a deep depression and never recovered. She did her best to hide it from Jack, but he still noticed the little things—the random tears around his birthday; the long, blank stares out the window; or how his parents switched off the radio when certain songs played. His father, Ben, filled his schedule with work and rediscovered religion. But no matter how much praying they did, the memory of their little girl never faded. Like a lost piece to an intricate puzzle, the focus was always on the hole she had left.

One evening when Jack was seven years old, as the family sat down to dinner, he noticed the familiar far-away look in his mother's eyes and correctly guessed that she was thinking about her lost child.

"Don't worry, Mom. Anne's OK," he said.

Blinking away tears, Diane looked down at her youngest son. "What did you say?"

"Anne's OK," Jack repeated. "Don't worry about her."

"Oh, honey," she said, clearing her throat and then pausing for a moment. "Why do you say that?"

"Because you look sad," Jack said.

"I am sad, sweetie. Just a little. I'm sorry."

"Don't be sorry, Mommy."

His mother took him by the hand and leaned down closer to his face, her eyes filling once again with tears. "Oh, that's sweet of you to say, honey. It is. I hope that's true."

"It's true, Mommy. I know it," Jack insisted.

"How could you know that, dear?"

"Because I talk to her, Mommy."

Diane cleared her throat again and looked at her imaginative little boy for a moment. "You talk to her?"

The others at the table sat in silence. Ben, who had been reading the newspaper, was now staring at Jack, bewildered. Jack's three brothers were watching with similar looks on their faces. The oldest, Shannon, sat frozen with a full fork of food still sitting inches from his wide-open mouth. Scott and Terry were looking at Jack like he a bizarre creature who had crawled in through an open window. Ben cleared his throat as if he was about to say something, but stayed silent.

Jack looked around the table and then back at his mother. "Yes, Mommy. I talk to her every day."

"Oh, honey, if only that were true."

"It is true. Anne comes to my room all the time. She's always with us."

"She's here with us?"

"Yes, Mommy."

Diane glanced across the table at her husband. Ben finally found his voice and asked, "She's here now, Jack?"

"Yes, Dad."

"Here in this room?" his mother asked.

"Yes."

"Where?"

"She's right over there in the doorway."

Jack's dad looked at the doorway and asked, "What's she doing, Jack?"

"She's watching us."

Jack saw everyone at the table tense up immediately. They didn't react the way he had thought they would, and his mom was still sad. He had said the wrong thing, the worst thing he could have said.

Jack looked at Anne. She lifted a finger to her mouth and whispered, "They don't understand. Remember when I told you we must keep this a secret? If you talk about me, you'll only worry them. Do you understand?"

Jack nodded, tears filling his eyes. He looked at his mom and said, "I'm sorry, Mommy. I was just trying to make you happy."

Diane reached out to him with both hands, snatching him out of his chair and into her lap. He could feel her warm tears falling down his cheek mixing with his own. He so wished he could make her understand. But Jack was too young to understand. He had summoned Anne to deal with his first creation.

Johnny.

Johnny was a mystery. When he first appeared, he seemed beneficial. If a ghost came into Jack's room, Johnny would sweep in and frighten it away with a clever song or an ornery laugh. Like a woodland sprite, magical and free spirited, Johnny invented a world of play and discovery, making each day an adventure.

"Why do the ghosts come to me, Johnny? Why don't they bother my brothers or Mom and Dad? Why always *me*?" Jack would ask.

"Because you're special," Johnny would reply. "You're the most special boy in all of Bettendorf—in all the world."

"It's not fair. I don't want to be special anymore."

"Oh, Jacky boy! There's nothing you can do about that. And why would you want to even if you could?"

In those days, Jack looked forward to Johnny's visits. They inspired him to dream, to imagine, and Johnny empowered Jack. But at some point, all of that changed as a darkness grew in Johnny. He became less of a friend and more of a troublemaker. Instead of protecting Jack from the ghostly visitations, he stirred them up.

Two months after his sixth birthday, as the October air fell into an early chill, Jack faced the biggest test of his young life. That night, as a thunderstorm moved into the area, Jack crawled into bed after a tiring day of two-hand touch. As soon as his head hit the pillow, he heard his closet door opening, followed by Johnny's familiar, mischievous laugh. Jack's heart raced with anxiety.

"Johnny, I don't want to play. I'm going to bed," Jack said, pulling the covers up to his neck.

Johnny kneeled by his ear and whispered, "Oh no, you're not going to bed just yet, my brother."

"I'm not your brother, Johnny. You're not even real."

"I'm real to you, Jacky boy."

"What's that matter?" Jack asked.

"I'd say it matters a lot to you. What else is there?"

Jack sighed. "That makes no sense."

"Anyway, I won't stay long. I've got things to do and people to see, ya know." Johnny sat on the bed rubbing his hands together.

"So, what do you want?" Jack asked, deciding it was easier to play along.

"It's not what I want. It's what she wants." A flash of lightning lit the room, and Jack saw an unusually pensive look on Johnny's face.

"Who?"

"My friend."

"What friend?"

Johnny stood up with a flourish, waving one hand above his head. "Now that would spoil the surprise!"

"What friend?" Jack asked again. "I'm your only friend."

"That's not true! I have lots of friends. Maybe you don't know about them. Anyway, she's a new friend—I met her today. And she wants to meet you."

"Why does she want to meet me?"

"Oh, she's heard so much about you. I've told her everything, and she thinks you're a very remarkable little boy." Johnny shuffled to the closet door and leaned against it.

"Why?"

"Well, because you are! Oh, you do not understand just how special you are, do you, Jack? But you're about to find out. And I promise, after tonight, you'll never second-guess yourself again. Come on, Jack, get out of bed and meet her. I swear she's a blast!"

Jack sat up and thought for a moment. "Where is she? It's bedtime. You know I can't go out at night."

"Not a problem! She's right here."

"Here? In the house?"

"Yep! She's right here. Right on the other side of this door, actually."

"Huh?"

"She's in your closet, Jack. I snuck her in, and she's waiting for you. Oh, you'll love her. She's the most amazing person! In fact, she's just like you! I know you will be best friends forever."

Jack sat there for a moment. "I don't like the closet."

"Oh, come on, you sissy!"

"No, Johnny. Leave me alone."

"Tell you what. Meet my friend and I will leave you alone for an entire month. And I won't bring any more friends here to bother you," Johnny offered.

"Really?"

"Really!"

"You promise?"

"And hope to die." Johnny stepped away from the closet and motioned for him to go inside.

Jack stood and walked to the closet door, putting his hand on the knob. "You sure she's in there?" he asked.

"Only one way to find out."

With a sigh, Jack opened the door and stepped in.

The entire upstairs of the home had at one time been a huge attic. Previous owners converted it into three bedrooms years before the Davies bought the house, and whoever designed the space decided each bedroom should have a walk-in closet. Jack's closet was almost large enough to be its own room. There was space for two large clothes racks and several shelves of storage for old clothes and camping equipment. The room was long and narrow, running the entire length of Jack's bedroom wall.

Jack pulled at the chain on a hanging light that came down from the ceiling to turn on the fifty-watt bulb that was barely bright enough to illuminate the front part of the space, leaving the back of the closet covered in shadows.

"Where is she?" Jack asked.

Johnny peeked his head inside and whispered, "She's back there. Go on, find her. She's rather shy, and her eyes aren't used to the light. But go on, Jack. Find her."

"Hello?" Jack called out.

He bent down to peer under the hanging clothes but couldn't see anyone. As he stood back up, he heard something and moved closer to get a better look, but the sound stopped.

"Hello? Johnny's friend? That you?" Jack asked.

A footstep sounded from the back of the closet and then another. Jack bent down once again to look under the rack and this time saw two pale bare feet, dirty and too large to be a child's.

"Hello? Who's there?" Jack asked. "This isn't funny, John—"

But before Jack could finish, the closet door slammed shut behind him.

"Oh, Jack, you are too trusting." Johnny laughed from the bedroom.

Jack ran to the door and tried pulling it open, but it wouldn't budge. "Stop, Johnny. This isn't funny!"

"It's not funny to you, maybe. But I'm dying over here!"

Jack froze as the sound of metal hangers slowly parting screeched behind him. Jack turned around to see a woman standing there, her eyes shooting back and forth, looking like she did not understand where she was or how she got there. Dark circles surrounded her eyes. Her rain-drenched hair lay plastered to the sides of her head. She had a soft, kind face that might have been pretty if not for the filth. She wore a soaking wet hospital gown with the words "One North" stamped on the top left shoulder. Suddenly, Jack realized something crucial, and his young mind reeled with the realization. Unlike his normal visitors, this woman wasn't a ghost; she was a real person. She looked like she was struggling against something—some great force within her. Her face was a mixture of confusion, terror, and pain.

All at once, she reached out and seized Jack by the shoulders.

"Please! Help me!" she cried. "My husband. Please find my husband. I'm in danger!"

Confused, Jack tried to escape. "Please don't hurt me!"

The woman fell silent and bowed her head, keeping hold of Jack's shoulders. After a few moments, a small wicked laugh, almost a cackle, came out of the woman, and her hands squeezed down on his shoulders with growing force. When he tried to wiggle out of her grasp, she gave him a yank and looked straight into his eyes.

Somehow her appearance had changed. She looked older now as if she had aged several years in a few seconds. The dark circles around her eyes had grown darker, and her hair had become gray. But the worst part, the part that chilled Jack, was her eyes.

Her blood-red eyes.

Her mouth hung wide open. A long line of saliva dripped over her lower lip and hung there below her chin. Bloody tears flowed down her cheeks as she forcibly pressed down on Jack's shoulders, slowly pushing him to the floor. Terrified, Jack lay on his back looking up at the woman as she squatted down and straddled him. The light above her swung back and forth.

"Please—" Jack tried to say before some unseen force wrenched his mouth open.

The woman lowered her head until her lips were upon his, covering his mouth as if she was administering CPR. But instead of blowing air into his lungs, she sucked it out. Great pain invaded Jack's body as he felt his strength being drained. It felt to him as if his soul was being pulled away from him. He closed his eyes and tried to fight against it, but to no avail. He tried calling out, but no sound came forth. Finally, with nothing else left to do, he called out in his mind with what might have been a prayer. He prayed to God, to the universe, to whoever would listen—even to Anne.

"Ha! Anne's dead. She's dead, and you are alone," a voice spoke into his mind. The voice sounded like Johnny's, and yet it didn't. It was deeper, like a man's voice.

Young Jack Davies felt himself slowly fading. But then, just as darkness overtook him, Jack heard a shriek from the other side of the door, and then moments later, a bright light broke into the closet, startling the woman. She pulled away from Jack's face, a great dread filling her crimson eyes, and she scurried behind a rack of clothes. The strange light grew in power, illuminating the entire closet with a bright-white glow, and Jack drifted out of consciousness as sounds of thunder raged on outside.

When Jack awoke several minutes later, he met his sister for the first time.

2.

"Hello, Jack," she said as she lovingly stared down at him. She had the bluest eyes he'd ever seen—mirrors of his own.

"Anne?"

"Yes."

"Are you real?"

"Do you see me?" she asked.

"Yes, I see you."

"Then I'm real to you."

"How did you get here?" he asked.

"You called me. Don't you remember?"

Jack thought about it for a moment. "I guess. Are you like Johnny?"

Anne smiled. "I suppose I am. Is Johnny the boy that was here before?"

"Yes. He used to be my friend. He's mean now." Jack fought the tears threatening to fill his eyes, remembering the trick Johnny had played on him.

"Yes, that boy is wicked Jack, more than you know. We must send him away at once."

"How?"

"Do you know where to find him?"

"No, he hides."

"Where?" she asked.

"I don't know. Someplace in the house, I think. He calls it the corner of the dark—says I must never go there."

"The corner of the dark?" Anne asked. The name seemed to concern her. It had always scared Jack, which was probably the point.

"Yes, that's where he hides."

"And you're sure it's here in this house?" Anne asked.

"I think so," Jack replied. Then he remembered something. "What happened to the scary woman, Johnny's friend? Did you make her go away?"

Anne's eyes held a touch of sadness. "Yes, I did. She will never come here again, I promise."

"Who was she?"

"I'm uncertain, but I believe she wasn't herself."

"What's that mean?" Jack asked.

"I don't know if I could explain it to you even if we had the time, but unfortunately, there isn't any. We have much to do before the night is over. We must find this Johnny and make him go away for good. I fear he has caused great mischief in his time here, and I can never undo some of it. We must rid this place of him. Are you ready?" Anne asked, standing up.

"I'm scared."

"Oh, Jack, I know you are. What happened to you tonight was terrible. But I am with you now, and that is a beautiful thing for both of us."

Her words comforted Jack, but he breathed a heavy sigh, for he knew where they had to look—the basement.

As if reading his mind, Anne whispered, "Jack, you have nothing to fear if I am with you. Let's go get him, shall we?"

Minutes later, after Jack had gathered the rest of his courage, they descended the basement's open stairs. Jack feared that hands might reach between them to grab his ankles as sometimes happened. The basement was mostly one open space with two small rooms built into it. There was a large old gas furnace in the center with pipes and tubes reaching out from its top like a giant metal octopus. Jack skirted past it with care.

In the far northwest corner of the basement, they saw something. "Something" was the only word for it, because it didn't exactly look like a person. It didn't look like anything really, more like the absence of something. A darkness, or a shadow in the shape of a boy. It was standing in the corner as if waiting for Jack.

"I told you not to come here, Jack," a voice said from the shadow. It was like Johnny's voice, but deeper and angrier. "You must go to bed now, Jack. Forget what you've seen. Do as I say and I'll bring you a treat in the morning."

"Silence!" Anne commanded. "Silence yourself now or I will silence you forever."

The shape recoiled, and fear seemed to emanate from its shapelessness, as if Anne did not figure in its calculations. Within moments, it regained its composure and put on a false bravado. It straightened itself and paused, then suddenly threw back its head with a laugh.

"Oh, Jack! You remarkable boy! You brought your dead sister here. I underestimated you. It's all true, every bit; you are the one. I almost can't believe it, but I can't deny what I see. Now, brother, you must listen to what I say."

Anne said, "You must go now away from this house forever."

"Do not listen to her. Come with me to my corner."

Those were the last words Johnny would speak. He hissed, then looked as if he was grasping at his black throat. Jack looked at Anne and saw she was holding out one hand toward the shadow. When she spoke, a brilliant light shone all about her, illuminating the cavernous basement.

"Silence, demon! I hold your voice, and you will speak no more. Leave this house and never return, or I will cast you into the abyss where you will spend eternity!"

Immediately, the shadow dissolved.

"Is he gone?" Jack asked.

"Yes. Gone forever," Anne replied.

Anne followed Jack upstairs to his bed and stood over it, singing a soft lullaby she called "The Hymn of Forgetting" as her brother drifted into the most peaceful sleep he'd slept in many months.

In the morning, Jack awoke with a tremendous headache and a large bruise on each shoulder. He was forgetting what had happened, but it didn't matter. The hymn was all he could hear; it was the only sound in the world and it washed away all worry, all pain. All the events—Johnny's trick, the woman with blood in her eyes, and the parting of Johnny—the hymn absorbed it all, cleaning it and turning it into make-believe. All of it was just another adventure, part of a game—a game he had won, with the help of his sister.

In time, he forgot about Johnny almost entirely. Within a few weeks, only fragments remained. What little he remembered seemed to him to be nothing more than fantasy—the wild imaginings of a strange little boy.

CREEPS

AN HOUR AFTER BREAKFAST, Jack and Randy were pedaling their bikes down Central Avenue toward Devils Glen Park. It was a golden sunny fall day, around sixty-five degrees. It was October 24, and the orange leaves were falling fast—perfect football weather. Still, Jack felt a strange tension in the air. He thought maybe Randy was feeling it too, and for each of them, the feeling grew as they drew closer. Jack hadn't been to the park since Stephanie Caine went missing.

It's only about Stephanie, that's all.

The game itself was a one-sided affair, as Jack and his friends all knew each other well, having played two-hand touch together since they were kids. Jack could give a nod or a wink, and Randy knew to break off his route and run a hook. If Mike Shore tapped his elbow, Jack knew he was going deep. Every trick in their book worked to perfection, and by halftime, the Pleasant Valley guys were already looking weary.

At the half, Jack jogged over to the drinking fountain just beyond a chain-link fence. As he bent down to slurp a few gulps, he saw a strange-looking man standing next to a barren oak, watching him. Then Jack noticed two other men sitting under a picnic shelter, clothed in dirty jeans and old T-shirts. There was something about them that felt wrong, though Jack did not understand why he'd think it. But the men seemed wild in some subtle way. The one in the white t-shirt looked particularly intimidating, like a mean drunk looking for a fight. He had scraggly dark hair with dark brown eyes peering out from under it. Jack shrugged it off and returned to the game.

After the game was over, the boys said their goodbyes, hopped on their bikes, and made their way back down the main drive back through the park. Though it was still only 3:00 p.m., it seemed like dusk, as new clouds darkened the sky. The leafy canopy of the enormous oak trees hovered overhead, swaying in the growing wind.

Then they both saw them. They were hanging out under one of the picnic shelters. The one in the white t-shirt was standing at the near side of the structure while the other two were hanging out near one of the picnic tables on the far side. All three were staring directly at Jack.

"Randy, do you know those guys?" Jack asked.

"Never seen them." Randy's voice cracked.

"They were watching us during the game. I don't know. I think we should get out of here."

"You got it."

The boys turned their bikes onto one of the side paths and, looking back, the three were now facing them, walking in their direction.

"Randy, I think those creeps are following us!" Jack cried out.

"Ah, shit!" Randy said as he looked over his shoulder to see the men running and gaining on them. "Dude! Come on! Hurry!"

Jack and Randy pedaled as fast as they could, not looking back until they reached the park entrance. Taking a left, they crossed over the Duck Creek Bridge and didn't stop to rest until they got all the way back to Jack's house and were safely in his bedroom.

"I think we should call the police and tell them what happened. Maybe those guys were the ones who kidnapped Stephanie," Jack said.

"Maybe, but I don't know. Something my cousin told me last week is bothering me."

"Leo?" Jack asked.

"Yeah, Leo. He told me some things that make me wonder about our Bettendorf cops," Randy said, rubbing the sweat from his eyes.

Randy's cousin was a strange guy named Leo Lourogen. He weighed almost four hundred pounds, sported a razor-short buzz cut, and wore tank tops that looked like they had just recently dried from being drenched in dirty sweat—on the rare occasion he wore a shirt. He rode around town on a motorcycle that strained under his enormous weight. Randy swore up and down he was harmless, but something in his actions and demeanor suggested otherwise. No one had ever witnessed him doing anything illegal. However, the kids of Bettendorf were on high alert whenever they heard his Honda 750 roaring down the street.

"So I'm with Leo, helping him fix his parents' garage roof and just keeping an eye on him 'cause Aunt Maggie and Uncle Red went to Peoria for the afternoon. It goes fine, as always, no problems all morning. We ate lunch, drank pop, and finished the roof around five. So I said to Leo, 'OK, see ya!' and I hop on my bike to go home. I look up at him, and he's got this weird look on his face. Like, weirder than usual, ya know? And I'm like, 'What's wrong?' And he's like, 'Which way ya going?' which was odd. I mean, he never gives a shit about which way I'm going or where I'm going, ya know what I'm saying?"

Jack knew exactly what Randy meant. Leo's perspective of the world was singular. He was the star of his own movie, and everyone in the world was just offstage, waiting for their cue. When an actor left Leo's vicinity, he or she returned to some universal green room until their next scene.

"I told him, 'I don't know. I'll probably go through Devils Glen,' and Leo gave me another funny look. Not his usual funny look, but something odd, like he didn't care for the route I was taking. Then he looked up at the sky and back down to the ground, and said, 'OK, but don't dillydally,

Sally,' and he went inside. So, I'm like, whatever, and I head toward Devils Glen, even though the vibe from Leo was still hanging over me and making me think about taking a detour down State Street. But then I'm like, Leo's nuts, so what the heck?"

"But as I'm going up the hill, I get this feeling like something just isn't right. I couldn't put my finger on it, but it felt like there was something wrong. It got stronger as I rode into the park. In fact, it got so frigging strong I turned around and went back out the other way. Took me an extra half hour to get home! Anyway, when I got home, I called Leo to see why he was acting so weird. He told me to stay away from Devils Glen—the whole area, if I can. He seemed to think the cops aren't telling the truth about Stephanie Caine's disappearance."

"Why would they lie about that?" Jack asked.

"No idea. I dismissed it as Leo acting weird. But now, after what happened today, I'm wondering."

Jack looked down at his bedroom floor, searching for answers in the old shag carpet. "Something's happening. I can feel it."

"What do you mean?" Randy asked.

"There's something I haven't told you, Randy. So many things. I don't even know where to begin." Jack rubbed his hand back and forth on his jeans as he took a few deep breaths.

"Yeah? What is it?" Randy asked.

Jack took one last breath and replied, "It's a long story."

Of Brother Jones's Gift

Jimmy Vance slouched his way down Devils Glen Road on his way to no place in particular. It had been a typical Sunday afternoon at the Vance residence, which meant it was time for Jimmy to take a walk—a long walk. When he left his house, his dad, as usual, was busying himself with a full bottle of Jim Beam and a rinsed-out mason jar. It was best to make himself scarce by the time his dad hit the bottom of that bottle, or it would be his ass. Unfortunately for his mom, Jimmy's leaving meant it would be her ass, or if she got wise and took off, it would be the dog's ass. Jimmy didn't care who took the beating as long as it wasn't him. His mom could die tonight and he wouldn't shed a tear. He had better things to think about, like who would be his punching bag today.

When Jimmy walked down the street, every kid under the age of fourteen, and maybe a few older ones, would find a good reason to go inside. For Jimmy, that was enough to make him happy, even if it meant he had no one to beat on. He was the undisputed bully of the ninth grade, and any kid who challenged him got sent home with a black eye and a bloodied nose—if that kid was lucky.

As he walked down Devils Glen Road, he finally came upon two kids to knock around. They were slightly on the young side, maybe fifth graders, but it didn't matter to Jimmy as long as he had a little fun.

As he approached, the kids, playing with their Star Wars figures, were oblivious to the danger. Jimmy jumped in between them, slamming his big boots on top of their toys. Both fell silent when they looked up and saw the cause of the destruction. Jimmy grabbed each boy by the collar and lifted them until they were choking.

"What do we have here? Two little girls playing with their dollies! You know what I do to girly boys?"

Jimmy took a quick look around and saw no one. There would be no interruption of his fun time today. The parents would find their brats beaten and scared, but they would learn from it. Never again would these two kids play alone in the front yard.

"You know what I do to girly boys?" Jimmy asked again.

"We aren't girly boys!" the smaller of the two screamed.

"You're not?" Jimmy dropped the kid and smacked him across the side of his head, knocking him to the ground. "You sure fall like a girl."

"You're bigger than us," the smaller kid protested.

"Shut up, Mikey!" the bigger kid said.

"Oh, your big brother here is smart! Don't run your mouth and maybe the big bully will let us go. Is that what you're thinking?" The kid nodded his head, tears running down his cheeks.

"Well, you're wrong. I don't care what you say, I'm gonna beat you all the same. Ya know why? I want to. So cry all you want. Talk back all you want or just sit there and take it. Either way, I'm gonna have me some fun," Jimmy said, commending himself for the dead-on impression of his old man. "Ya know what I will do first—"

The blaring sound of an old school bus cut Jimmy's threat short. The bus was ancient and purple, with the words "Valley Baptist Church" painted on the side. When it stopped, a cloud of exhaust billowed forward. The doors opened slowly with an ear-piercing squeal, and down stepped a middle-aged man in a cheap gray suit with a pearly smile and greasy hair.

"My word, what is happening here, boys?" the man asked in a melodic southern drawl.

Jimmy dropped the boy he was holding. "Nothing, Mister. We were just having fun. Huh, kids?"

"He's gonna beat us up!" the smaller boy cried.

"For shame, for shame," the man in the suit said. "That's not a good way to spend the Lord's day now, is it? It seems like someone here needs a lesson."

"Yes, sir!" the bigger boy added. "He's a big fat bully!"

Jimmy glared down at the kid.

"Well, boys, I think you two should run inside and let me handle this. Now run along and leave your parents out of this? I want to give this here bully a chance to redeem his-self."

The boys looked at each other and then back at the man before hurrying off. The man glanced down at Jimmy and shook his head. Jimmy wasn't sure what to make of him, but he sure as hell would not let the guy think he feared anyone, let alone some weird Bible-thumper.

"The fuck you looking at?" Jimmy asked.

As soon as the last word left his lips, the man backhanded Jimmy across the face, sending him straight to the ground. Instinctively, Jimmy touched the side of his face and fought back the tears welling up in his eyes. "Jesus," was all he could mutter.

"No, I'm not Him, though I imagine He'd give you a couple more smacks were He here. Picking on them poor boys. They're not even old enough to have their first wet dream, and here you are in what, high school? You's a cruel boy, I take it."

"What's it to you?"

"Oh, I'd watch your tone, boy. I already showed you once what I do when I'm disrespected. I'd hate to show you again, you being on the ground and all. But I promise to smack the living sin outta you if you go running that mouth again, ya hear?" The man took a step closer and stared down at Jimmy with a wicked grin.

"Yes, sir," Jimmy replied, still fighting tears.

"That's a good boy. You know who I am?"

"No, sir."

"Ah, look at them manners there," the man called back to the bus driver. "And you said this boy wasn't worth spit, Carl. I imagine if someone just spent a little time with this one, he'd be a right proper little bastard. Wouldn't you—uh—what's your name, boy?"

"Jimmy. Jimmy Vance."

"Ah yes, Vance. I believe I've seen your old man running around these parts. I'm new to the area, mind you, but I've had occasion to do my research on the town reprobates. He seems like he'd be a hard man to live with."

Jimmy shrugged.

"Well, my name is Reverend Billy Jones, but I like folks to call me Brother Jones."

"Hi."

Jimmy suddenly noticed that on his right hand, and only his right hand, Jones was wearing a black leather glove.

"Do you know I am the preacher at that little white church just down the road here? Valley Baptist?"

"No, I didn't."

"No?" Brother Jones asked. "What exactly do you do on Sundays, Mr. Vance?"

"You're looking at it."

"Yes, I can see how you've chosen to occupy your time. Such a waste of your given talents, bullying those stupid little varmints."

Jimmy smirked and then glanced at Jones, making sure he wasn't about to get another smack. "But I have no talents."

"Sure you do. You don't recognize them, or maybe you don't appreciate them. The Lord has an eye on you, Mr. Vance. He surely does, and He wants you to know a thing or two, which is why He sent old Brother Jones out here this afternoon to find ya. He wants you. He wants you on His team, so to speak. Are you looking to be on His team, or are you gonna keep wasting your weekends like this?" As he spoke, Brother Jones's voice became as smooth as maple syrup in his Southern drawl.

"You mean church? I'm not really a church-goer."

Jones squatted down close to Jimmy, looking him directly in the eyes. "Oh, son, this ain't no church you have ever been to before, and that's a fact. Why don't you come with me? I promise you a meal, and maybe some of my world-famous chocolate-chunk brownies. How about that? Do this and I promise you, that old man of yours will never lay another hand on you, so long as I live."

Jimmy squinted at Brother Jones. If he was offering to lay a smack down on the old man, Jimmy had no problem with that, and it couldn't hurt to see what this church was all about and find out what this guy saw in him. Few people in Jimmy's life saw *anything* in him.

"OK, I'll go. But if you turn out to be a pedo, I'll rip your junk off."

"Heh, heh, no problem there, my young friend. I promise you I am one hundred percent heterosexual and not at all tempted by the fruits of young flesh. I like them around my age if you take my meaning. My intentions with you are purely spiritual, I assure you of that. No degenerate worth his salt would admit to being a pedophile, so I understand if you're reluctant to take my word for it. Tell ya what, I have here a little old pocketknife my granddaddy gave me years ago. How about I loan it to ya?"

Brother Jones reached into his pants pocket and produced a medium-size pocketknife with a black-and-red handle and then presented it as though he were offering a precious gem. Jimmy tentatively reached out and took it, rolling the knife around in his hands as he inspected it. It looked old and used, but would do. He closed the blade and stuck it in his pocket, saying, "Thanks, Mr. Jones."

"Brother Jones, son. Got it?"

"Yes, Brother Jones," Jimmy replied.

"Good boy. Now climb aboard the Valley Baptist Express. This here's your pilot, Mr. Carl Hickson. He doesn't say much, but he can drive through the gates of hell and never scratch an inch of paint. Done it a few times, ain't ya, Carl?"

Carl said nothing, but turned and looked back at Jimmy through glasses that looked like someone had cut them from the bottom of a pair of Coke bottles. His eyes were devoid of personality, emotion, or any other sign of humanity. Likewise, there was neither malice nor judgment in them. The strange man turned back to the road as the bus lumbered along.

Jones laughed and said, "Ah, don't you worry about Carl. He's a good old boy, and that's a fact. He has the eyes of the dead, as they say, that's all."

Jimmy wondered what Brother Jones meant, but the sudden jerk of the bus broke his attention as they approached Valley Baptist. On Devils Glen Road, about halfway between Central Avenue and Middle Road, it wasn't a church very many people attended. Most probably passed by without so much as a glance at the little white church. As they pulled up, Jimmy heard singing and shouting like an old-fashioned revival coming from inside. "Is there a service going on?"

"Yes, indeed!" The preacher's eyes burned with a white hot fire.

Carl turned the bus into the gravel driveway, jostling around the right side of the church and stopping it at the back. He opened the door and once again turned to look at Jimmy with the same dead stare. This time Jimmy immediately looked away and exited the bus.

Jones led him inside the back entrance and up a short flight of stairs to a door marked "Sanctuary." He could hear the congregation inside singing an old-time Southern gospel hymn:

When you feel a little prayer wheel turnin'
You will know a little fire is burnin'

Brother Jones glanced back with a big grin and opened the door, pulling Jimmy with him into the sanctuary. The door they came through opened at the front of the church, just to the right side of the altar. An older man stood behind a large oak pulpit, leading the congregation in song. Every one of the two hundred congregants looked at Brother Jones and Jimmy as they entered, singing and clapping even louder than before. In fact, it seemed to Jimmy like they were working themselves into a frenzy.

Finally, the old song leader stopped and raised his hands. As one, the congregation went silent. "Ah, my brothers and sisters, Brother Jones has returned!"

The congregation roared a lot of "Praise Jesus" and "Hallelujah." Brother Jones waved his hands and did a little dance to the rollicking sound of the baby grand piano as he led Jimmy up the steps and straight to the pulpit. Jones adjusted the microphone and began his sermon.

"Thank you, Brother Rollie. That is one of my very favorite hymns as I'm sure I've mentioned before."

Jimmy noticed Carl stealthily slipped into the sanctuary from the main doors.

"Oh, my brothers and sisters! What a sweet day it is!" Brother Jones called out, his voice reverberating with a profound power that seemed somehow magical, almost hypnotizing. "The Lord is good, yes. I can see His works every day, and they are surely getting stronger, my brothers and sisters! There is a power growing in this here little church. Yes, there is! And I feel you, my brothers and sisters. I feel your power, the power in each one of you that comes directly from the Lord!"

Sounds of agreement and "Amen" sounded out from several congregants.

Brother Jones continued. "But that power is hidden, my friends, when it should be out in the light. We cannot deny the Lord His sacrifice, though He asks for much, maybe more than we want to give. But the day will come, my dear friends, the day will come when all shall be judged, when all men and women, black and white, saint and sinner, shall be judged and found wanting! We all have hardships and burdens; this I know. Some of you have suffered. And some of you cry out to the Lord. You ask, 'Why? Why, oh Lord, have I been given this burden? Why am I cursed, dear Lord?' But I say unto you: the Lord is good!"

Then, as the congregation's response exploded with a chorus of "Hallelujah," Jones took the microphone from the pulpit and stepped down one step with his hand rubbing his forehead in a sign of deep thought or prayer. Jimmy smiled to himself, amazed, and perhaps slightly admiring, at the preacher's bogus display of emotion. The congregation lapped all of it up with a growing fervour.

Jones raised his hands to silence the crowd. "So I say come, brothers and sisters! Leave your burdens right here at this altar. Leave them right here, and the Lord will use them to His will. He needs us, my friends! He needs us to give Him an army! Are you ready, brothers and sisters? Are you prepared to give unto Him your burdens?"

The congregation responded with an "Amen" that rattled the rickety windows of the church. Jimmy now noticed people were moving down the aisles, pushing wheelchairs and leading old folks using walkers. Some were carrying sick children, and others were leading mentally ill family members. At the front of the line was a couple that was holding each arm of their teenage daughter. Jimmy recognized her—she was Lucy Doyle, a girl from his elementary school class who had some mental disorder. He had picked on her mercilessly when he was in first and second grade. Eventually, her parents had sent her to a Catholic school. Jimmy had to keep himself from rolling his eyes as the realization of what he was witnessing dawned on him. Brother Jones had miscalculated this one—Lucy had a disorder, one Jones would not cure with powerful preaching and flowery words.

"I see this girl has been suffering her whole life, is that right?" Brother Jones called out to the congregation.

Her parents nodded affirmatively. Their daughter seemed confused, as though heavily medicated. Slowly, she lifted her head and looked around quizzically. Jimmy saw fear in her eyes when she looked at Jones. She struggled.

"Ah, hold her now, Mom and Dad! Keep her there. The Lord has a plan for this girl. This girl who has suffered this terrible affliction shall be free. I tell you, I shall liberate her! She will be a soldier in the Lord's army, and your family shall live in a peace you haven't known in many a year."

Brother Jones lifted his right hand, and two of his deacons stepped forward wearing leather gloves of their own. Carefully, they removed Jones's glove. Jimmy, still trying not to roll his eyes about the whole spectacle, noticed again that Lucy's eyes were wide with horror. Her mouth hung open in a silent scream, and the vessels in her forehead popped up under her increasingly red skin.

"Oh, there is a demon inside this girl, and I am here to release him! Sister Lucy, you will be free! I call to you Lucy and command you to be free, in the name of the Lord!"

Brother Jones slapped his hand down on Lucy's face, gripping it by the sides and holding it there for a few moments. He bent his head in silent concentration, then he released her face and stretched his arm up above his head with a flourish. Lucy shook almost uncontrollably in her parents' arms. They looked down at her, crying tears of joy, praising the Lord. Lucy's seizure continued for nearly a minute, and doubt crept into Jimmy's belief that what he was witnessing was a mere sideshow. He could feel a strange energy in the air.

Suddenly, Lucy's body went limp, her head rolling to the side until her lifeless eyes were staring straight at Jimmy. A chill ran up his spine as he realized what had just happened. The girl wasn't healed—she was dead.

As the Doyles dragged their dead daughter away, praising the lord and weeping tears of joy, the next couple approached: a middle-aged man and his wife, pushing an old woman in a wheelchair who was reaching out and begging the congregants for help. The worshippers ignored her, drowning out her frail pleas with a rollicking rendition of another Southern hymn.

Brother Jones glanced over his shoulder at Jimmy, smiled, and gave a small wink.

Jimmy Vance grinned back at him, thinking, *I'm home.*

The Woods

1.

On Monday, Jack awoke with an unusual feeling—a feeling that only grew as the day progressed. The air was electric, and he could barely keep his mind on lessons or lectures. In each class, he focused more on the clock than anything else until the lunch bell finally rang out. When he entered the cafeteria, he hoped his friends would provide a distraction. He was wrong.

As he set his food down at the table, he heard Mike Shore making plans. It seemed Randy had told their friends all about their encounter at the park and Leo's theory about Stephanie Caine's disappearance. This got everyone riled up, especially Mike.

"Look, we have to do something," Mike said. "We can't just sit here on our asses."

"Dude, we're not cops. What are we supposed to do about it?" Joe Lambert asked, kicking his enormous feet on the table.

Jack chimed in, "Joe's right. What can *we* do they can't do?"

"The police?" Mike asked. "Jesus, guys, it's not what they can or can't do, it's what they *aren't* doing! Leo might be onto something here. Have you seen any searches in town? Doesn't that seem weird to you guys? Aside from the 'Wanted' posters and the news reports, have you seen *any* sign that the BPD is doing a thing about this? I mean, this is a teenage girl. Why isn't this all over the news on every TV station? Why isn't the mayor giving press conferences? It's like they gave up before they started. Now they're saying Stephanie just up and took off with some guy. Total BS!"

Jack asked, "How do we know she didn't?"

It was a reasonable question. Stephanie was a beautiful girl, she always had been, and it wasn't only because of her bright red hair. She had a perfectly defined face and large, dark brown eyes. Her looks alone intimidated most of the boys. When you added in her confidence and the fact she stood about five-nine, and it was amazing any of them had the nerve to talk to her at all.

"Well, for one, none of her friends have heard from her. I mean, look at Mindy Luden," Mike said, pointing across the cafeteria to a girl who was weeping with a small group of friends. "She's a wreck! If Stephanie had taken off with some guy, don't you think she would have called her best friend? And then you guys get chased by some weirdos at Devils Glen, the same place Brad Loman says he left her! That's a coincidence?"

Joe took a swig of his orange juice, most of which promptly flowed over his lower lip and dribbled down his shirt. He wiped it away with his hand and said, "Yeah, I get it. It's all weird, but it still doesn't answer my question. What can *we* do? We're not cops! We can't search people's homes, we don't have frigging bloodhounds, we don't even know where to begin. The only thing we can do is run around like idiots. Maybe get ourselves in trouble."

"He's right," Randy said.

"Thank you," Joe replied.

"No, I mean *him*," Randy said, directing a thumb at Mike. "We need to do something, doesn't matter what. The police have dropped the ball on this thing, or they don't care, or hell, maybe they're in on it, I don't know. But we have to do something."

"Excellent," Mike said.

"But *what*, exactly?" Jack asked. "I mean, I'm all for saving Stephanie if we can. But *how*? What do we do?"

"Look," Randy replied, "Here's what we do. We go out and search the town, street by street, or maybe we search the parks. I mean, if I was a killer, that's where I'd go to dump a body. If we see something suspicious, we group text with information."

"And then what?" Jack asked.

"We call the police or we take matters into our own hands. Either way, we must try. I don't know why, but I think it's what we're supposed to do. It *feels* like the right thing." Randy shrugged and looked around the table. The other guys were silent for a moment, but they had arrived at an unspoken decision.

"OK," Jack said. "What's the plan?"

2.

There were four major parks in Bettendorf—Middle Park, Devils Glen, Crow Creek, and Sunnycrest. The boys split into three groups of two, and they assigned each pair an area of town to search. Mike and Brian Westerdale would go to Crow Creek, a sprawling park on the northeast edge of the city bordering on Pleasant Valley. Besides the softball fields and picnic spots, it had a large wooded area with a flooded quarry. Joe and Shaun Porter would investigate Middle Park and the Lagoon, a quaint little duck pond in the middle of town. It left the remaining two parks for Jack and Randy—Devils Glen and Sunnycrest.

To avoid the creeps who had chased them, they agreed it would be best to enter the Devils Glen from the southern end, which meant that they would have to hop fences and sneak through some yards to get there. It didn't have an entrance on that side, but it was worth the extra effort to approach from that end. It offered the safety of tall rocky cliffs that overlooked Duck

Creek. From that vantage point, they could survey the entire park quickly, and if discovered, the cliffs would provide a natural barrier for a quick retreat.

Running on adrenaline, the boys made it to Devils Glen early. As they broke through the brush, carefully feeling their way toward the edge of the cliff, Jack saw there was plenty of moonlight peeking through the oaks to light their way. The park itself seemed to glow. At the cliff's edge, they crouched down and scanned the area.

The creeps were still exactly where they had been on Saturday afternoon—under the picnic shelter at the top of the hill. The one in the white T-shirt was staring down the main road, looking at nothing much in particular, while the other two were skulking on the far side of the shelter. Then, as Jack's eyes further adjusted to the light, he could see that the white-shirted creep was interacting with someone away from the shelter in the shadows of some trees. Randy leaned forward, noticing the same thing.

"You see that?" he whispered.

"Yeah," Jack replied. "Who are they talking to?"

"Don't know. I can't see who it is. Maybe we should try to get a better look. Over there, there's a spot—"

Randy took another step to the edge of the rock cliff. His foot knocked a pebble down into the water, causing a small but echoing splash in the creek below. Horrified, the boys looked at each other and back at the creeps, all of whom now were searching in their direction. The creeps ambled down the hill toward the creek.

The white-shirted guy scanned the rock wall, his eyes slowly drawing up to the ridge until he appeared to be looking directly at the spot where Jack and Randy hid. He let out a laugh that sounded like death itself and pointed straight at Jack. Randy raised a finger to his lips and, motioning for

Jack to follow, the two backed away from the cliff's edge. They held their breath as they made their way back through the park and to their bikes.

Once they were finally peddling back down Central Avenue, Jack checked behind them and then called for Randy to slow down. "So what do ya think?" he asked.

"I don't know," Randy replied. "Something isn't right about those guys, that's for sure."

"Yeah, but we still don't know they had anything to do with Stephanie's disappearance. They're just sitting around looking weird. That's not a crime."

"Yeah, I don't know what to think," Randy said. "I mean, these are the same dudes who chased us the other day."

"True. If they are the kidnappers, maybe they've got her held up somewhere. Those caves over by the creek? That would be the perfect place. Maybe that was why they chased us—to keep us away."

Randy sighed. "But how do we *know*? We don't. Plus, if they had her in a cave, why would they draw attention to themselves by hanging around?"

"You're right," Jack said.

"We need to be patient. We got information tonight—that's worth something. Don't you think?"

"I suppose."

They concluded there wasn't much to do about the men, at least not at that moment. Satisfied to be putting a distance between themselves and the creeps at Devils Glen, the boys continued their way back down Central Avenue toward the second of their two assignments.

3.

Sunnycrest Park was quiet and bathed in the light of a quarter moon as Randy and Jack rode across the field to a small picnic shelter at the edge of a small one-acre patch of trees, known to the neighborhood kids as "the woods." Thinning branches swayed slowly in a light breeze. Jack doubted they would find much of consequence. Sunnycrest was a quiet little place, rarely used by anyone aside from Jack and his friends. He hoped the peace would give them a chance to brainstorm.

Suddenly, out of the eastern end of the woods came the sound of someone walking through fallen leaves.

"Holy shit, you don't think those guys followed us all the way here, do you?" Randy asked.

"I don't see how. No, I'm sure no one followed us," Jack whispered, looking back to the trees.

"Yeah, could be," Randy replied. "But I don't think so."

To be safe, the boys quietly lowered their bikes to the ground and hid behind two trash cans. After a moment, a figure passed through an opening in the trees as it made its way west into the deeper part of the woods. The figure looked to be a man, a rather large man at that. It was hard to make out much else, except for a slight limp. Both boys could easily see it was not one of their friends. They crept into the woods and followed the lumbering figure, keeping him in sight as he made his way through the brush.

Randy whispered, "Looks like he's heading toward the cellar."

Jack nodded and continued along the path. In the center of the woods was an old cellar, the only structure that remained of an old farmhouse demolished decades ago. The term "cellar" was too generous a word. It was little more than a big hole in the ground with various bits of old furniture and appliances haphazardly piled into it. As they approached, they saw that the man was slowly climbing down into the cellar. He was older, probably in his fifties or sixties, but well built for his age with thinned-out, unkempt white hair.

The boys crouched behind a pair of trees at the edge of the cellar. From their vantage point, they could see the man was approaching a discarded freezer—the kind people keep in their garages for extra meat and frozen foods. It had a small hole in the door. The man peered in, chuckled vulgarly, then pulled a set of keys from his pocket, unlocked the door, and opened it wide. What the boys saw inside brought a gasp from Randy. However, the man was so preoccupied with what he was doing, he didn't hear a thing.

Inside the freezer was a girl, chained up and gagged. For a moment, Jack thought they had found their prize, but he soon realized this girl wasn't Stephanie Caine. She appeared to be in her mid-teens, about Jack's age, perhaps. She was conscious and obviously in some discomfort as she tried to communicate with the man through the duct tape covering her mouth. Oddly, from the look on her face, she didn't seem scared. She looked angry. There was a fire in her piercing eyes as they peered through strands of long dirty black hair. She kicked at the man, hitting him full in the chest, and he responded with a grunt and a punch to her face.

"What did I tell you about that?" he snarled. "More of that and I'll add another chain, but this time I'll tie it someplace that won't feel so good." The man, huffing and groaning, reached into the back of his pants. "I got one right here in my pocket." He produced a shiny metal chain from his pants. It didn't seem like anything that would hold a person in place for long.

The shock of what he was seeing quickly faded. Jack glanced at Randy and motioned with a nod toward the scene below.

As Jack slowly led the way down into the cellar, the girl in the freezer noticed their presence. She craned her neck, sniffed the air, looked back at her captor, and kicked him hard once in the chest with one dirty bare foot and then again on his shoulder with the other, which produced a sharp cracking sound. The kicks sent the man reeling backward several feet. He cursed once and whipped the chain at the girl. Blood and flesh splattered into the air and back across the man's face.

As the man wiped his face, Jack seized the opportunity. He grabbed a large stone, ran as fast as he could across the cellar floor, and in one swift motion, struck the man in the back of the head. Before the guy could respond to the unexpected attack, Randy tackled him from behind and hit him with the stone.

Jack rushed to the girl and pulled on one chain, thinking he would use it to yank her out of the freezer. Instead, to his astonishment, the chain came away freely. The remaining chains on her legs and wrists came free just as easily. He helped her out of the freezer and untied her wrists—and then their eyes met.

—her red eyes.

They were red from lid to lid and filled with fury. When she returned his gaze, he felt time stop, and a swirl of lights and colors raced around the pair as they stood there for several moments, staring at each other in a daze. Her eyes changed to blue. Jack stood awestruck by her gaze.

At first, the girl seemed equally mesmerized, but then her expression changed to something very different. Was it fear? Uncertainty? Shock? All of them at once? Yes, all those emotions crossed her face as she pulled back, staggering for a moment beside the freezer. With some effort, she shook her eyes away from Jack's and looked down at her captor, who now lay under Randy's knee. Her lips peeled back, showing white sharp predator's teeth, and gave him a low growl. She took a step forward, but Jack instinctively stepped toward her, blocking her path. Rage flashed across her face, but when she looked into Jack's eyes once more, anger morphed into uncertainty.

She let out a long sigh, growled under her breath, "I don't believe it," turned, leaped out of the cellar in one smooth motion, and was gone.

"What the hell? Where did she go?" Randy asked.

"Oh, you fools," the man cried. "What have you done?"

The boys asked him many questions before calling the police, but his only response remained, "You fools! What have you done?"

The BPD

1.

Something confused officer Mark Warren. The two boys who stood before him were telling a bizarre story about a girl held captive in a freezer by the large old man they somehow had bound with silver chains. Both seemed honest in their descriptions, right down to the kidnapped girl and the clothes she was wearing. Their story about how she had somehow leaped ten feet into the air out of the cellar seemed fantastical, but the old guy denied nothing.

"OK, wait a minute guys," Mark said, interrupting the louder of the two boys. "What's your name again?"

"Randy Wall."

"And you?"

"Jack Davies."

"And you both say you saw this man keeping a girl locked up in that freezer over there?"

"Yes, sir," the boys answered simultaneously.

"And she wasn't the missing girl? Stephanie Caine?"

"No."

"And your name, sir?"

"Richard. Richard Loomis."

"And where do you live, sir?"

"Four forty-five Twenty-Third Street. Right over there, past them apartments."

"OK, and you deny nothing these boys say?"

"No, I don't deny a word. I don't want to answer any more questions."

Mark's eyes widened. "Oh, is that right? Well, I hate to break it to you, mister, but you're gonna have to answer a lot of questions by the time tonight is through."

"Uh huh," the old man said casually.

"These are some severe charges here."

"I understand," Richard replied.

"Let me ask you, Loomis: you spend much time over in the Sunset Circle area?"

Richard briefly glanced at Mark with a hint of surprise lingering in his eyes. "Nah. Why would I want to hang around those stuck-up richies?"

"Dude, he doesn't even care he got caught. You believe that?" Randy cried out.

"Quiet!" Mark snapped. "What exactly were you boys doing out here in the middle of the night, Mr. Wall? A school night, no less."

The one named Jack answered, "I'm sorry, Officer Warren. We were just hanging out when we saw this guy walking through the woods. I mean, no one walks through these woods at night, so we followed him. With Stephanie Caine getting kidnapped and all, everyone's been on high alert."

As Mark considered the boys for a moment, another police car pulled into the park, and two officers strolled to the woods.

The first officer said, "Heya, Warren, we'll take it from here. Thanks, buddy."

"What do you mean, Jim? I was the first on the scene."

The other officer replied, "Hey, no problem, buddy, but the chief wants to see ya down at the station. Says it's important. Sent us out here to take care of this thing, so I guess he wants to see ya bad."

"What? The chief?" Mark asked.

"Yeah, sorry, Warren," the other officer said.

"The chief is still at the station?"

"Oh yeah, he's working late, I guess." Jim flipped through his notepad to take down statements. "You better get a move on. Don't worry about his whole thing. We got this."

As Mark stormed back to his cruiser, he heard one officer ask, "What the hell were you doing out here in the woods? Don't you know it's a school night?"

When he arrived at the station, Mark saw one of the few cops on the force who would still speak to him, Paul Wojakowsky.

"Heya, Mark," Paul said.

"Hey, Wojo, how's it going?" Mark replied.

"Not too bad. Back already?"

"Yeah, I guess the chief wants me."

Paul hesitated for a moment. "Ah," he said finally.

"Know anything about it?" Mark asked.

"No idea. Didn't know the chief was here. You do something you shouldn't have?"

"That depends on your point of view, I guess."

"Mind if I give you a word of advice, as your old mentor?"

"Your advice is always welcome."

"Tread lightly, Mark. Things are tense around here if you haven't noticed. You're a good guy, probably the best cop on the force. We need all the good ones we can get around here, ya know? So watch your back. Got it?"

Mark smiled appreciatively. Paul was a good guy, one of the few. "Thanks, Wojo. I'll be careful."

Paul grabbed him by the upper arm and looked around to make sure no one was nearby. "I mean it, buddy. You gotta watch your tail. I'm only telling you this because I'm worried about you. You know me, I don't worry easily. People are talking, and they ain't talking sweet."

"What are they saying?"

Paul let go of his arm and considered the question for a moment. "Let's talk about this another time. Just be careful and do me a favor. Lie low, OK? Don't go nosing around Sunset Circle, or whatever it is you're doing these days. Make them think you're wising up, at least for a while."

"OK, Wojo. Thanks for looking out for me. I appreciate it."

2.

A few minutes later, Mark was sitting in front of Grover Lane, Bettendorf's soft and squishy chief of police. Chief Lane had no neck to speak of, and his large round head looked like it was sitting directly on his shoulders, the skin from his double chin pouring over the top of his uniform collar. His chair squeaked as he sat there staring at Mark, obviously uncomfortable with confrontation.

"Hey, Chief, did you have a reason you wanted to talk?" Mark asked finally.

"Oh yes, I do. I was just thinking about how to put it. Mark, we all know you've been under a lot of stress these past ten years."

"Now hold on there, Chief. I think I know where you're going with this. There's nothing to say about that. That's all years in the past."

"Well now, Mark, I don't think that's true. I believe that you're underestimating the effect that whole—thing had on you."

"Thing, Chief?"

"Yes, Mark. I mean, come on—you lost your wife. That's just not something you can shake off like a twisted ankle. You gotta deal with the loss, that's what they say. You gotta come to terms with it, I think. Not to mention her condition all those months before she passed."

"Her—condition?" Mark sat up in his chair and forced himself to keep from walking out of the office.

"Yes, well, you know. Your wife's mental condition." Chief Lane squirmed in his chair.

"Her condition was just fine!"

"Look, Mark, no one is saying she was crazy! You must understand, we're all just concerned for you. It's been ten years now, and, well, it seems like you should put all this stuff behind you, that's all. I know it's difficult."

"You know what that's like, do ya, Chief? And it's been nine years, Chief. Nine!" Mark was leaning forward further in his seat, his hands throttling the arms of the chair.

"Easy now, buddy. I'm not looking for trouble here. I need you to ease up, that's all." The chief reached out for a drink of water from a glass with the words *World's Greatest Boss* emblazoned on the side.

"Ease up? How?"

"Well, ya see, there's grumbling from on high about you. There are concerns about your recent interests, I guess you could say."

There it was. Mark sat back in his seat. "On high? Who would that be? You're the chief of police, aren't you?"

"Oh, well yes, I am, but I have bosses, Mark. I still must answer to people, just like you must answer. You know how it goes, buddy."

If he calls me "buddy" one more time, I'll punch him in the nose, Mark thought. Instead, he said, "OK, I get that. So what are they grumbling about?"

"Well, there's concern about your off-duty, or should I say, *extra*-duty activities. You're spending an awful lot of time around the Sunset Circle area these days, I'm told." Chief Lane's statement was unusually direct. He was apparently getting information from someone.

"I like the area. I might look to buy." Mark smirked and crossed his legs.

"I'm told you're harassing residents. What's that all about?"

"Since when is asking a few questions harassment?"

"I'm just telling you, Mark. I'm not arguing with you. You need to be careful. People are watching, and that's all I'm gonna say."

3.

Ten minutes later, Mark drove his cruiser up Eighteenth Street to Central Avenue and, hesitating for only a moment, turned onto Sunset Circle. He could feel eyes upon him while he sipped his coffee and took a bite from a double chocolate energy bar. Mark looked at the worn photo clipped to his dashboard and read the words at the bottom—words he'd written years ago.

Seek the gates and save the boy.

The Possession of Jennifer Warren

1.

They married on June 7, 2002, on the banks of the Mississippi River just off River Drive near the 74 bridge, with fifty close friends and family in attendance. Just out of college, the couple had little money, though their prospects weren't too bad. Mark took his criminal law degree and got himself a job at the Bettendorf Police Department—his academy training would start only a week after the wedding. Jennifer got her credentials and taught English at Saint Mark's School in the old Bennett mansion off Eighteenth Street.

With some help from Jennifer's parents, they put a down payment on a nice little brick house on Bellevue. The home wasn't extravagant, but Jennifer loved it and that was all that mattered to Mark. Iowa was a place where a young family could get a house without selling their souls. The house was within walking distance from Saint Mark's on the other side of Sunset Circle, north of Central Avenue, making it easy for them to manage with only one car.

They were well-matched in every way. Mark was tall and handsome with a strong masculine face and broad shoulders. She was average height with a pretty face and warm green eyes that lit up whenever she smiled. They shared the same tastes in most things and each challenged the other just enough to keep them on their toes.

One Sunday evening that July, after both Mark's and Jennifer's parents had left the couple's home, the young couple sat on their patio listening to the chorus of cicadas as they finished a bottle of wine.

"Wow, families. Ha!" Mark laughed.

"Wow, is right. Does it always have to come down to politics whenever we get together?"

"Good Lord, I know. How did my family get so damn conservative?"

"Iowa, perhaps?" she asked, snickering. "Just kidding! Honestly, I don't remember my parents being so liberal about everything. Is the entire world suddenly turning political?"

"I swear it is," Mark replied. "I think everyone should be moderate and modest."

"I agree. The middle is far more attractive."

"To the middle?" He raised his glass.

"To the middle!" Jennifer replied.

They laughed together for longer than the situation warranted and then sat for a while, listening to the evening sounds. Mark looked at her and asked, "How ya doing, buddy?"

"Honestly? I don't think I could be better," Jennifer replied. "I feel like everything is falling into place so easily."

"Yeah, it is. It's like we're naturals at this," Mark said.

"I know, right? I can't believe I get to live like this for the rest of my life!" Jennifer threw her head back and giggled.

"Ha! I couldn't agree more. It all seems like a dream. The house is perfect and living with you is so—effortless."

"I love our life," Jennifer said.

"Nothing else you could say could make me happier."

"We've chosen the middle path, Mark," she said as she kissed his hand. "And I love it. We could have made our way to Chicago or New York or sunny California, but we chose Iowa. Right in the middle. I think from here on out, for the rest of our days, we should always take the middle path."

Soon the pair fell asleep on the patio and didn't wake until the first rumblings of a midsummer thunderstorm nudged them from their dreams.

Jennifer started her teaching job in August, and for a while, things seemed to go well at work. The administrators were all happy with her, and the other teachers had nothing but kind things to say. If they noticed her struggling with a difficult student, one of them came to her with helpful advice. *There couldn't be a better situation for a fresh-out-of-college teacher,* Jennifer thought every afternoon as she graded papers or filed lessons.

The school was in an enormous old mansion, previously owned by one of the illustrious founding fathers of the town, William Bennett III, a railroad investor who made a massive fortune at the turn of the century. Jennifer's classroom was the former master bedroom, and the view looked out over most of downtown Bettendorf and the Mississippi River.

"It's the most beautiful place, Mark!" Jennifer exclaimed over dinner one night. "I can't believe it was once a family's house! Can you imagine being that rich? It's crazy!"

"Yes, I've seen it. Quite a place to go to work every day."

"Oh God, it's so beautiful, with all the trees and old stone staircases. There are these amazing statues of wolves in the back—and the trees! There are giant oaks everywhere you look. I can't wait to see it in the fall. And best of all, Mark? They say it's haunted!" Jennifer said joyfully. She had always been a lover of the paranormal, and she religiously watched every ghost hunting show on cable. In fact, she claimed to be sensitive to such things.

"Well, that's not a shock. The place looks creepy as hell. Didn't I hear there's a mausoleum on the property?"

"Oh my God, yes! It's so beautifully creepy!"

"Who's in it?" Mark asked as he poured two glasses of wine.

"Mr. Bennett's wife is in there. Griselda was her name."

"Griselda? Wow, what a handle!" Mark laughed.

"I know! From what I'm told, she was totally into the occult. She made her husband pledge to build her mausoleum right next to the house when she died." Jennifer's enthusiasm was contagious. Mark smiled at her, loving the moment. "How did you find out all this stuff?" he asked.

"Our librarian, Mildred Helmsley, told me. She's ninety-three years old and sharp as a tack. She used to work at the mansion back when it was still a functioning estate."

"So you work in a haunted house?"

"Oh my God, yes! There's Mr. Bennett and Griselda. People see him in various parts of the house, but they mostly see her outside on the grounds."

"Well, be careful. Those old places have all kinds of halls and tunnels. Don't go getting yourself lost." He laughed at the thought.

"It's so fascinating. Who knows? I might just write a book about it."

"I think that's an excellent idea, buddy," Mark said, picturing her hunched over a laptop, plunking away at the keys. He thought he might make room for her to do her writing. Maybe the front bedroom—at least, until it was a nursery.

"You know that Sunset Circle area over there by the school? It seems like all the residents enroll their kids in the school. The families are all super-involved too. Kinda weird."

"How is that a bad thing?"

"I don't know—the intensity of their involvement seems odd. It's hard to explain. And they seem oddly interested in me—us. They're always asking when we're gonna start our family, what our plans are. Stuff like that."

"Well, I guess it's not surprising. We are newlyweds."

"Yeah, I know," Jennifer replied. "It seems intense. I'm not used to strangers asking me about personal things like that."

"I think you might be a little paranoid from all the spooky stuff you're finding out about the place. I'm sure they mean no harm. People love babies, that's all. Babies and puppies."

Jennifer sighed. "I suppose you're right. My parents sure are asking a lot about it."

"Well, maybe we should think about it. We're doing pretty well, and there's no sign that's changing soon, except for the better."

"Are you ready for that?" Jennifer wore a smile that came from happiness, but also from surprise. "It's a pretty life-changing thing."

"Uh, yeah, that's for sure. But I think I'm as ready as I will ever be. I mean, who's ever ready for that? You make it work, ya know?"

Jennifer smiled again and laid her head back against her chair, staring at Mark with so much love he thought he could never look away. Taking his hand and kissing it, she closed her eyes and seemed to say a silent prayer. Her hands gripped his palm, squeezing his fingers between her own. Then her eyes opened, and it seemed to Mark like a cloud passed over his wife's face. She shivered once, gazing at the ceiling as if listening to some unheard sound.

"You OK?" Mark asked. "Hey, I was just talking. We have plenty of kids—there's no rush."

"No, I loved what you said. I feel a headache coming on." She leaned her head back against her chair again, and her smile returned, though this time with a measure of something else beneath it.

2.

The screaming began at 4:00 a.m.

Mark woke up to his wife crying out so loudly it seemed she would tear out her throat. Jennifer was still asleep, crying out and struggling against something. She was having a nightmare. Mark nudged her on the shoulder, but she didn't wake. He tried again, but she continued to fight as if someone was on top of her, holding her down by the shoulders.

"Hey, buddy! Wake up!" he cried.

Jennifer's eyes popped open, red and tearing. She was apparently disoriented because she balled up her fist, punched Mark in the side of his head, and jumped out of bed, looking around the room as if she was readying herself for an attacker.

"Hey, Jennifer," he said, holding out a hand. "It's OK, calm down. You had a nightmare."

She glared over at him and let out a brief hiss. Then a change came over her and she calmed. She held a hand over her quivering lips and fell to her knees in tears. Mark rushed over and held her there on the floor, kissing her head as she lay under his chin. She wrapped her arms around him and squeezed until Mark thought she might knock his wind out.

"Shh—hey now, just how bad was this dream?" he asked.

"Oh, Mark, it was awful," she replied, tears trailing down her face. "Like no dream I've ever had before. What happened?"

"You woke up screaming. Don't you remember?"

"The first thing I remember is standing here. I don't even remember getting out of bed."

"You don't remember screaming or hitting me in the head?" he asked, chuckling.

"I hit you? Oh my God, I'm so sorry! Are you OK?"

"I'm fine, though I'll think twice before I argue with you. You've got quite a left hook there." Mark stretched his jaw and rubbed his temple.

At that moment, a great pounding rang throughout the halls of the little house. The sound reverberated, rattling the old windows and knocking knickknacks from shelves. It continued for more than a minute, increasing in volume but not rhythm. Over and over it repeated until it became so loud that the Warrens covered their ears, each of them wide-eyed with shock. Then, just as quickly as it started, it was over. Silence. Mark ran to the closet and grabbed his service revolver.

"Buddy, I'm gonna go check around the house, OK? You wait here. If you see anything, call out!"

Mark checked every room, the basement, and the attic, but found nothing. After exhausting every place a person could hide, he gave up and returned to bed. Jennifer was awake with the covers pulled up to her nose. The two of them lay together the rest of the night, unable to sleep. The next day, Jennifer seemed somewhat better in the morning and though exhausted, she felt well enough to go to work.

"You sure about that, honey? They won't fire you for taking a sick day, ya know?"

"No, I'm fine. And I think I'd rather not be alone." She gave him a small, half-hearted smile.

"Yeah, I understand. But if you feel ill, get yourself home, OK? I can always get someone to cover the rest of my shift or the whole day if I need to."

There were no more nightmares that week. The Warrens tried to get on with their day-to-day lives, hoping it would all blow over. Jennifer worked late more and more, and Mark wondered if she was avoiding their home.

The nightmares returned the next week, worse than before. Jennifer described dreams where someone was crawling on top of her in bed and trying to suck the life out of her. Violent convulsions overcame her, and Mark thought maybe he should restrain her at night. When he suggested this idea, Jennifer begged him not to do it. "No, Mark! If you do that, she'll take me. I won't be able to fight back!"

"What do you mean? There isn't anyone in bed with you, buddy. You're just having nightmares. You know that, don't you?" Mark asked.

"Oh, Mark. In those moments, I can't tell what's real. It feels like this old woman is actually on top of me."

"Old woman? What old woman?" This was the first time she'd described the attacker from her nightmare.

She paused for a moment, like she was trying to decide how to answer the question. Finally, she replied, "I don't know who it is. She's horrible. She says awful things. And she has no eyes."

"No eyes?"

"Just two big dark sockets. And her mouth is always open like she can't close it. But she somehow she speaks through it. The sound comes out, but her jaw never moves."

"Jesus Christ! This is crazy. What does she say to you?"

"It's too awful. I don't want to think of it."

"Honey," Mark cautiously said, "I think maybe we should see someone. A professional, maybe."

"You mean a psychiatrist?" she asked.

"Yes."

"I'm not crazy, Mark. But I agree we should seek professional help."

"Good," Mark said. "A therapist?"

"No, not a therapist. We should bring in a parapsychologist, someone who deals with the supernatural. I know it sounds crazy. Something unnatural is happening. It's not in my mind!"

Mark considered it for a moment. Though he usually might have scoffed at the notion, what they'd been through seemed unnatural even to him, and he couldn't explain the pounding on the walls from that first night.

"OK, you got it. But on one condition: if this doesn't work, you gotta seek therapy."

"Agreed," she said.

3.

After an hour of Googling, Mark had a name and the number of a man in Davenport who taught religious studies at Saint Ambrose University. Dr. Martin Truman was his name. On the phone, his voice sounded like he'd been chain smoking for thirty years. Mark made it clear just how desperate he and his wife were, explaining the violence of Jennifer's dreams and the precarious position of their respective sanity.

Within days, Dr. Truman came to their home with two assistants, two tomboyish females, and an ancient man Truman referred to as "the seer."

"Don't mind us," Truman said. "Just go on about your business, and we'll try to do our thing without being too much of a pain in the ass for ya. Mikki and Rachael are usually quiet as church mice. You won't even notice they're around. And the seer—well, he does what he does."

The seer stood in the dining room, staring down the hall toward the master bedroom. He closed his eyes and cocked his head as if he was listening to something. After a few moments, he walked down the hall and did not return for thirty minutes. When he finally came back, the seer walked into the living room, sat down on the sofa, and fell asleep.

"Ah, don't mind him," Truman said. "He sleeps like that every now and again. When you're as old as the hills, you get that way. He'll wake up in about ten minutes, and we'll all have a little talk, OK?"

Truman instructed the girls to set up cameras in the bedroom and then pack everything else up.

"What are they doing?" Mark asked.

"You told me her episodes happen at night while she's sleeping. It only makes sense for us to record her sleep cycle, just to see what we can find. Nothing big, mind you. Just some infrared cameras, heat sensors, EMT recorder, and a video camera. Standard stuff."

Mark asked, "Is that necessary?"

Truman shrugged. "Well, I suppose that depends on how bad you want to find out what's happening around here. Hell, say the word, and we can pack up our shit and get the hell outta your hair. But if you're at your wit's end, like you said on the phone, I'd say you should let us do what we do. We're not a bunch of pervs here. None of us will get our jollies from watching you catch Zs."

"No, I didn't think—"

"We're only in this to help you people. So far, we haven't seen a damn thing in here," Truman said.

The seer woke up and looked around the room. He sat there for a few minutes, looking like he was trying to remember something, and then he held up a finger and motioned for Truman to come closer. Truman leaned in, and the old man whispered in his ear. When he finished, the seer stood and left the house.

"Well, I've got good news and bad news," Truman said. "The seer says the problem isn't with the house itself. He felt no haunting signs, no ghosts, so far as he could tell. The bad news—it seems he's not sure how or why. You work at Saint Mark's, right?"

Mark and Jennifer looked at each other. "Yes," Jennifer replied. "I teach there."

"Well, ya see, that mansion and the entire area around it are unusual, I guess you could say. A lot of rumors about that place. I know little about it, but if I were you, I'd keep to myself. Maybe get another job if you can. Might not be a bad idea."

"Did the old guy say something about the mansion?" Mark asked.

"In so many words. I need to think about it to get more details out of him. It's hard because he's old and stubborn, but when he mentions something specific, it's best to take heed."

After they finished setting up the bedroom equipment and instructed Mark how to turn everything on, Truman's team left, leaving the Warrens to sit and wonder about what had just happened. That night, Mark turned on all the sensors and cameras, then got in bed with Jennifer, who lay there staring at the various contraptions surrounding their bed.

"Oh, Mark, when you married me, I bet you never thought you'd have to put up with anything like this," she said.

"Ha. No, I guess I didn't expect to go to sleep in a reality show." Mark laughed, and Jennifer joined him.

At 3:00 a.m., Mark awoke to screaming unlike anything he'd heard before. Jennifer thrashed and flailed about, tossing the covers off the side of the bed. Her entire body tensed, and she seemed to strain against a dominant force with all of her strength. Finally, she sat up and let out a long piercing scream. Then, just as suddenly as it had begun, it was over.

It went on like this for the next week: terrible fits during the night, followed by relative peace and silence. Dr. Truman's team picked up their equipment, promising to give the word of any findings by Saturday. On Friday morning, Truman called Mark with news that none of the sensors or equipment picked up anything unusual.

"What does that mean?" Mark asked.

"It means that as far as our equipment goes, there's no evidence of a haunting in the classic sense. I honestly don't know what to think. Do you know if your wife has ever had any mental illness or a family history of it?" Truman was trying to be tactful. It didn't come naturally for him.

"Not that we know of. Nothing like this."

"I see. Well, if I think of anything, I'll let you know. One of my girls will drop off the audio and video recordings later this evening. It's yours, and we don't keep copies."

"What should we do with it?" Mark asked.

"Up to you. There's nothing important on any of it, so you can trash it. Sorry again, Mr. Warren. It's a hell of a thing you're dealing with. I can't imagine anything like it. Good luck, my friend."

When Mark got home that evening, the house was empty. He tried Jennifer's office, but the call went to voicemail. Mikki and Rachael dropped off the audio and video recordings and a large stack of readouts that meant absolutely nothing to Mark. He put it all in an upstairs closet and made himself a bourbon. Exhausted, he put on Frank Sinatra's In the Wee Small Hours, sat in his favorite chair, and fell asleep with the half-empty glass resting next to him.

Hours later, he woke up with a start and saw a dark figure standing before him in the dimly lit room. Instinctively, Mark reached for his revolver but then realized the figure was Jennifer. He sat back and let out a sigh. She made no sound or movement but stood there, still as stone, staring down at him.

"Buddy? Where were you? Why were you so late?"

She remained still, saying nothing. Shadows covered her face. Mark could barely see the reflection of the dining room light twinkling in her green eyes.

"Hey, you OK? What's going on? Jennifer?"

She startled him with her response. "The boy," she said.

"What?"

"The boy."

Mark leaned forward and took her hands. "Boy? What boy?"

"You must save him."

Mark stood up, keeping her hands in his. "Save who? I don't understand, Jennifer."

"I'm slipping away, Mark. I can't fight anymore."

"What do you mean?" Mark grabbed her by the shoulders. "Fight! Whatever you say, fight!"

"Mark?" she cried, almost pleading.

"Yes! What is it? What's wrong?"

"I have little time," she said, sounding like she was a hundred miles away. "You must find the gates. You must find them, Mark. It's what you must do. I know this now."

"What gates? Honey, you're not making sense! What are you talking about?" Mark shook her by the shoulders, trying to bring her to consciousness.

"I'm sorry, honey," she said. "I made a mistake."

"Mistake? What mistake?"

"I stuck my head where I shouldn't have. I found something I wasn't supposed to find. Or maybe—maybe I did what I had to do. Yes, perhaps that's it, maybe that's my part. You can save him. Seek the gates and save the boy. No one can find them but you, I'm certain of that."

"What gates? What boy? Jennifer? Jennifer! Jennifer!"

"Seek the gates and save the boy."

Jennifer's head fell forward, and Mark hugged her to his chest. She was still alive and breathing, but she wouldn't respond. He held her up by his arms and stood there with her for several minutes until he heard a soft sound. At first, Mark thought she was crying, but soon he realized it was laughter. He stepped back.

She stood there looking up at him with a smile on her face, a smile he'd never seen on her face before. Jennifer opened her mouth and whispered.

"She's with me now."

Then she turned and leaped through the large living room window, crashing through in an explosion of shards. She kept running, barely dazed by the jagged glass that cut her flesh into ribbons. Stunned, Mark stood there for a second, watching her run off into the night, unable to believe what he'd just seen. Then he came to and ran out the front door and into the front yard. There was no sign of her. Shaken, he felt the first migraine of his life coming on. It darkened his vision and made everything around him look fuzzy. Vertigo hit him hard. He fell to his knees.

"Jennifer!" he feebly called out.

As his world spun around him, Mark pulled out his cell phone and dialed 911.

4.

The police found her at 3:00 a.m. wandering the grounds of the Bennett mansion, naked and bleeding from the deep cuts all over her body. At the hospital, a young doctor told Mark that Jennifer had experienced an emotional breakdown. Mark was silent as he filled out the paperwork to have her involuntarily admitted to the Davenport Hospital's One North unit for observation and therapy. The doctors told him that with therapy and effort, she might get out in seventy-two hours.

She didn't.

Days turned into weeks, the weeks into months, and the months into years, until over two passed with no improvement. Mark refused to sell their home—he wanted her to come home to familiar surroundings. But for him, things were never the same. No barbecues. No family gatherings. No quiet evenings listening to the cicadas. Friends advised him to seek a divorce, to abandon her, and get on with his life, but Mark refused. He visited her every other day, which only brought more heartache and migraines. She was no longer the woman he'd married.

One night in early October, Mark received an uneasy call from a therapist at One North. A nurse had inadvertently left a door open earlier that evening, allowing three patients to escape the facility. Jennifer was one of those patients.

"How can that be?" Mark asked. "She's hardly moved or said a word in over two years!"

"Yes, we're shocked too. The Davenport Police have been in contact with your station. I'm sure you'll get a call soon. We are all very sorry, Mr. Warren. We'll let you know if we hear anything on our end."

Lightning flashed as a storm moved into the area. Loud booms of thunder rattled the windows, and rain poured down from the sky. Mark put on his uniform in a hurry and ran out to the cruiser. He drove from one end of town to the other, following the main roads between Davenport and Bettendorf—any route she could have taken on foot. The nurse explained that Jennifer was wearing nothing but a thin hospital gown. She would be wet and freezing in this weather.

After three hours of searching, Sergeant Wilkes of the BPD called Mark to tell him to go home. "We've got plenty of officers on the job, Mark. We don't need you out there. It's better if you're home in case she heads there."

He agreed and spent the evening sitting by the window, listening for any sign of movement outside. His head pounded, and he went to the kitchen for one of his pills. When he returned to the living room, something outside the window caught his eye. A flash of lightning illuminated the front yard. On the other side of the window, staring in through the window at him, was Jennifer. She was still wearing her hospital gown, soaked from the rain, and her eyes looked like they were bleeding.

Bleeding!

She stared at him for a moment, then turned and sprinted up the street. Mark rushed out the front door and chased after her through the rain and lightning. As he ran, he glimpsed something in her right hand, something shiny and metallic. She continued running straight through the entrance of Sunset Circle. Once there, she stopped and turned, screaming into the rainy night, holding a kitchen knife in her fist. Mark slowed, holding out a hand.

"Buddy! Calm down! Take it easy. Please, hand me the knife," Mark pleaded.

"Oh, Mark, I'm sorry for what they've done to us!"

"Who? Who's done something to us?"

"These people, Mark!" she screamed, pointing to the houses of Sunset Circle. "They're rotten, Mark! They sent her Mark! These people in their stuffy homes with their shitty names. They sent her and now she owns me!"

"Who? Who did they send?" Mark asked.

"Griselda! She's using me, Mark. I must stop her! I can't let her win!"

Jennifer held the knife up to her stomach and froze there for a moment. She closed her eyes and looked as if she was preparing for a great pain. "Mark, please forgive me!"

"No!" Mark cried. "Don't do it, Jennifer! We can stop them together! Whatever they're doing to you, we can fight it together. Just give me the knife!"

As he took a step toward her, she opened her eyes and said, "There is nothing else I can do. Please look away, Mark."

"No, Jennifer! No!"

Before he could reach her, she plunged the knife into her stomach and pulled it across her abdomen, slicing through her body with great effort. Jennifer collapsed to the ground as Mark reached her a moment too late.

He held her in his arms and wept. "Oh, what did you do? Oh, Jennifer, what did you do?"

She looked up at him, bloody tears running down her cheeks, and asked, "Remember what I told you before?"

"What do you mean?" he asked, choking back tears.

"Mark, you are the only one who knows. Only you can do it."

"What do you mean?"

"Seek the gates and save the boy."

5.

Months later—after the funeral, after the wake, after people stopped sending baked goods and precooked meals, after the horrific crying fits gave way to bitter loneliness, after he'd run out of family leave, after the songs on the radio stopped tearing his heart out, after the last of his belongings were boxed and ready for a move, Mark found a forgotten box of recordings. Dr. Truman's recordings from the investigation of their home—video recordings of the Warrens sleeping.

A thought came to him.

Mark carried the box into what used to be his office and hooked up the computer he'd just taken apart. He took out a disk marked "Warren Video" and slipped it into the drive. Within seconds, a video popped onto the screen of Mark and Jennifer sleeping. It was all that he wanted—to watch himself sleeping with his wife like he would never do again.

Then the nightmare began.

When he saw the telltale twitching and flailing, Mark almost removed the disk, but something told him to wait. He watched as Jennifer's nightmare intensified. He saw himself wake up. Jennifer was convulsing violently until finally she froze, her back arched, her hands clenched. Then all at once, she sat up and let out a terrible scream, a scream that sounded like it came from a wild animal.

Mark's blood froze and his muscles tensed. He saw something. Truman was wrong—the camera caught something that night, something the team had missed.

There was a flash, like an insignificant blip on the screen just as Jennifer sat up in the bed. It happened so quickly Mark had missed it. They all had missed it. Hands shaking, he moved mouse and brought the cursor back slowly, stopping it right at when Jennifer had come to a full sitting position. And to his horror, there it was, hidden in a fraction of a second. Just for the tiniest fraction of a moment, his wife's face was not her own. There, frozen on the screen, Mark saw someone else's face, almost as if someone had switched places with his wife for an instant. In that second, in that smallest point of a moment, Jennifer's face had changed.

It was the face of an old woman—an old woman with no eyes.

Of Darkness

THE TWO HOURS AFTER the rescue at Sunnycrest were a blur in Jack's mind. He remembered calling the police and waiting for them at the park. He remembered being asked lots of questions, most of them having more to do with why he and Randy were out there at night rather than about the kidnapper kneeling next to them. Eventually, the officers sent the boys off, reminding them to go straight home. When he made it to his bed, Jack's head was cloudy and full of the strangest questions.

What happened in that cellar? He asked himself over and over as he lay under the covers. Then his mind drifted to the girl and her ocean-moon eyes. Who was she, and where did she come from?

A breeze swept into his room from the open window, and for a moment he saw a shadow barely visible through the rustling curtains. It startled him out of his daze, and he instinctively pulled the covers up to his chin, thinking it was yet another ghost entering his room.

Slowly, Jack rose from his bed and crept over to the window, staying low. He ventured a peek outside but couldn't see a thing. He drew closer and scanned the areas to the right and left of his house. At first, he saw nothing, but just as he was about to go back to bed, he spotted someone in the alley behind his house—a girl looking up at his window.

She stood in the alley directly behind the neighbor's house, looking right at him. She stayed in place as if frozen. A sudden urge overcame him, and he stepped to the window as though he were being pulled out. He caught both sides of the windowsill, never breaking his gaze. He had to go to her.

He lifted a finger and whispered, "Wait there."

To Jack's surprise, she replied with a nod.

He moved downstairs and through the dining room to the kitchen, trying his best to be quiet. Anne stood in the kitchen, hands on her hips. Jack's heart leaped in his chest. "Jesus, Anne. You scared me half to death," he whispered.

"What are you doing, Jack?"

"Don't worry, I'll be right back," he replied, continuing through to the back door. He felt bad for ignoring her, but then again, imaginary sisters didn't have feelings. Once outside, he jogged out the back gate and past the driveway.

She stood in the alleyway, her feet spread apart as if ready for a threat. Their eyes met again, and an incredible surge of incoherence flooded Jack's brain. She took a step back, giving him a sideways glance.

"Who are you?" she asked.

Her voice was melodic, yet sad. Its tones, almost visual, floated in the air like animated fireflies. The exhilaration of the sound caught Jack's breath, and his eyes widened from the impact. His face reddened, and there was nothing he could do to hide it. He stood there before her, naked in his vulnerability.

"Jack Davies," he replied. At that moment, he hated his voice and wished he had not spoken. However, she seemed to have the same exhilarated reaction to the sound of his voice as he'd had to hers. Her head tilted imperceptibly fast. She seemed like something other than human. She had the form of a girl, but there was something different about her—something otherworldly.

As if sharing the same thoughts about him, she asked, "What are you?"

"A teenager?"

Her lips twitched into the slightest hint of a smile, taking a step closer. Jack retreated a step, sensing something dangerous about her. She shot a look at the back of the Davies house as if listening to a voice Jack couldn't hear.

"Are you a vampire?" Jack asked, embarrassed by the question.

She laughed. "What a boring notion."

"Not really. Vampires are kinda cool," Jack replied.

"Wait till you meet one."

Jack laughed, but she shushed him. She froze and looked again at the back of his house, as if someone had spoken to her. "Who lives with you?"

"My mom and dad," Jack replied.

"Do not take me for a fool, boy. Who else lives in that house? Someone is speaking to me."

"What do you mean? No one, I swear. My brothers have all grown up and moved away. One's in Chicago, one lives in Rockford, and the other lives in Davenport. I'm the only kid left," Jack said, and though what he said was true, somehow it felt like a lie.

Her gaze shot back at him in the blink of an eye with an accusatory glare, which slowly softened to a smile and a look of pity. She came to him slowly, saying, "Ah, he doesn't know, does he? Or he knows, but he has forgotten. Or is he pretending?"

Again, she stopped and looked at the house. She threw back her head. "Ha! And if I wanted to, what could you do about it? But don't worry. At this moment, there is no one on earth I would less like to harm."

"What are you talking about?" Jack asked.

The girl turned, striding confidently straight at him, stopping only inches away, her eyes dancing over the skin of his face. "Jack," she said.

"Yes." His voice cracked.

"Jack Davies? A simple name."

He laughed at himself, and she seemed hypnotized by the sound. "Well, it's the one they gave me. What's yours?"

"I have many names—some known by many, and some by none. However, I think you will know them all in time." She moved closer still and lifted herself onto her toes, leaning into his neck, sniffing his skin.

"I will?"

"In time."

"What can I call you?" He could barely form the words.

"Ava," she replied as she moved her face directly in front of his, their lips almost touching. Finally, she gave him a soft kiss, holding it for a few moments as electricity poured back and forth between them. With some effort, she stepped back, her pure white skin flushed in the moonlight.

"Oh my," she whispered, then shot another look at the house, smiling. "I think you will have no choice."

"Who are you talking to?" he asked. "No one's there."

"Oh, silly boy, you're asleep. And that silly hymn still plays in your mind. But you'll remember soon enough. It is time for you to wake—I think that's why I'm here. To wake you. Something is coming, and you must wake before it's too late."

"What do you mean? What's coming? Is it something bad?"

Her eyebrows lifted with a mixture of sadness and resignation. "Oh, yes."

"What is it?"

"I will not speak of it at this hour of night, but even I do not know all it will be. It has grown for many years, right here in your little town. But I am here now, and it is time for you to wake."

"Am I asleep? Is this a dream?"

"Everyone in this tired town has been sleeping for years, but this is no dream. It's time. Time for you to remember what you have forgotten. Look back through the seasons of your life and find what you have lost. Travel, young Jack."

"Travel? Where?"

"Unless I am mistaken, there was a time, not so long ago, that you can half remember, though you half forgot. Start there. You must travel to the land of the half-forgotten. Bring it back." She withdrew, turning to leave down the alley.

"The land of—what? What am I looking for?" he asked.

"Only you will know," she said over her shoulder.

"Wait! I don't understand a thing you've said. I have questions!"

Ava looked back at him with a mixture of sadness and love. "I wish I had the answers. But I will return. I doubt I could stay away from you even if I desired to do so, which I must admit I do not."

She gave a short laugh, tilted her head, and flew up the alley in a flash.

PEREGRINATING

1.

THE NEXT MORNING, JACK entered his first-period English class, still in a daze. He moved through the halls of Bettendorf High School, scarcely aware of the other students. When friends greeted him, he could hardly reply coherently. Jack took his seat next to Randy while the teacher wrote notes on the board.

"Dude, how ya doing? Did your parents take it easy on you?" Randy asked.

"Yeah, I guess."

"What's up? You seem out of it?"

"I swear to God, I feel like I'm floating or something."

"Looks like you hardly slept. I guess I didn't either. I'm still blown away by that whole scene. We gotta find that old guy. I heard the police just let him go. Do you believe that? A kidnapping and they let him go? And that girl too. We gotta find her."

"Don't worry about that. She found *me*," Jack said.

"The hell you talking about?"

"She came to my house last night after I got home."

"Shut up!"

"I'm serious." Jack told him all about the post-Sunnycrest activities that transpired outside his window and in the alley behind his house. Randy looked positively dumbfounded, and by the end of the story, he was the one who looked like he hadn't slept. Randy sat back in his chair, staring up at the ceiling. It was hard to tell if he was frightened or envious.

They could not talk any further because the teacher, Mr. Burton, directed the students to open their books to the next short story, "The Cask of Amontillado." Jack had read this one a few times on his own from a well-worn Poe collection, so he daydreamed instead.

His thoughts went immediately to Ava. For most of his life, girls had seemed to be a puzzle. Lucky for him, most of the other guys of that age were just as useless in that department.

Am I crazy, or did it seem like she was into me? Jack wondered.

Suddenly, he felt a cold sensation on the back of his neck. It started out almost like a slight breeze, but then grew until he finally looked over his shoulder to find the source, but could see nothing. The chill ran down his back, and the hair on his arms stood on end. For a reason he couldn't identify, he perceived that something was in the hall just outside the classroom. Jack got permission to go to the bathroom and made his way out.

The hallway was empty. The voice of Mr. Burton reading from the story faded out as he made his way toward the bathroom. In fact, all sound and awareness of others faded away. Jack got the sensation he had somehow left the school. Reality had changed, and he was no longer in a building full of students. He was alone. The halls had darkened, and a growing wind was now whipping through the tiled halls.

A moonlight glow was the only illumination as he made his way past many lockers and the occasional fire extinguisher. As he continued, Jack noticed a strange clicking sound, not rhythmic, but almost guttural, as if made by some strange creature. He heard footsteps behind him, just a few slow steps. When he turned to look, at the end of the hall he saw a dark shape of a man, tall as the ceiling, with arms like a spider's stretching out to the sides, his long bony fingers spread wide like the spokes of a web. The creature's head cocked from side to side, and though moonlight shone all around him, it did not illuminate him.

Then a voice came from the creature—a voice that creaked and wailed. Jack grew dizzy.

"Who are you?" the creature asked. "How did you find this place?"

Jack gasped and struggled for air. Slowly, he regained his equilibrium while the creature stood at the far end of the hall waiting for a reply, its head weaving from side to side and its arms almost beckoning.

Jack replied, "I don't know."

"Difficult to believe. One does not wander into this place by chance."

"I don't know how I got here," Jack gasped and took a step back. "I was heading to the bathroom."

"You lie!" the creature screamed, the sound piercing through Jack's body and sending him to his knees. "Only a traveler may find this place."

He moved toward Jack, singing a dark song. It sounded like a thousand organs clashing together; the words were of some language never heard by man, hideous to the ear, full of screeches and barking—low notes so deep Jack could feel them in his chest. The reverberations shook the walls of the school, causing the locker doors to burst open and rattle back and forth.

Jack threw himself to the ground, plugging his ears with his fingers, but the song remained in his mind. Through the song, there came a dark laughter soaring above the melody. Then, just when all hope had nearly fled from his mind, a powerful voice cut through the song—a voice that uttered just one word, but through that one word came hope and rescue, love and strength.

"Jack," the voice said.

It was Anne.

The creature hesitated, unaccustomed to being challenged in such a way. Could the creature hear her too? Jack wondered. How could that be possible? Anne isn't a real person.

"Who is there?" the creature inquired, his head craning anxiously this way and that. His erratic movements stilled, as if he was straining to find the source of this intruding voice.

With the creature distracted, Jack returned to his feet. But suddenly, an explosion shook the tiled floors, and he lost his balance, landing on his back. Jack pulled himself up to his knees when he heard a new song. Like a hymn, it soared over the cavern ceiling and silenced the dark aria, knocking back the diabolical creature a full three paces. This new song, though less overbearing than the monster's scream, held a quiet power that pushed back the darkness.

Jack turned his head, and there behind him stood Anne, clothed in a dress made of silk and clouds and flowers, bathed in a glowing light that shone all about her. She stretched her arms out to him and called in a voice that rang like the chimes of a thousand bells, "Come, dear brother. I have revealed myself to the creature, and you must come now!"

Jack pulled himself up, gathering every bit of strength to take one lurching step toward his sister. Her arms reached out, and he could feel a kind of energy rush to him, flowing through him, lifting his spirits, though he could still feel the influence of the creature's darkness behind him. Jack was being pulled in two different directions. He knew it would not be long before the creature regained his power and doubled his efforts. Jack broke into a wobbly run, barreling straight into the bright arms of his waiting sister just as the creature began another hideous wail.

The world turned white. Nothing but pure light filled Jack's vision, even when he closed his eyes. It felt as though his body was floating in a void. It seemed to Jack that he hung in that void for eternity.

The material world came back into focus. The tiled halls and locker-lined walls of Bettendorf High School came into view, and he could see that he was right back in the hallway just outside Mr. Burton's English class. Though he had been away for at least twenty minutes, apparently only a few moments had passed since he left the classroom. He could hear his teacher reading from "The Cask of Amontillado," perhaps a paragraph further than he had been before Jack had lost time. A gust of wind rushed into his face. Ava suddenly appeared before him in a flash, her eyes wide with fear.

"There you are! I felt you go—someplace. Where were you?" she asked, looking like she didn't know if she wanted to scold him, kiss him, or both. He still couldn't believe how fast she moved.

"I don't know. One moment I was walking down the hall, and the next I was in a dark world with a monster trying to kill me. Wait—what do you mean, you felt me go?" His voice was shaking, and he could barely keep from bursting into tears.

Ignoring the question, Ava asked, "What creature?"

"I don't know. Anne called him a creature." Jack said it before he could catch himself. Anne couldn't have been real; she had died sixteen years ago. He looked at Ava, cringing.

"She was probably right. But how did you go there? Do you remember entering? Did you go through a gateway? A door, maybe?"

"No, not that I remember," he replied.

He quietly explained to her how he had been in class and felt the cool breeze on the back of his neck and how he went into the hall to investigate. He couldn't recall the exact moment when he crossed over. "It was like everything changed and I was someplace else. What the hell is going on? And how did you know?"

"We have a connection, Jack, as I told you last night. I think it happened the minute we saw each other. Lucky for you, someone is watching out. You must protect yourself. Protect your thoughts and keep yourself grounded to this world, or the next time, she might not find you."

"Who?" he asked.

"Anne. Didn't you say she was the one who found you?"

"Yes. I mean, no. It's impossible! She doesn't exist!"

"Oh, Jack, you need to wake up. Tonight, when you are asleep, blow out that hymn like a candle, wake yourself, and dream."

"That makes no sense. How can I sleep and be awake?"

"It's easy. It is just the opposite of what you've been doing all along. Wake in your sleep and remember. You're a traveler, Jack. You must travel tonight. If you do, you'll remember what you've half forgotten." And with that she was gone, leaving him forming the words to another frustrated question.

He decided he had better return to class and try to make sense of what was happening. Jack's mind couldn't wrap itself around the idea that what was happening to him was real, so he did his best to pretend it was all a hallucination—Ava, the creature, the creeps, the old man in the park, all of it!

Randy looked up at him briefly and then back down at his book, saying, "Geez, where were you?"

"Just went out in the hall to get air," Jack replied.

"Did you fall into a pit or something?"

"Huh?"

"You've got dirt all over you."

2.

Jack lay in his bed that night, exhausted from the events of the past few days. He wanted nothing more than a full night of uninterrupted sleep. Unfortunately, Ava's words kept ringing in his mind.

Wake in your sleep and remember—you're a traveler!

He did not understand what that meant. And "The Hymn of Forgetting"? No matter how hard he tried, it made no sense. As he finally drifted off to sleep, a thought occurred to him and a voice spoke in his mind.

Now, Jack! You're almost asleep. Take control of it!

It all became perfectly clear. Jack was in charge of his subconscious, if only he could find an in-between place, somewhere between dreaming and waking, between the fantasy and the reality. That's where he'd find the power to travel into his memories. He didn't fight the sleeping feeling. Instead, Jack dove further into it, while keeping control of his thoughts.

Soon, he felt himself floating into a darkness unlike anything he'd ever experienced before. But he sensed something else beyond it—a place he needed to be. A shimmer beyond the black veil holding the answers and the key to all he had forgotten.

And so it was that Jack Davies finally entered the land of the half-forgotten and walked down the streets of Bettendorf on the night of a half-forgotten Halloween not so long ago.

THE HALF-FORGOTTEN

1.

IN THE MEMORY, THE sky is dark gray, and Jack is with his best friends Luke and Dan. All three boys are in cheap costumes, carrying large sacks of candy. Luke lives just down the street, and Dan is Jack's next-door neighbor. They are all ten years old—the first Halloween the boys could trick-or-treat without parents or a sibling tagging along.

As the hours passed, the number of young revelers dwindles until Jack and his friends are the only ones still roaming the streets. The wind picks up, blowing leaves and Halloween decorations across the sidewalk as they make their way up to Twentieth Street and then to Mississippi Avenue. Jack almost wishes he had worn his jacket, as his mother had advised.

"OK, you guys ready to do this?" Dan asks.

"What time is it?" Luke looks at the darkening clouds above.

Dan punches him lightly in the arm. "Why? You chickening out?"

"Heck no! I can't be home late is all. Plus, it looks like it's gonna rain." Luke appears every bit like someone who wants to chicken out.

"You afraid of a little rain, chicken?" Dan says.

"No way, I'm no chicken," Luke says.

"I'm ready too," Jack adds, trying to sound convincing.

"OK," Dan says. "Remember the plan. We go to the Bennett mansion and run up the back stairs, touch the wolves, and then come back down. Got it?"

The others nod, and the three of them make their way down Mississippi Avenue. There was a distinct feeling in the air that this was no doubt the witching night. Jack glances at the ominous sky just as a slight flash of lightning brightens the world around them. The boys stop and look at each other, increased anxiety present on all their faces.

"It's just lightning," Dan says.

"We can do this," Jack says. "We've been planning this thing too long to let a little lightning scare us."

The boys continue until they come upon the old wrought-iron fence that encircles the entire Bennett estate—all five acres. The street curves around to the right, and the great old entryway to the estate comes into view. Two stone pillars guard each side of the gateway with dimly lit gas lamps faintly glowing in the misty fall air. A cobblestone road runs past the gates, winding up a wooded hill lined on each side by gnarled oak trees. To the right side of the road, a tiny creek runs down the hill, passing through the mouth of a stone lion further up the drive.

The gates are, as always, wide open. To the left is a broken staircase leading up a steep hill to the former garden area and the grand stone staircase behind the mansion, upon which sit two colossal statues of wolves.

A light fog rolls along the hills and leaf-covered grounds of the old estate. The bony arms and fingers of tree branches arch over the broken staircase, and mist rolls along the undergrowth. Dan leads the way and Jack follows, with Luke keeping watch behind to make sure no one notices their entry. As soon as they cross the gates, Jack gets the distinct feeling that their entry has not gone unnoticed. The entire area is whispering.

Just then, something moves in the corner of Jack's vision just north on the other side of the primary drive.

"What?" Dan asks.

"Nothing. I thought I saw something."

"Dude, don't screw around. I'm freaked out enough as it is." Dan's voice sounds shaky.

"I'm not screwing around," Jack protests. "I thought I saw something over there on the other side of the road, but it must have been nothing. Come on, let's get this over with."

"Yeah, come on guys," Luke adds, stepping forward and taking the lead the rest of the way up the stairs.

More lightning flashes, and Luke's small silhouette seems overwhelmed by the gothic scene around him. It looks to Jack like they are journeying into some fairyland, into the heart of Halloween. Thunder rumbles in the distance, followed by a change in the wind. From the east comes a swift breeze carrying moisture with it and the smell of a rainfall soon to come. A few drops of water fall around them, and instinctively the three boys quicken their pace up the stairs.

As they reach the top, Jack steps into a large flat yard where the estate gardens had once stood. Some broken sculptures and parts of what must have been some stone structure are all that remain of the former gardens.

Again, a flash of lightning cuts through the darkness, illuminating the entire back of the mansion so that the boys can now see the massive stone wolves sitting on the railings at each end of the top of the grand staircase. The wolf on the left is looking to the west, while the one on the right looks east and, incidentally, right at the boys.

Suddenly, Dan yells out, "OK, here we go! On the count of three. One! Two! Three—now!"

The boys sprint as fast as their legs can take them. They quickly climb the stairs, two at a time, until one by one they find themselves at the top. Jack reaches the first wolf, touches it, runs to the second, and touches it too. The others do the same, and then they fly down the stairs as quickly as they came up them. When they finally reach the bottom, they stop to relish their victory and catch their breath. After a moment or two, the boys giggle. Dan leans on Jack's shoulder and attempts to say something, but the words can't get past his fits of nervous laughter.

Another flash of lightning hits, but Dan and Jack are laughing so hard they don't even notice. However, Luke lets out a gasp, staring wide-eyed back at the broken staircase to their right.

"Luke? What's wrong?" Jack asks after a moment. Following Luke's gaze, he sees it too.

At the top of the broken staircase stands a man, tall and well built. He appears to be watching them. All three boys freeze where they are. Jack gets a sudden urge to call out for his mom.

We're caught! This was a stupid idea. What were we thinking?

Jack's jaw rattles, and though he tries to speak, he can't form words. All he can do is stare at the man as though his mind and actions are under someone else's control.

"Guys! We gotta get out of here!" Jack finally whispers with great effort.

"Yeah, we'd better," Dan replies as if waking from a dream. "Must be the groundskeeper. I've heard he's mean."

"I don't think it's him," Luke says. "This guy looks scary."

"We should run," Jack says.

"OK, but let's split up," Dan says. "He can't catch us all. Luke, you go down the hill by Eighteenth Street. There's a hole in the fence there. Jack, you run around the far side of the house to Sunset Circle and then over to 21st. I'll go back up the wolf stairs and around the east side and meet you, OK?"

"Yeah," the boys reply in unison.

"Go!"

Jack takes off running around the west side of the mansion. The lightning continues to flash, and now he can feel the first drops of rain hitting his cheeks. He glances back before he rounds the corner and sees that the man is still standing at the top of the stairs, and he's looking in Jack's direction.

Jack continues around the corner of the mansion, making his way toward the servants' quarters, when he catches sight of the old mausoleum. Something about it makes him stop in his tracks. Usually, the sinister tomb itself would be enough to make a person want to turn around and go back the other way, but this time it isn't just the nightmarish ghouls on the corners of the facade that fill Jack with terror. On tonight of all nights, Jack sees that the mausoleum's massive stone doors are open wide.

Lightning strikes somewhere behind him, and the sound rings through his ears. Jack peers into the crypt as another bright flash of light illuminates the inside of the mausoleum. He sees the figure of a person covered by a thin white sheet lying on a stone slab. Griselda Bennett's lifeless body lies under that sheet.

A smell of rot and decay wafts from the dark resting place, crashing into Jack's face. He stumbles right and left, overcome by fear and the rancid smell. Before he finally falls, a cold black hand clutches his left shoulder, steadying him.

Jack looks at the hand, but cannot perceive any form or detail. It is twice the size of his little shoulder, and from it emanates pure dread. Another bolt of lightning strikes the roof of the mausoleum, producing an explosion that drives Jack backward ten feet. Gently, he lifts his head from the ground and peers again into the crypt. More lightning laces its way across the sky, once again brightening the entire world and illuminating the inside of the crypt. Jack spots something that nearly stops his heart.

At that moment, while a chain of lightning dances around the black-and-gray October sky, Jack sees the damned old woman, Griselda Bennett, sitting upon her bier facing him. The white shroud has fallen to her waist, and she is naked above it. Bare breasts, rotting and misshaped, droop downward like two dead geese. The woman's hair is a tangled dreary mess, and her mouth hangs wide, exposing two lines of long razor-sharp teeth. Her skin is pale and pristine but for several decaying wounds around her shoulders and neck.

Paralyzed, Jack lays his head back on the ground, staring at the flickering clouds above, waiting for the inevitable. A dark shadow of a man moves into view above him, and a devilish laugh falls from his mouth.

Then Griselda enters his field of vision and stands next to the dark man, her mouth still hanging wide. She methodically squats so that her face is directly over Jack's, a few inches above his nose. A putrid liquid leaks over her lips and hangs there on a string until it snaps free, dripping onto his chin.

As Jack loses consciousness, he hears a whistle followed by the sound of wolves' paws padding toward him across wet leaves.

2.

Jack awoke from the dream with his head pounding and a sense of suffocation clutching his chest. The vision he'd just lived through was something much more than a mere dream—it was a memory. But why had he not remembered it until now?

The hymn! Ava told him "The Hymn of Forgetting" that Anne sang was the reason he couldn't remember what had happened to him that night. It was why Jack had so many holes in his recollection.

If Ava knew something more than she was letting on, he had to make her talk somehow. The girl was a mystery, one of many that seemed to have taken over his life. The world as he knew it was fading into the background as a world of make-believe entered the fore. He decided at that moment he would take control of his life and figure out whatever forces were working against him.

Eventually, he fell back into a dreamless sleep.

Shadow Plans

Jimmy Vance stood behind Brother Billy Jones under the oaks of Devils Glen Park. Jones had never brought him along to one of his meetings. The preacher could be a bastard, but he treated Jimmy better than his father did.

"Now Jimmy, I need not remind you not to say a word, right?"

"Not a word, Brother Jones," Jimmy replied.

"Good. My friends might be a little put off by your presence, so try not to give them any reason to take notice of you. Understood?"

"Yes, sir. I ain't big on attention."

"Well, that's real good, Jimmy."

"I am eager to learn, sir."

Brother Jones smiled, reached back, and patted Jimmy on the head. "That's a good boy. I hope you're well rested. Tonight is liable to be a long one."

Three men approached from the main road. Jimmy was used to creepy people, but there was something altogether different about these three. A dark aura cloaked them—the air seemed to thicken as they approached. The first, the one wearing a white T-shirt, noted Jimmy and appeared displeased.

Brother Jones said, "Now don't you mind old Jimmy over here. He's a good boy. You can trust him, same as Carl and me."

The one in the white T-shirt stepped directly in front of Jones, the other two flanking him. He paused for a moment with a blank expression and said, "You are to come alone."

"I am? That's not anything we've ever discussed before. Look, I need help. I can't do it all myself, and I promise, my boy here is fine. After tonight, he's gonna be even better."

"Your people are ready?" the man asked.

"Yes, we are! Things are working out just like you said they would."

White T-shirt looked at Jimmy for a moment, then back at Jones and asked, "Have you found the key?"

"Not yet, but I'm sure it won't be long now. I can feel a change in the air. It's everywhere, focused right here in this shitty little town. Ain't that something?" Jones's Southern charm appeared wasted on these three. They seemed unmoved by it.

"The creature has escaped.?"

"The girl?" Brother Jones asked. "Ah yes. If you'd given me that task, she'd be dead by now. Old Carl would have taken care of that one."

White T-shirt raised an eyebrow at this. "She is not a girl, but she is meddling."

"Who is she?" Jones asked.

"It matters not. When we have the key, she will fall in line," said White T-shirt.

"And those boys? The ones spying the other night?"

"They have not come back. One of them has power, though somehow he hides it. We sensed it the day we chased them on this road, but outside our natural form, we could tell little," White T-shirt replied.

"So he could be important," Brother Jones said.

"He most definitely is important—though we cannot yet tell if he is the key. Powerful humans are rare. We feel an awakening, and our time is at hand. Leave the boy alone for now—deal with the constable first."

"The constable? I don't know how things work where you're from, but around here, folks don't like their law officers getting killed."

"His meddling keeps my people from their tasks, so we must risk the exposure. Kill him and make your army. My brothers and I will draw the key into the open."

"Yes, sir. And the girl? Want me to send my boys out to get her back?"

"No. Be watchful. The key draws her. Keep with your orders."

The three men turned as one and walked back down the main road back to the creek, seeming to disappear in the darkness.

"Now Jimmy, there go the three weirdest dudes you're ever likely to meet. But I'll tell you what—they hold the future in their hands," Jones said.

"So what do we do?"

"It's time for us to move on with the plan, my boy. You know that fiery little filly we got down there in the basement?"

"Yeah."

"Well, she's about to get herself some company."

Babysitter's Nightmare

As Jack Davies was beginning his journey through the memory of a forgotten Halloween, Lara Fanning was across town lounging on a recliner in the Dawson family home. The seventeen-year-old had babysat for the Dawsons on most weekends since she was fourteen. She wasn't the best babysitter in the world, but she was honest and dependable, and she never fell asleep, no matter how late Mr. and Mrs. Dawson stayed out drinking.

The home itself was a double-wide in the Devils Glen Trailer Park, located just south of Devils Glen Park and a half mile west of the giant mile-long Almira aluminum factory, where Mr. Dawson worked as a tool fitter. Like most trailer homes, it was a modest dwelling, but well-maintained and relatively clean.

As the time on the microwave snapped to eleven o'clock, Lara's phone rang in her pocket. Seeing it was her best friend, Emily Scott, she answered, "Hey."

"Hi, what are you doing?" Emily asked, sounding pensive.

"Just sitting for the Dawsons."

"Cool! I'm sitting for the Watsons!" Emily exclaimed, a little too joyfully.

"I know. You told me this morning."

"Oh, that's right. Sorry. So hey, what are the kids doing?"

"They're sleeping. It's like eleven o'clock," Lara replied. "Is everything OK?"

"Oh yeah. I mean, I don't know." Emily sighed. "Do you think I could bring the kids over there?"

"What do you mean? They're not in bed yet?" Lara asked. Their usual bedtime was at least two hours ago.

"Well, no. The kids can't sleep."

Lara stood up and walked over to her purse, removing a small bottle of nail polish. "Geez, give them some warm milk or something."

"It's not that. Someone keeps banging on the doors and the walls every ten minutes. It's freaking me out!" Emily sounded like she was trying not to cry.

Lara peered out the back window. "I don't see anything. Did you look outside? It's gotta be one some idiot pulling a prank."

Though she struggled to sound nonchalant for her friend, Lara remembered the man who had been watching the Dawsons' trailer the other night. She decided it would be best not to bring that incident up right now. Stephanie Caine's disappearance was something neither of them had to bring up—it was item number one on the mind of every resident of Bettendorf.

"No," Emily said. "At first, I thought it was Ryan playing a joke, but I called his phone and he's at his house. There it is again! Did you hear that?"

"Emily, this is giving me the creeps. You better not be effing with me!"

"I swear to God, I'm not! I'm scared, Lara!" Emily had never been a great liar in the first place, and she was terrible at keeping secrets. If you wanted to plan a surprise birthday party for someone, you had to keep Emily Scott out of the know or your plans would surely go awry.

"Look," Lara said, "just call the cops, and I'm sure whoever it is will high tail it lickety-split. In fact, why didn't you call the police in the first place?"

"I don't know. The cops around here do nothing, you know that."

"Don't be silly. They are the ones you call when you fear for your life, not me. OK?"

Emily sighed once again. "Fine."

"Good," Lara said. "Call me back right away."

Lara hung up her phone and stared out the back window toward the Watson trailer. She still couldn't see anything outside. After a few minutes, she went back and finish her toes. She glanced toward the back window now and then until she finally saw red-and-blue lights flickering from the other side of the trailer.

"Finally," she muttered to herself.

She sat on the couch and waited for Emily to call back. Ten minutes later, Lara noticed a patrol car driving slowly around the corner and up the street in front of the Dawson trailer, its searchlights aimed all around the neighborhood. She decided she should give Emily a call. After a few rings, a male voice answered, "Hello?"

"Um, hi," Lara replied. "Is Emily there?"

"No, she isn't. May I ask who's calling?"

"Is this the police?" Lara asked, becoming genuinely alarmed.

"Why, yes, it is. This is Officer Warren. Who am I speaking to?"

"Lara Fanning. I'm Emily Scott's best friend. I was talking to her before she called you guys. I'm babysitting right around the corner at the Dawsons' place. She's not there?"

"No, she's not. Do you know where she might be? We received a call about a disturbance. When we arrived, no one was here but two young children."

Lara was silent for a moment as she tried to process. If the kids were alone, where was Emily?

"No, like I said, the last time I talked to her, she was about to call you guys. She called me because something scared her. She said someone was pounding on the walls of the house. That was like twenty minutes ago. What happened to her?"

"I wish I could say, miss. But we have a car searching the neighborhood, so I'll call you if we find anything."

Lara stood a while in the living room of the trailer, trying to work through exactly what was happening. Soon, the Watsons' car came screeching down the street. Not knowing what else she could do, Lara returned to her former position on the recliner and tried to relax while she waited for Officer Warren to call back.

Eventually, another patrol car pulled around the corner and stopped in front of the Dawsons' trailer. A handsome cop in his thirties emerged and approached the front door as Lara came out to meet him. "Are you Lara Fanning?" the officer asked.

"Yes, I am."

"I'm Officer Warren; we spoke on the phone. I'm sorry, but we still have had no word from Emily Scott. If you hear or see anything unusual, please call us. We're gonna patrol the area. We won't be too far away. I suggest you contact Mr. and Mrs. Dawson and ask them to come home."

"OK," Lara said, doubting that either of the Dawsons would be sober enough to drive home at this point in the evening.

"How will you be getting home?" Officer Warren asked.

"I drove here. I'll be fine."

"OK. Just be careful. Here's my card."

"Thank you, Officer. I'm sure I'll be fine," Lara replied.

Lara stood like a statue, staring at the worn linoleum floor. A chill ran up her back and she felt anxiety creeping into her chest. She glanced out the back window and then flew to the front door, but could see nothing and no one outside.

Knowing there was nothing she could do, she checked on the kids. Satisfied that both were sleeping, she returned to the living room and turned on the TV to distract her thoughts, which was futile under the circumstances. She gave the Dawsons a call on their cell phones but both calls went straight to voicemail.

The fall air came flowing into the trailer, smelling of fallen leaves and bringing a slight sting of chilliness to the room. Lara returned to the living room and jumped with a start.

The front door was wide open.

"Hello?" she called out, her voice cracking.

She flew to the door and just as she swung it almost shut, glimpsed someone down the street. It was a small person standing under a streetlight on the corner between the Dawson and Watson trailers. It looked like he was wearing a cape.

"What the hell?" Lara said.

Just then, a motorcycle rumbled into the trailer park. Lara watched as the caped figure backed away from the street and faded into the shadows. The motorcycle pulled up to the exact spot where the man had been standing and stared into the shadows beyond the picket fence.

"Leo!" she cried as she zipped up her hoodie against the chilly air and waved for him to come to her.

Leo Lourogen turned his Honda around and drove back up the street to meet her. "Hey, Lara. You shouldn't be out here. Better get back inside, OK?"

"You shouldn't either. My friend Emily was babysitting at the Watsons, and now she's missing and some weirdo in a cape was standing right over there where you stopped."

"Uh huh, I saw him too. You get back inside. I'll keep an eye out. Don't worry: old Leo is here now."

Lara smiled and asked Leo to come inside with her until the Dawsons got home. She even offered to make him popcorn and put on a movie, but Leo refused as politely as he could, saying he had "things to do and people to see."

When the Dawsons returned home and Lara, at last, could leave, Leo returned to escort her. Though she didn't like him putting himself out—her home was on the other side of Bettendorf—it gave her some comfort to see him watching over her as she went inside.

The Fenno Cemetery

The cruiser's wheels were loud this late at night. The droning sound seemed to grow as the evening went on until Mark thought it would wake the entire world. He'd been up and down every street in the area, looking for some sign of Emily Scott. "It's in the hands of the detectives now," Chief Lane had said.

He rubbed his eyes and turned up Twenty-Third Street. With all the strange goings-on around Sunnycrest the past couple of nights, he thought he'd give it a look-see from a different angle. As he passed the eastern end of the Sunnycrest woods, he slowed his patrol car down to get a good look into the dark trees. As he could have guessed, it was too dark to see anything going on at this time of the night.

Like everywhere else in the town of Bettendorf, the woods were sleeping quietly in the darkness of a typical Iowa weeknight. Mark pressed the gas and continued up Twenty-Third Street until he came to the Cumberland Square shopping center—a strip mall mostly composed of mom-and-pop restaurants and shops. Happy Joe's Pizza and Ice Cream sat on the western end of the shopping center parking lot. It was one of the most popular pizza joints in the entire Quad City area. At 3:00 a.m., the parking lot was empty.

As Mark steered into the lot, he saw two of his colleagues parked next to each other in their cruisers, conversing between rolled-down windows.

When he pulled up next to them, the officers halted their conversation and the one closest to him, Jim Meadows, opened his passenger-side window.

"Hey guys," Mark said.

"Hey, Warren," Jim replied.

The other officer, Teddy Rodin, gave a small wave and said, "How's it going?"

"Eh, crazy night again. No sign of the Scott girl."

Jim grunted something and Teddy replied, "Yeah, but aren't you supposed to be out in Pleasant Valley by now?"

"Yeah, I went by the office to drop off paperwork."

"Ah yeah, that's a terrible thing. Poor girl." Teddy's tone sounded far from sympathetic. "You saw nothing?"

"Nope, not a thing." He sensed an accusation in Teddy's look, like he thought Mark had dropped the ball somehow.

"Hope you're staying away from Sunset Circle, buddy." Jim spat out the word "buddy," like it was an insult.

"Oh yeah. I'm just doing my job now. Toeing the line, as they say." Mark tried to ignore the patronizing tone, but Jim's words grated on him.

Like most of the other guys on the force, Teddy and Jim both observed him with a mixture of pity and hesitation in their eyes—the same look you'd give to someone who was cursed.

Making excuses to get back to work or down to the station, the other officers left, leaving Mark alone in the Happy Joe's parking lot.

What am I doing? Mark gripped the steering wheel like he wanted to choke the life out of it.

He looked once again at the picture on the dashboard. Every memory rushed through his head, the good and the bad. He tried to keep focused on the good ones, the happy memories, but inevitably horrific images would infiltrate his mind—the blood running down her face, the old woman's face on the video, or carrying Jennifer's coffin up the stone steps of the cathedral.

I felt her body shift inside the casket.

Mark shivered. He looked at the picture again and read the words at the bottom. Seek the gates and save the boy.

"Please let me know what I'm supposed to do. Show me the way," he whispered up to the stars.

A screech on the radio startled his thoughts. Dispatch had a call for a disturbance on Belmont Road in Pleasant Valley, Mark's patrol for the night. Someone saw a girl walking down the middle of the road, refusing to move. *Probably just some drunk teenager walking home from a party,* Mark told himself.

Ten minutes later, he was making his way down Belmont, almost to the T-intersection at Valley Drive, when he saw something moving in the ditch by the opposite lane just outside the old Fenno Cemetery. He stopped the cruiser and shined his spotlight along the shrubs and weeds growing next to the road. Slowly, his light moved further out until it caught a startling sight. A girl dressed in a black skirt and a soiled white blouse stood just off the road, barefoot and half-hidden behind a bush. Her dark hair hung down in filthy strands, and one visible eye peered through it, glowing in the spotlight.

"Hey!" Mark called out. "Are you OK, miss? What are you doing out here?"

The girl didn't move, but kept her one visible eye fixed upon Mark's spotlight. He opened his car door and stepped out onto the road, his police lights flashing a bright red and blue into the crisp night air. He reached down and unsnapped the restraint on the holster of his Smith & Wesson. The girl looked harmless enough, but there was something unsettling.

"Don't be afraid, honey, it's OK. I got a call you were walking down the middle of the road. How about you hop in the cruiser and I take you home?"

The girl blinked once but said nothing.

Mark took another step toward her, saying, "It's OK, you're not in trouble. I can take you home if you need a ride. You shouldn't be out here alone at night. It's dangerous."

The girl gave a caustic laugh, setting the hair on the back of Mark's neck on end. He stopped immediately.

"Who are you?" she finally asked.

"I'm Officer Warren. What's your name?" Mark regained his courage and took another step toward her. She didn't respond, but stepped behind the bush and out of sight.

"Shit!" Mark cursed and jogged over to where the girl had been standing. He pulled out his flashlight and pointed in the direction she had gone. Soon he found a one-lane dirt driveway that led up a little hill into a small cemetery. Mark sighed.

It was Fenno Cemetery, one of the oldest cemeteries in the entire state. The newest gravestone was from the 1890s, but most were from no later than 1850. As expected, in a cemetery with such a history, mystery surrounded the place. Stories of bizarre occurrences and ghostly sightings were common throughout the years. In the sixties, a group of five Girl Scouts took on a project to restore the Fenno Cemetery, which had fallen into disrepair. The girls went to the cemetery one evening to finish cleaning the headstones and clearing out debris, and no one ever saw them again.

Real or not, these stories were on Mark's mind as he looked up the overgrown drive. After everything he'd been through, he would not dismiss any supernatural legend. He approached the place with caution.

"Hey! I need you to come back down here right now! You're trespassing on private property! Come back down here, and I can take you home!"

Mark heard the girl giggle once or twice. He thought about calling for backup, but given he was already as much of an embarrassment as he could be, Mark decided against it and hoped he could persuade the girl to come with him peacefully. Just to be safe, he drew his sidearm and stalked up the drive, flashing his light right and left. As he came up the small hill to the graveyard, he saw the girl standing in the middle of a bunch of old weatherworn headstones. The skin on his neck tightened.

She isn't hiding. She's waiting.

It didn't help matters she looked like a ghost herself. Her pale skin and darkened eyes gave off an undead appearance.

"Why did you come here?" the girl asked. It sounded less like a question and more like a threat.

"I was called here," Mark answered.

This time, it was the girl who took a step toward Mark. Shaking, he raised his sidearm and pointed it straight at her, stepping back and shifting his weight onto his right foot.

"Young lady, stay where you are. I need you to raise your hands and slowly lower yourself to the ground."

"But why? Don't you see I'm just a lonely girl? What could I do to you?"

"I told you to get on the ground. Do it, now!"

"I asked you a question," the girl sad. "What could I do to you? Do you know what I could do to you, Officer—Mark—Warren?"

"Please do as I say. I don't want this to get out of hand."

How does she know my name? He studied her for several moments, and then it hit him. He knew her!

Through the dirt and greasy hair, he recognized her. She wasn't some random drunken Pleasant Valley girl walking down the street.

"Stephanie," he said. "You're Stephanie Caine. We've been looking for you. Please come with me, Ms. Caine."

"Oh, Mark, this is not your night. You shouldn't have come to this place, though I guess you had no choice. You know so much, but you don't *understand*, do you?" She took another step toward him and lifted her arms out to the sides. Her fingers spread open wide, illuminated by the flashing lights on Mark's cruiser.

Then from the bushes behind Stephanie came five figures—girls dressed in uniform—Girl Scout uniforms. They made no sound as they strode over the leaf-covered ground to stand on either side of Stephanie.

Mark tensed his finger around the trigger of his gun and readied his body. "What the hell! Do not take another step! Get down on the goddamn ground and lay on your stomach! Now! All of you!"

Stephanie froze and for a moment, he thought she might finally follow his orders, but then her eyes focused on something behind him. Mark looked down at the grass, and in the flashing lights, he saw two shadows—his own and that of someone else.

Before he could turn around, he felt a flash of pain at the back of his head. He immediately fell to the grass, dropping his flashlight and his weapon. He felt some hard object bludgeoning his head, over and over, until blood splattered on the ground around him and his vision faded.

Just as he released his last breath of life, Mark heard someone above him speaking in a melodic Southern accent, "Praise be to the Lord!"

The Keeper of Lost Souls

Jack awoke the following morning, drenched in sweat and with aching arms, after his first traveling dream. Before last night, he'd had zero recollection of the events from that night, but now he remembered it all as if it had happened yesterday. He knew there was more to the dream, but something blocked him from seeing the rest.

Then there was the question of Dan and Luke. Did they remember anything about that night? The answer was surely no. Somehow they must have forgotten it, too. Suddenly, Jack noticed Anne's presence.

"So you know," she said.

"I don't think I know anything!" Jack said. "I've seen a lot of things, but none of it makes sense. You need to tell me everything you know, Anne. It's time."

"I can tell you I don't know everything. I'm sure I don't know as much as you'd like me to know."

"OK, then let's start with something you do know. What are you?" Jack asked.

Anne paused for a moment, then answered, "I don't know that either."

"What do you mean, you don't know what you are? How is that possible? You've been with me half my life, but I was the only one who could see you. I thought I was crazy!"

"I know. There was nothing I could do about that."

"What do you mean? Couldn't you have told the truth? You couldn't have told me I wasn't insane?"

"You were young. There's no way you could have understood. It seemed best for you to think I wasn't real, at least until you were ready for the truth. I'm sorry, Jack. I did the best I could."

"OK, well, how about what happened at school? You rescued me the other day from that thing. It seemed like you had some kind of power. How did you do that?"

"I don't know how I did that—I'd never done it before. How can I describe it? I guess I sensed you were in trouble, and so I searched for you. I searched for you in my mind, and presto! I found you."

Her explanation, though not satisfying, seemed genuine. "You mean to tell me you have power, but you didn't know it?"

"All I can tell you is that for as long as I have been here on this earth, all of my existence has centered on you. You are destined for something great, I think. They sent me here to aid you."

"Who?"

"This story is long. Go to school. You'll be late."

"There's time. And if I'm late, I'm late. There's no way I can go to school before we have this out. Please, Anne, I must know."

Anne took a breath and began.

"When you and I were born, I had a heart condition and died, as you know. However, it wasn't so simple. There were forces at work—dark forces attempting to block our birth. I don't know who or why, but I believe someone made some kind of choice. You were the choice—the chosen.

"My spirit passed out of my body and into another world, just as yours was born into this one. I wandered for an eternity. My infant spirit was new, so I couldn't comprehend much. Gradually, over a period longer than many years in this world, I became conscious of myself and aware of others around me. I was in a strange land where multitudes of souls waited."

"Waited for what?" Jack asked.

"To grow—to evolve."

"Like a giant nursery?"

"It was something like that, but I don't think I could describe it to you adequately. You wouldn't comprehend it. Just know that it was a place where lots of souls were waiting. Time ran differently there, but I think many years passed. Things happened in those years—some good and some terrible—but I'm not ready to talk about the terrible things. I lived those years as best I could and I survived. Along the way, I learned to travel, though I never became as adept at it as you. However, I made my way to Faelia, a place you and I have gone together, though you may not remember.

"One day, an old man came. He had an enormous beard that wound throughout the entire world. Many creatures lived within it, some by force and some by choice. The old man had bright eyes the color of the most brilliant sunset—he seemed sad and joyous at the same time. When he spoke, which he rarely did, the entire world went still and all the lost souls hummed as one.

"Person they named Anne Margaret Davies," he said. "Do you know who I am?"

"No, sir, I'm afraid I don't,' I replied.

"You do not, for I have not told you. I am the Keeper of Lost Souls, and it has been my charge to hold you here for a time. Did you know this?"

"No, sir, I did not," I replied again.

"You didn't because I did not tell you. I took your soul from the world of your spirits. Do you know why?"

"No, sir, you have not told me," I said.

"He smiled and laughed for a moment and stared out into the abyss beyond his world for what seemed to be many hours. Eventually, he returned his attention and asked, as if only a moment had passed, 'Do you want to know why?'

"Please, sir. Little else has occupied my mind these many years. I don't know why I'm here."

"I will tell you. Anne Margaret Davies, I brought you to wait until the appointed hour. That hour is now upon us. You will now go back to the world of your birth."

"I cried out to him, 'Am I to be reborn?'"

"No, my young one." He shook his head with sadness. "You cannot be but who you are. You will go back in spirit only."

"The Keeper told me of my purpose. He described my place in the world as your watcher, advisor, and protector. He told me many things, some happy, some sad, and then he sent me back. I have guarded you these years since. Protected you from the spirits who would seek you out within our home.

"The forces of darkness gathered in this place, this town of Bettendorf, long before you or I came into the world. The Keeper explained these forces were leftovers from a time when our world was part physical, part magical. A powerful spirit drove them out long ago and sealed it, to be inhabited solely by the children of the stars—Earth, they called it.

"The seal was too great for the most powerful spirits to enter, but the smaller ones—called the Bel-Atast—found their way in. The strongest of the Bel-Atast affected the lives of the people of this world, and some even became flesh, though at great expense. Sometimes the transformation turned them mad, and they lived out their physical lives caught between both worlds."

Jack asked, "Are some of these spirits good and some evil?"

"Yes. Some are of the light, and some are of the dark. Those of the light do good for the people of this world. They come here to keep the dark spirits from overrunning it."

"Are you one of these spirits of light?" Jack asked.

"I don't know what I am, though I don't think I'm a spirit like these others. I believe I'm more like a ghost, though even that doesn't explain what happened in the creature's den.

"The Keeper of Lost Souls didn't tell me what I was and wouldn't tell me exactly why I was sent back here to protect you or why you are so important. I can assume you have a destiny, one I must protect. I'm not confident he knew much more than that, or if he did, he'd forgotten. He seemed oblivious, at any rate. I'm sure one soul out of an infinity of souls tied to one world, out of an infinity of worlds, mattered little to him. All I know, Jack, is that this world is under siege and has been for a good many years. We must discover how you fit into all of this."

Jack put his head into his hands and tried his best not to scream from the madness of everything he had just heard. "Last night, I traveled back in time and relived a memory from a Halloween when I was ten," he said. "Something happened that night."

Anne looked at the floor and became still for a moment. Jack looked up at her and saw that a tear had left her eye and rolled down her face.

"What is it, Anne? What happened that night? I only remember part of it. Please, tell me what you know."

"I only know you were beyond my protection. An ancient and powerful force had you for a time. The rest, you must find yourself. The memory haunts me to this day, but I do not know what happened. I could *feel* your pain, Jack, but I couldn't do anything about it." Anne composed herself for a moment. "You came back, and you are alive. Nothing more than that matters."

Jack nodded.

Anne leaned toward him. "But there is one other thing I have to tell you—this Ava is not to be trusted."

"Why?" At the mention of her name, Jack's eyes lit up involuntarily.

Anne noticed his reaction but continued. "She is a spirit from another world. She crossed over somehow. I don't know how long she's been here or anything else about her, though I suspect she has been here for some time. Jack, I urge you to be cautious about her. Something connects you to her—that's obvious to me. But we need to learn more about her intentions."

"Well, if I'm connected to her, isn't that a good thing?"

"I'm not sure it's a good thing, Jack. A person can be tied to many ideas, events, places, people, or spirits, both light and dark. Some we must avoid. Ava might be something like that."

"Why do you think so?"

"Because, Jack, many things in the world are mysteries to me, but there are things I understand very well. Ava is a spirit of the darkness. Of that I am most certain."

Visions

At school a host of girls bombarded Lara with questions. Most of them told similar stories of their own. Susie Michaels was certain she saw the same caped man standing outside her parents' house just a month ago, while Jen Graver told a story of how a Bettendorf police officer shot a man in a cape last weekend, but when he looked for the body, it had disappeared. Theories and speculations abounded, but most of the girls were certain Leo Lourogen was behind it all.

"Guys, he's not behind any of this, believe me. I trust him," Lara said during lunch as she and her friends sat at their usual table in the middle of the cafeteria.

"What?" Susie asked. "You're an idiot if you trust that creeper. I've caught him staring at me like a bazillion times. He totally has that kidnapper-in-waiting vibe."

"Yeah, Lara," Jen chimed in. "My dad won't even let me ride my bike down the street if he sees that perv around."

Lara rubbed her eyes. "Look, you guys can be creeped out all you want, but he has been nothing but kind to me. Last night, he protected me. And as soon as he pulled up, that guy in the cape took off like a bat out of hell. Plus, how could he have kidnapped anyone on that motorcycle?"

Jen nodded. "OK, I guess that makes sense. Still, I wouldn't trust him until we know for sure what happened. And what about this Dracula guy?"

"I don't know," Lara said. "It's all confusing."

"I'm just scared," Jen said.

Lara put her hand on Jen's shoulder. "Oh, honey, I am too."

"I'm frightened for Emily," Susie said. "And I'm worried about us. As if babysitter stories aren't scary enough. I heard the varsity football team is gonna go looking for Stephanie tonight."

Lara raised an eyebrow. "With torches and pitchforks, I suppose? A lot of good that's gonna do. Now, instead of focusing on finding Emily, the cops will have to worry about a bunch of doofus jocks running around like a bunch of idiots!"

"Hey, someone has to do something, Lara," Susie said. "We have two missing girls—first Stephanie, and now Emily. The police aren't doing shit about this! I hope those jocks go out looking. Who knows, maybe they'll find something. Anyway, it can't hurt."

The girls sat for a while, staring off into the cafeteria. Kidnappings were things they read about or watched on crime shows like America's Most Wanted. They didn't seem real, not to a bunch of girls in Bettendorf, Iowa.

Tears fell from their eyes, and the girls leaned into a silent group hug. Lara looked up over the backs of her friends as they continued to cry. She felt a strange protective instinct set in at that moment.

Across the cafeteria, she saw a girl sitting by herself watching Lara and her friends, or at least she was looking in their general direction. She had blue eyes, long dark hair, and was stunningly beautiful. Lara had never seen the girl before in her life, but there was something familiar about her all the same. She stared at her as if she couldn't look away. Lara thought for a moment she might be losing her mind, but she couldn't keep from looking at the girl. "Do you guys see that girl sitting over there at that table in the corner?"

Susie looked to where Lara was pointing. "You mean the new girl? Yeah, I met her this morning. She's beautiful, isn't she? Her name is Ava. Have you met her?"

"No, I hadn't seen her until just now. But—"

"But what?" Jen asked.

"Oh, nothing. I should introduce myself, that's all," Lara said, keeping her real thoughts to herself.

"Ha! Since when have you become the school welcome wagon?" Susie laughed, making Jen laugh too.

Lara allowed herself the opportunity to laugh. Laughing wouldn't bring back Emily, but the moment of levity felt good, nonetheless.

Lara's respite ended as Jack Davies enter the cafeteria. The sight of him sent a wave of electricity through her entire body. Lara's head spun, and she thought she might faint like one of those ladies from an old black-and-white movie. She knew Jack only in passing, given he was in a grade lower than she was, and though she'd probably seen him hundreds of times, she'd seen nothing like this. A strange blue aura shone all around him from head to toe. It surrounded his entire body in a kind of halo. Lara was not prone to visions, so she didn't trust what her eyes were telling her. Initially, she thought the stress from the previous day had impacted her eyesight or her mind, but she then realised the aura focused only on Jack. When she glanced at anyone else in the room, she didn't see it, but when she looked back at Jack, there it was.

Is anyone else seeing this?

Lara peered around the room and saw that almost no one else seemed to take any notice of Jack. Only a table full of freshman girls noted his entrance, but from their giggling and blushing, Lara could tell their reasons for noticing him were entirely different.

Jack meandered past their table, oblivious to them, and joined Randy Wall at the lunch line. Though she couldn't hear what Jack was saying, she could tell his face was flushed. He was speaking in a rushed but muted tone. Did he have a secret? Was he in trouble?

Why do I care?

Jack left Randy and crossed the room straight to Ava. They spoke like they had met before. There was something strange about their connection.

How does he know her? Are they flirting? Why does Jack have a blue aura, and why am I the only one who sees it?

"Hey, do you guys see that?" Lara asked the other girls.

"See what?" Jen asked.

"Look at Jack. What do you notice about him?"

Susie gave him a once-over. "He's cute—for a sophomore. Why? You like him?"

"No!" Lara replied.

Susie quickly switched to an apologetic tone. "Seriously, it's OK if you do. He's cute. I mean, you're usually into older guys, that's all. Hey, I know his best friend, Randy! I could set you up, though it kinda looks like he's hitting on the new girl."

"No, that's not it! I mean, do you notice anything weird about him?"

Lara's friends gave him a good once-over again, but both concluded that aside from being cute for an underclassman, he looked exactly like he always did.

Suddenly, the entire room shook. The windows rattled until half of them shattered from the force. Lara's books fell off the table in front of her, and her friends fought to keep their lunches from dumping onto the floor. Jen screamed and reached out to hold on to her friends. Lara held on to her chair for dear life. She had never once felt an earthquake in Bettendorf, and she took several moments to comprehend what exactly was happening. When she looked across the room, it made sense.

The aura around Jack Davies wasn't blue anymore.

It was bright red.

Discovery

1.

JACK MADE IT TO school only a little late. He thought the schoolwork load was getting easier, though it could have been that he was learning to handle the load better with a year of high school under his belt. Either way, he felt good about his chances this year. Algebra 2 would be problematic; math was always Jack's weakness. Jack's dad advised him to make a game of it.

"Turn it into a puzzle. Try to make it fun if you can," his dad would say. Unfortunately, Jack could never make that happen. Instead, he had to suffer through it and deal with the sometimes overwhelming frustration that went along with mind-numbing work, combined with racing teenage hormones.

At that moment, a new distraction walked into the classroom—one he knew immediately would prove almost impossible to resist. The wary part of him screamed in his head, *Run, you fool! Run now!*

There would be time for running later. For the time being, he wanted to sit and stare at the girl standing at the front of the room. Mr. Polaski looked over her paperwork and wrote her name in his grade book. He said something quietly about introducing her, and that she could pick whichever seat she preferred. The seat next to Jack was open. *Of course!*

"Attention, everyone," Mr. Polaski announced. "We have a new student in the class, Ava Von Tassen. Please make her feel welcome when you have a chance."

Jack heard snickers and boyish remarks, all amounting to a lot of "Hubba-hubba." In fact, Brad Loder said those exact words as Ava made her way across the room looking for a seat. Each boy and girl in the class watched Ava stride confidently down the center aisle. Jealousy and lust were thick in the air. Every one of them was wondering the same thing—where she would sit—that is, everyone but Jack. He knew exactly where she would sit, and he was probably the only boy who wished she wouldn't.

As if fulfilling Jack's hormonal prophesy, Ava sat in the vacant chair next to him. She chuckled as she heard him let out a long sigh.

"Was that a sigh of relief or anxiety?" she asked.

"Maybe both," he replied.

"Should I feel flattered or insulted?"

"That's up to you. You're going to BHS now?"

"Yep," she replied.

"Where are you from?"

"That's a long story for another day. Class is starting," she whispered with a wicked grin. "Just relax and take your notes. Let's talk at lunch, OK?"

Mr. Polaski cleared his throat and began his lecture. The class settled into the usual routine, but Jack didn't think he'd be able to pay attention to a thing his teacher said. He could see from the corner of his eye—the only safe way for him to look at her—that Ava was smiling to herself.

2.

Three hours later, Jack entered the cafeteria and joined Randy in the food line, cutting in front of several freshman girls. Randy turned and slapped Jack on the back.

"Well, my friend, I've got some great info. You'll never guess who joined in my bio class," Randy said proudly.

"Ava?"

"Nope, Ava—wait, what? You know?"

"Yep, she's in my algebra class."

"Ah. Where did she sit?"

"Right next to me."

"Really? She sat by herself in biology. Mr. Jensen had to give her a lab partner. He chose Neil Lammers! The kid was so nervous he looked like he wanted to hurl in their sink."

The previous few days had been a roller coaster of odd happenings and narrow escapes, so it was a relief to have something to laugh about. As they came out of the line, Jack saw Ava sitting at a table by herself against the southern wall of the cafeteria. She waved, and butterflies leaped through his abdomen.

"Hey, Randy, save me a seat. I'll join you guys soon."

Randy looked and saw Ava too. "Oh, man, that's how it is, huh? You're gonna ditch us for that crazy girl?"

"Yeah, just for a minute. I'll be right back."

"Yeah, right," Randy grunted as he stormed off to join their friends.

Jack made his way to Ava, taking the seat across from her to keep the table between them. She laughed and gave him a mockingly indignant look.

"Ah, I see how it is," she said. "You're unsure of me. Good."

"How is that good?"

"Caution is good, especially in times like these—particularly for you. These are times that call for caution."

Anne's words of warning kept replaying in Jack's head. He didn't feel comfortable letting Ava know too much about what he was thinking. She was already far too good at reading his thoughts. He didn't need to give her any extra help.

"Maybe I'm just not as easily charmed by you as these other guys." Jack glanced around and saw that half the male students were staring in their direction.

"Are you jealous?" she asked.

"No."

"Of *course* not."

Ignoring her tone, he asked, "Why did you change schools in the middle of the year?"

"It's not the middle. It's the first semester, isn't it?"

"It's the middle of the first semester. But either way, why did you do it?"

"Why do you think?"

"Jesus, is everything a frigging game with you? Just answer the question."

"I'm playing with you because the answer to that question is none of your business—at least, not yet." Her eye color flashed from dark blue into a snow blue, almost white, and her lips peeled back over her perfectly white teeth, revealing four sharp canines. Her voice became low, with a rumbling bass that shook Jack's nonchalant act. "Do not mistake me, Jack Davies. I am not one of your silly teenage classmates."

Jack's eyes widened, and he sat up in his chair, looking around to see if anyone else had noticed her dramatic display. When Jack looked back at her, Ava's eyes had changed back to dark blue, and her lips had returned to their normal state of smirking fullness.

He leaned over the table and whispered, "I knew it! You're a vampire! And a liar!"

"I told you before; I am not a vampire. And though I will lie when it suits me, I have not yet lied to you. I don't think I could, even if it suited me."

"Oh yeah? Then what are those teeth? They sure look like fangs!"

"Vampires are not the only creatures with fangs, boy."

"Are you human?"

"Sometimes."

"Anne was right. You're not of the light. I can feel it."

"*Of the light?* Is that what Anne told you? What kinds of stories has that little dead girl been feeding you? Of the light! If only she understood an ounce of what she thinks she knows, but alas, she is double the fool. She knows nothing, but thinks she knows all."

It was Jack's turn to show his anger. "Watch what you say about Anne."

"Or—you'll do *what*, exactly?"

"I'll walk away from this table and never speak to you again."

Ava watched him for a moment. "Oh, really? And then where will you be? If not for me, you won't survive to see November. Who do you think will protect you? That dead sister of yours? She can't. She's stuck in that shabby house for the rest of her existence, doomed to be your shadow."

Jack felt a rage swell up from deep within him. All the stress and revelations of the past week finally caught up with him and flowed into his mind like a river of pain and confusion. He wanted to lash out and make Ava feel the terrible humiliation he was experiencing—he wanted to make her stop speaking.

His eyes closed, and his arms shook with tremendous force. Then Jack opened his eyes and focused his gaze directly on Ava, whose natural confidence had given way to surprise and shock. Though his reaction to her words happened involuntarily, he was doing nothing to stop it. The power felt good.

Ava choked and coughed before finally spitting out, "Jack! Stop!"

The entire room swayed. Tables shook violently, and lunches came crashing to the ground. Jack could hear screams from the other students as they fell to the floor and ducked under their tables. Most of them had never experienced an earthquake before in their lives, so they did not understand how to respond.

Ava cried out, "Stop, Jack! Please stop, you're hurting me!"

Ava's eyes went back to that snow-blue color, and her lips again curled up over her sharp white teeth. She leaned in, looking deep into Jack's eyes. Though he couldn't hear what she was saying, he suddenly felt her presence in his mind. A calming sensation flowed into his thoughts, and his anger quickly subsided. Above the cool river of peace, a commanding voice ordered him to cease.

"Jack. You must stop. You will reveal yourself and lose everything, my love. Come back. Follow my voice back here now. Follow my voice and be at peace."

Jack relaxed his mind, and the anger drifted away until he couldn't remember what caused it.

"Good, Jack," Ava whispered. "Keep going. You're doing well. Return. Relax."

The room stopped shaking. Students across the cafeteria were crying and calling out to one another.

"What happened?" Jack mumbled, looking around at the chaos.

"*You* happened," Ava replied. "Never do that again."

"I don't even know what happened," Jack said. "I did all this?"

"Yes, you did."

"How?"

"You have more to you than meets the eye, Jack Davies. All these years you had a secret—a well-kept secret—until now, that is."

"Until now?"

"Oh, every power within a hundred miles will know that someone in this town can do something that hasn't happened in this world in a very long time."

Jack swallowed back a wave of nausea. "I take it that's a bad thing."

"Oh yes. You've revealed yourself to them. And you've put us all in danger."

The Devils of the Glen

1.

After school, Jack and Randy rode their bikes down to Devils Glen after stopping at Whitey's Ice Cream, both of them needing to get out after the stress of the past few days. Jack was particularly out of sorts, and even Randy knew not to bug him. It's rare for a guy to cause an earthquake in the middle of a high school cafeteria. Jack clamped his eyes shut as the scene played out in his mind again.

What is happening? He wondered as he peddled his bike faster down the road. Ava had been no help to him after the incident, other than repeatedly telling him to control his anger until he knew how to use his powers. *Powers? Who has powers? Jack Davies, that's who!* Jack peddled even faster.

"Hey! Dude, slow down! Hey!" Randy slammed the brakes on his bike. Jack swung his bike back around and joined him at the side of the road.

"Sorry, I need to let off steam," Jack said.

"I get it. It's been a weird week, but—"

"No, you don't get it!"

"Jesus, what's your problem?"

"My problem? Do you have any idea what I'm going through right now? Ya know that little earthquake we had today? The earthquake that happened in the middle of frigging Iowa?"

"No duh," Randy replied.

"Well, it wasn't an earthquake."

Randy looked at him sideways. "What do you mean?"

"It was me," Jack said. "I did that."

"You?" Randy asked.

"Yeah, me. And I don't even know how I did it. I got mad and suddenly everything went crazy."

"What the hell are you talking about?" Randy asked.

Jack leaned down on his handlebars and tried to gather his thoughts. "Remember the other day when I told you about my ghosts and all that other stuff?"

"Shit yes, I remember."

"Did you believe me or not?"

"I believe you. Two months ago I might not have, but with all the weird crap that's happening around here, it didn't seem that far-fetched, I guess. But an earthquake? That might take a little convince—"

Randy was cut off by the sound of singing and praises coming from a small white church across the street.

"Wow, I thought no one went to that church," Randy said. "Since when do that many people go to church on a weekday afternoon?"

Jack looked at the church. "Yeah," he agreed. Then he realized something was wrong about it. "It looks different, doesn't it? Like something's missing."

"Hey, someone stole the cross," Randy said.

"What cross?"

"On the steeple. There used to be a gold cross. My sister used to dare me to go up and steal it. She said it was worth like a zillion dollars, but now it's gone. See?"

Randy was right. There had been a gold cross on top of the steeple. "Who would steal a cross from a steeple?" Jack asked.

"I don't know," Randy replied. "Hey, what d'ya say we praise us some Jesus?"

Jack noticed something going on inside the church, and not just the singing and clapping. He sensed electricity or a power. He stepped off his bike, letting it fall to the ground, and started across Devils Glen toward the church.

"Hey, I was just joking. What are you doing?" Randy asked.

"Stay here," Jack said.

As Jack approached the steps leading up to the massive wooden front doors, a darkness seemed to cloud his mind. As he stared at the building, a vision came to him. In his mind, he could see dark vines crawling up the walls, doors, and windows of the church. Some evil force corrupted the ground all around the place.

Stepping to the front doors, Jack looked back at Randy, who raised his hands in a gesture as if to say, "What the hell?"

Jack reached out and clasped his hand around the shining door handle. Immediately, a rush of images flooded his mind, and he stood frozen in place, unable to let go of the handle. He felt death inside this building. Murder was everywhere. Something inside was draining life, not giving it. This place was a lair of darkness and mayhem.

For what purpose? Jack asked himself.

Another vision flashed into the forefront of his mind: a line of people willingly offering their sick loved ones to a tall man at the front of the church. He spoke words of freedom and forgiveness, promises of salvation for all who entered and gave of themselves. The poor people thought they were releasing their loved ones from pain and suffering. But the poor souls offered up were not released. Jack could see them—stranded here on earth, sealed in a sacrificial prison. Jack could feel each one, and, likewise, all the lost souls sensed his presence. They called to him.

The vision changed. It flashed to Devils Glen Park. Here were the creeps under the shelter and a dark figure walking among the oaks. Another flash. Here was Duck Creek flowing through the park, red with blood. Here were living things deep in the caverns running beneath the rock cliffs. Here one warped creature sniffed the air and appeared to sense his presence. It cocked its head and screamed a piercing wail that cut across the park. Other creatures lifted their heads, joining the dreadful alarm.

Here a great beast emerged from the cave, heavy feet stomping down on the smooth stones of Duck Creek, crushing them. The creature reached out with its mind, and Jack felt it enter his thoughts. It sifted through his mind as if leafing through the pages of a book, uncovering all the boy's secrets. Then the beast reared back its head with a bellowing laugh that rattled the earth and sent the other creatures scurrying away.

Another flash. Here was a strange world that looked like his own, yet different. Here was the inside of an old house and a police officer lying lifeless upon a large canopy bed. Here a frightened woman stood outside the bedroom window, peering in at the officer with bloody tears streaming down her face.

Another flash. Here a young girl with jet-black hair sat on her bedroom floor drawing piles of strange images.

Another flash. Here was the sanctuary of the little white church. Here was the dark ceremony being held inside.

The preacher smiled and called out, "Come all ye sinners into the house of the Lord! Bring your burdens to the altar and let them be free! Perhaps you have an ailing parent or—a *sister?* Yes, bring your sister! All who come shall be with the Lord!"

Jack took every ounce of his strength and pried his hand from the church door. His momentum sent him tumbling down the front steps and onto the vile ground.

Randy was running across the road toward him, but Jack stopped him in his tracks, screaming, "Stay where you are!"

Randy ignored him, sprinted all the way across the yard, grabbed Jack by the arm, and lifted him to his feet. "What happened? Are you OK?"

"Yes, but let's get out of here. I'll explain later. Go!"

They made it to their bikes and were pedaling once again down Devils Glen Road before Jack looked back to see that the church was still ringing with the sound of hymns and hallelujahs. He could see no sign of anyone watching them from the fake stained-glass windows.

The boys continued down the road, slowing their pace only after they were certain they weren't being followed. Jack's head had been pounding ever since he had wrenched his hand away from the church door, and the pain grew as they fled. Suddenly, just as he brought his Schwinn to a halt and slammed his hands to the sides of his head, the pounding ceased. He held his hands out a few inches from his temples and waited to see if the awful feeling would return. When Jack realized he was free, he looked up and took notice of where he was.

They had stopped directly outside the entrance to Devils Glen Park. Red, yellow, and brown leaves blew across the narrow winding entrance. More leaves fluttered in the air as a chorus of branches swayed back and forth. Jack could feel something happening in the park—he sensed a presence and power that was growing with each moment. All of Jack's new senses were on alert.

"Dude, you gonna tell me what the hell happened back there?" Randy asked, his whole body shaking.

"That church has a new minister," Jack replied.

"Yeah? And?"

"And he's not a good one. I think he's part of everything that's been happening to us, to this town. I don't know how, but he's part." Jack continued looking down the park road, getting a sense of something he had to do. First, he had to get rid of Randy. He didn't want him around for what he was planning. "Look, I need time to think alone. Why don't you go on home, and I'll call you later, OK?"

Randy looked at him suspiciously. "You kidding me? I'm not leaving you alone to do something dumb."

"I won't, Randy. Seriously, I only need a little time. Please, just go home, and I'll call you when I have my head on straight. OK?"

Randy stared at the ground like he might refuse, but eventually sighed and replied, "OK. But don't you do anything dumb. If I don't hear from you in an hour, I'm gonna come looking. Got it?"

"Got it. Don't worry, I'll call you."

Jack watched Randy ride all the way up the hill until he made his turn onto Central Avenue. When his best friend was no longer in sight, Jack returned his attention to Devils Glen Park.

2.

Jack made his way across the road and into the park. To his right, he could see Duck Creek running parallel to the road, and to his left was the steep hill up to the picnic shelter where he had seen the creeps. He decided he would go there first. As he slowly ascended the hill towards the shelter, he promised himself if he caught any sight of the creeps, he'd turn around and leave.

Silence loomed over everything as Jack made his way up the main road to the shelter. It was empty. *Maybe they took off for good,* he told himself, not believing it.

He headed back down the hill. When he got to the bottom, he laid his bike on the grass next to the road and walked along the north bank of Duck Creek. The water flowed quietly this time of the year, making little sound as it wound its way toward the Mississippi. Leaves floated atop the water, slowly turning in small groups, twisting with the various changes in current.

Jack continued until he came to a place where the creek jogged to the right. On the other side of the water were three dark openings in the rock, spread out with about ten feet between them. He would have to make his way across the creek if he wanted to investigate the caves. Fortunately, there was a line of rocks cutting through the small rapids leading to the other side. He had done plenty of rock-hopping while on family camping trips, so in a few seconds, he was across, standing just outside the first cave.

An intense energy seemed to flow from it, and a rotten smell emanated from the opening. No wonder none of the neighborhood kids were brave enough to come within a hundred yards of the place. The entrance was low, and Jack had to duck as he passed through it, climbing across a barrier of jagged rocks and shifting stones. Once inside, he found himself in a large cavern with moist, rough walls. An army of stalactites jutted down from the ceiling like giant fangs, dripping water on the cold stone floor. The sound of running water bounced around throughout the chamber. Jack sat for a moment to gather his thoughts.

Why am I here? he asked himself. *Something drew me here, but what? And why?*

A small sound like a pebble dropping into water echoed through the cavern. Jack got the distinct sense he wasn't alone, though he couldn't see anything in the shadowy recesses. Through the echoes of the creek water reverberating all around him, he could make out the sound of soft feet splashing across the wet ground.

"Hello?" he called into the darkness.

The skin on his neck tightened, and his heart raced—the first pangs of panic rose—yet he couldn't move. Jack now regretted coming to this place. *It's a trap!*

Looking into the darkness as his eyes adjusted, he could just make out a figure crouching at the far wall of the cave. Jack froze, fixing his eyes upon it and trying not to breathe.

A second and a third figure, both smaller than the first, crawled in from openings to his left and right. The first figure was manlike in form but naked, hairless, and dark-skinned, with sharply pointed ears sticking up that gave the illusion of horns. The creature on the left appeared to be skinny and dwarfish with long limbs and walked on all fours. The one on the right was a small, almost infant-size creature with a withered body and enormous eyes that glowed in the half light. It let out little croaks and grunts as it scrambled over the stones.

Jack's heart pounded like an alarm. He glanced back at the entrance. It was only ten feet away, but the opening was awkwardly small with a pile of stones under it. He wouldn't be able to get through with any kind of speed. He had a feeling that these creatures had much more experience navigating the area than he did. *Just how agile am I?*

All of them were facing him, crouched and bobbing side to side as if trying to decide what to make of him. They were as uncertain of Jack as he was of them. Three devils were watching him in the dim light of the cave. The Devils of the Glen.

"Hello?" Jack called.

The creatures snapped to attention at the sound of his voice, mesmerized by it. The larger one reached out one of his arms and crawled a few steps closer, sniffing at Jack through the misty cave air. It arched its neck and then made a long moaning sound, causing deep vibrations across the cavern walls.

The other two devils moved wide to the right and left, stalking along either wall like lizards. They were heading toward the entrance, apparently trying to block any chance he might have to escape. Jack brought himself into a crouch and moved closer to the opening.

"Hibicht thak tul mik solack!" the larger creature said, the words boiling from its mouth like a slow-moving flow of lava.

Though Jack couldn't understand the words, he felt a power in them and involuntarily stopped immediately in his tracks. The two creatures on the walls stopped as well; they too seemed frozen by the command.

"I'm sorry," Jack said, unable to control the fear shaking through his voice. "I apologize for trespassing. I would like to leave now."

"What are you?" the creature asked.

At the sound of its voice, Jack's heart grew dark, as if a deep shadow had moved over it, blocking out all hope. He had a desire to lie down on the cold floor of the cave, curl up into a ball, and weep. It was all he could do to keep himself crouched on his toes. He took another step toward the opening but doing so felt to him as if he'd hiked for hours. At that moment, he wanted nothing more than to take a nap. Waves of exhaustion poured over him, and for a moment, he almost gave in.

"What are you?" the creature asked again.

"Jack Davies," Jack replied. "Who are you?"

"Surgat," the creature said, and a sharp pain twisted in Jack's stomach at the sound of the name. "These are my brothers, Onoskelis and Bukavac."

Onoskelis and Bukavac eyed Jack hungrily as they moved a few steps closer. The two devils appeared to be gathering themselves for another quick run that would bring them close enough to block Jack's escape. Surgat crept toward Jack and craned his neck forward, opening his misshaped mouth.

"Sleep, young peregrinator. Stay here with us," Surgat said.

Clouds returned to Jack's mind, and he slumped back onto the floor. The devil's words reverberated in his brain, muffling all other sounds and making it impossible for him to think of anything else. He felt himself drifting off as his vision became fuzzy. Faintly, he could see Onoskelis scramble the remaining yards to the cavern's opening just as Bukavac arrived at the same time.

I *am coming,* a girl's voice said, softly cutting through the haze of Surgat's spell.

Who? Jack asked in his mind as he heard the sounds of Surgat's feet shuffling toward him.

The voice called out, *Remember who you are, Jack. Find your strength and run!*

Jack felt renewed strength rising within him. This new voice speaking in his mind was like a beacon shining through the darkness, pointing the way home. But more than that, the voice stirred something inside him—a memory of a talent, a power he possessed. He reached out in his mind and tried to seize onto it, like grabbing water with a fist. Still, he knew a great weapon was there if he could only remember how to find it, how to use it.

Bringing himself back into a crouch and up onto his toes, Jack took several labored steps toward the entrance and the devils waiting there. Their confused faces told him he was doing something right. They weren't expecting him to move toward them. They glanced back to their leader, who was now in pursuit, though visibly shocked by the boy's ability to break his charm.

With his strength and faculties returned, Jack crossed the few yards to the entrance without tumbling over the scattered rocks and holes on the cave floor. As he approached Onoskelis and Bukavac, the devils reach out to seize him, and from behind he heard a high wail that rattled the earth. But Jack was no longer afraid, and he quickly reached out in his mind and touched a power he'd never felt before. As he did so, energy burst forth from his hands, smashing into the devils and sending them back into the jagged walls of the cave.

He burst back into the daylight, and just like that, Jack was hopping over the stones and across the creek. Looking back, he could see that the devils hadn't followed him into the light. At first, they seemed to struggle just inside cavern's opening, but then Jack realized they were transforming, reshaping themselves into something more humanlike.

Then Jack recognized them. These devils were changing into the three creeps who had chased Randy and him last week. They were the same.

Jack hopped onto his bike and pedaled frantically as one demon caught up to him, punching him in the back with almost enough force to knock him off. He coughed and groaned but kept his feet pumping until he got up enough speed to put some distance between himself and the devils. He glanced back and saw that one of them had called off the pursuit and was strolling behind him, laughing.

Then, out of thin air, Ava appeared. She leaped past him and came to a halt, placing herself between Jack and the devils. With her legs spread out in a fighting position, Ava growled low and flashed her sharp white teeth. The devils stopped in their tracks and slowly backed away.

"Jack Davies," Surgat called out, and Jack recognized him as the creep in the white t-shirt. "Night is drawing near, and we will find you! You cannot hide any longer."

Sweat streamed down Jack's face as he hopped the curb onto Devils Glen Road and turned left toward Central Avenue, not daring to look back. Once they made it a safe distance away, Ava stopped him, grabbing the collar of his shirt.

"What in the hell were you doing in that cave?" she asked.

"I'm sorry," Jack replied. "I was trying to take back control, that's all."

"By 'control,' do you mean suicide? Do you have any idea how foolish that was? How did you find them?" she asked.

"I don't know. I felt something in this park—I think I have always felt a darkness here. But today I was drawn to it—I couldn't help myself."

"Why did you go alone?" she asked.

"I feel like a blind man being led around by the hand. So many things have been happening. I wanted to take control of something—handle it myself for once. I'm sick of feeling like a pawn."

"I get that Jack, really I do," Ava said with more sympathy than he was expecting. "But for your first test, did you have to go into a den of devils?"

"I promise, if I'd known what I'd find, I would never have gone there. Did you know about them?" he asked.

"No, I didn't. But I must admit, their presence explains a lot."

"What does it explain? Because I'm still pretty effing confused," Jack said, still shaking.

"It explains why this area has so much happening that shouldn't be happening. So how did you come to be in that cavern? Tell me everything."

Jack told her about the visions he'd had at the church and the power he'd sensed within the park. She listened and nodded as if some of it was known to her and asked questions about the parts that were not. When he described the activities at the church, she looked back toward Devils Glen for a moment as if considering something.

"I didn't mean to cause trouble, really I didn't. I was just mad after what happened today. It's just so frustrating to be in the dark all the time," Jack said.

"When you're in the dark, you can't go running about without care. You must feel your way, slowly and cautiously. Please, Jack, if you didn't understand it before, you must get it through your head now. Things are changing in your world. You must take nothing for granted. I will look into what's happening at that church. But you must promise me you won't do anything else as foolish as this."

"I promise," Jack said.

3.

When he finally made it back home, he ignored his parents, stumbled up the stairs to his room, and collapsed on his unmade bed. Despite how exhausted he was, sleep was not in the cards. Almost as soon as he had fallen into bed, Anne glided through the bedroom wall with a look of exasperation that rivaled the one he had just seen on Ava's face.

"What happened?" she asked. "I sensed you were in danger."

"I was at the park," he replied.

"Which park?"

"Devils Glen."

"Oh my God, Jack! Did you go there alone? Why would you do that?"

"Because it's *my* life! You hear? Today I caused an earthquake, and I don't even know how it happened. An earthquake!"

"You did that," Anne said. It sounded like a confirmation.

"Yes! All my life, shit has happened. No one has been there to teach me, only to protect me. And Anne, I am thankful, very thankful. You got rid of Johnny, and you scare away the ghosts whenever I need you to, and I love you for it. But now I feel like something bigger is happening, and I want to do something about it. I don't want to just sit around in the dark and pray it all goes away. I need to know what I am!"

Anne bowed her head and nodded. "I understand, Jack. And maybe you're right. Maybe it's time for you to learn."

"Can you teach me?"

"No, Jack. I wish I could, but I can't. I told you this morning I know a little more than you do. I think it's time for you to search."

"Where?"

"Faelia."

"The land you went to when you died?"

"Not exactly, though I went there from time to time while I waited. From what you described when you were younger, I think you and Johnny may have gone there too, when you played make-believe games with him."

"I don't remember that," Jack said.

"No, I suppose you wouldn't. There is still a lot you don't remember. But now I think it's time."

"Will I learn what I am?"

"Perhaps. But first you must travel someplace else," Anne said.

"Where?" Jack asked.

"You must go back to that Halloween night and remember the rest of what happened to you. Something powerful took you that night, but here you are, alive and well. I think it is important for you to discover how you escaped."

Jack thought about it for a moment. "Yes, I believe you're right. It might be the key to everything. Stay with me, please?"

Anne nodded and held up her hands, whispering words of prayer, as Jack lay down in his bed and traveled back into memory.

THE GUEST

MARK WARREN OPENED HIS eyes but couldn't see a thing. His head was pounding, and when he placed his hand on the back of his neck, he touched what felt like dried blood. Panic set in as he thought for a moment his vision wasn't returning. However, his eyes slowly adjusted and focused until he could finally discern the features of his surroundings.

"Thank God," Mark whispered, attempting to get to his feet.

He fell back onto the bed as his head felt like it might explode. Mark rubbed his temples and took in the surroundings. He was in an old bedroom. An antique fireplace with an ornate mantel loomed on the wall opposite him, and two tall windows, hidden by large velvet drapes, stood on the wall to his left. The room was dusty and drab, though appointed with what looked to have once been rather lavish furniture. The chairs, tables, dressers, and lamps were of another era. He was no expert in antiques, but he thought they looked Victorian. The bed he was lying on was a solid oak four-poster, with dark velvet curtains tied to its posts. A few dim gas lamps illuminated the room.

Who lit them? How did I get here?

Slowly, he slid himself to the side of the bed and struggled to bring himself to his feet. His head still pounded, though slightly less than before. He pressed his thumbs against his temples and reached into his pocket for his migraine pills, but found nothing—no wallet, no keys, no change, no meds. He quickly reached for his gun, but found an empty holster.

Mark moved to the windows and pulled open one of the heavy curtains. He couldn't make out much of the surroundings save for a few gnarled trees and a thick fog billowing across the dead ground, but he realized he was on the second floor of the house. Nothing about his surroundings looked familiar. In fact, he couldn't see another house anywhere.

I must be out in the country somewhere, maybe Leclaire—a lot of old houses like this out there.

Turning from the window, he spotted a door next to the fireplace. His vision was always blurry during a migraine attack. Only through pure willpower was he able to keep himself from doubling over and vomiting on the floor—that and the fact he probably hadn't eaten a thing in several hours. He reached the door and leaned his forehead against it to gather himself.

A woman's voice suddenly cut through the silence of the old house, startling him and sending chills across his back. It was a familiar voice—an impossible voice.

"Mark, my love! I've found you at last!"

Jennifer!

Mark turned, thinking he'd see the face of his late wife. Instead, he saw the rotting face and naked body of an old woman. She clawed at the window with crooked fingers and black nails. Mark's blood chilled, and though he tried with all his might, he could not turn his eyes away from the woman at the window.

"Mark Warren, I see you are a lost soul, just like your wife!" the old woman said.

"You!" Mark cried. "I've seen your face before!"

"Yes, I believe you have," she said, laughing.

"What have you done with Jennifer?"

"Would you like to see her?"

"Yes," Mark replied, tears welling up in his lower eyelids.

"The girl has amused me, but I'm afraid she has become rather tiresome. At first, she offered sport. Her spirit was strong, and her breaking did not come fast, but alas it came, and her suffering no longer brings me joy as it once did. If you do not come retrieve her, I will have to pass her on to others, others who may not be as kind as old Griselda."

"You lie!" he screamed.

"You know in your heart what I say is true."

"Why should I believe you? I've never met you before in my life, and every fiber of my being tells me you are evil!"

"Ha! That I may be, but I speak the truth, regardless. See for yourself!"

Griselda reached around behind her and dragged forward a woman in a torn and ragged dress. It was Jennifer. She stood there staring in through the window, looking like something broken. Mark's strength crumbled at the sight of her.

"Mark!" his wife cried weakly.

Her face battered and bruised, her will had long since left her. She existed at the whim of this cruel old woman. As much as Mark wanted to break through the window and rescue her, an alarm sounded in his mind. He had the feeling his wife was bait.

Why? Why would this woman want me?

"Jennifer!" Mark wept. "I'm so sorry!"

"My love," she cried. "Why have you come to this place? You shouldn't be here! Run! Seek the gates and save the boy!"

Griselda shoved her down to the balcony floor and held her there with one dirty foot. "Shut up, you little rag! I will deal with you later. As you can see, Officer Warren, she is with me. Come outside and join your dirty little wife."

"Why don't you come in here?" Mark asked.

Griselda paused for a moment, and though she didn't have eyes or any ability to make a facial expression, her manner conveyed a hesitation. She did not expect this question.

"What do you mean?" she asked.

Mark cleared his throat. "Why don't you break through the glass and come inside if you want me so badly? Why don't you walk into this house right now?"

Griselda's silence told Mark all he needed to know. Griselda, for whatever reason, could not enter this place. She needed Mark to come to her. Mark felt the power emanating from this foul creature, and though he didn't know where he was, something told him exiting the house was the worst choice he could make. As mighty as the urge was to run to his wife and take her in his arms, the alarm in his mind told him this was not the way.

But my Jennifer!

If it was truly his wife lying out there under the rotting foot of this madwoman, Mark could hardly bring himself to think of the horrors she had faced. Her eyes told but a hint of a terrible story he knew would break his heart if ever he heard it. Tears involuntarily trickled down his face. How could he simply walk away from the love of his life? After all this time, how could he make the choice he knew he had to make?

"I promise you, my love. I will find you again, and I will set you free." Turning to Griselda, Mark said, "And you, you nasty bitch, you will burn for this. I swear to you. You will burn."

Mark looked once again at his wife, then turned his back on them both and ran out the door, slamming it behind him, as Griselda screamed into the night.

The hallway was dimly lit and musty. The old paintings hanging on the walls seemed to change each time Mark looked away. One moment there would be a still life of a bowl of fruit, the next there would be an ocean scene with a lone sailboat, and the next a vase of flowers. With the muted colors and dusty rooms, and it felt to Mark as if he had stepped into an old sepia-toned photograph.

The hall ended at a window on one end and the top of a staircase on the other. Mark went to the window to see if he would have any better luck figuring out where he was from that angle. The view was of the back of the home, and he could see an old carriage house in the driveway. The drive wound down a hill, swallowed by a thick fog less than a quarter of a mile down the hill. There was an immense amount of fog encircling the entire property, making it impossible to tell much about his surroundings. However, as he looked further, he saw an enormous mansion sitting at the top of a hill less than a half mile away. He immediately recognized it as the Bennett mansion. That meant that he was inside the guesthouse. He couldn't see much else from this window, so he continued exploring.

There were two doors on either side of the hall—the one he had just exited and a door directly across the hall from it. Mark went to the second door and cautiously opened it. A smell of dust and mildew hit him in the face as he pushed it open.

The room was like the one in which he had awakened. In fact, it was a mirror image. There was the same fireplace and similar furniture. Two large windows stood opposite him, and another four-poster bed sat in the corner, though this one had its curtains drawn closed. As he crossed to the windows, he prayed Griselda would not be out there waiting for him.

Mark pulled aside one curtain a few inches. Seeing that the dead woman was not out there, he murmured thanks and opened the curtain all the way. To the right, he could see the Bennett mansion illuminated in pale white lights.

I'm in Bettendorf!

The mansion's windows were mostly dark, save for one. In one small window of the upper east wing, a solitary candle flickered with a pale glow. Mark paused for a moment, wondering. Then, looking at what should have been downtown Bettendorf, he saw nothing but fog, trees, and leaves scattered everywhere.

That doesn't make sense, Mark thought. *Where are all the houses? The churches? Heck, the 74 bridge should be visible from this window.*

It was as if something transported the Bennett estate and all its surroundings into a dream world. The thought crossed his mind that perhaps he was dreaming. That thought had crossed his mind a few times since he'd awakened in this house. Where was everyone? Why was he alone?

As he made his way back to the bedroom door, he heard a weak voice from the corner of the room. "Hello?" it called out, faintly.

Startled by this unexpected utterance, Mark turned toward the sound and saw the covered four-poster bed in the corner. He heard movement behind the curtains.

"Hello? Who's there?" he asked.

"Come closer, dear, I can't see you," the voice called. It sounded like an old woman, frail and soft.

"I can't see you either," Mark replied. "The bed curtains are closed. Pull them back, and we can see each other. I've never stepped foot in this house, so I'm not sure who I can trust."

"Whom, dear. And you're wise to be cautious, especially here. This place is full of tricks and traps. Only the wise will find their way out, though I cannot say if out is a direction you will be heading. I will use what little strength I have left to open this curtain so we may talk like civilized people."

After much struggling and groaning, an old bony hand reached out from the curtains and firmly grabbed one side, pulling it back to reveal an old woman in an ivory gown. Her wavy white hair flowed across the bed behind her. There was a strength in her eyes, and Mark sensed she could read his every thought just by looking at him. She laid her head on a large pillow and gazed out at Mark, her gray eyes glowing in the reflection of candlelight. Her gaze held him for a moment before she spoke.

"You're a police officer," she said.

"Yes," Mark answered.

"And you say you don't know how you came to be here?"

"No, ma'am. I don't remember a thing about it."

"What *do* you remember?" she asked.

"Uh, well—I remember I found that Caine girl. Stephanie Caine."

"Don't know her, dear."

"Oh, she's a missing girl. She'd been missing for days. I found her at a cemetery, I think. Yes! The Fenno Cemetery on—what's that street? How odd I can't remember that. Anyway, I found her—and then she was different, I think. Then someone hit me over the head, and here I am."

"Perhaps her captor hit you?" the old woman offered.

"I don't think so."

"Why not?"

Mark rubbed his temples again; his headache was returning. He sat down in a soft reading chair next to him. "I don't know. There was something strange about her—something she said. What was it?"

The old woman narrowed her eyes, and she lifted her head off the pillow. "What, dear? What did the girl say to you?"

"I can't remember."

"Yes, you can. It only happened last night. Think!"

"I don't know. It wasn't so much what she said but how she said it. She told me I shouldn't have come there, or something like that. It was like a warning—no, more like a threat. I don't know. None of this makes sense."

Suddenly, Mark thought of something the old woman had just said to him. "Hey, how do you know it happened last night?"

"Oh, didn't you mention it, dear?"

"No, I didn't."

"I suppose it was a fortuitous guess? I've always had a gift for such things." The old woman smiled.

"I don't believe you. Who are you? Are you a friend of that Griselda woman?"

At this accusation, the old woman grew cold. "What do you know of that one?"

"Who? Griselda?"

"Do not speak her name!" the old lady shouted with more force than Mark would have expected from someone who looked so frail. "She is an abomination. The mention of her name brings evil into this house as she brought evil into that one!" She pointed a thin finger in the mansion's direction.

"Sorry, ma'am," Mark whispered. "I know nothing about this place—I don't even know where I am. And that woman had my wife and was using her as some kind of bait just now. She tried to lure me to join her outside, but something told me that was the wrong decision. I had to turn my back on the love of my life. I'm lost, and my head is killing me."

The old woman's eyes slowly softened as she listened to his tale, and at last, she tenderly patted the bed. "Please dear. Come sit."

Mark studied her for a moment. "What's your name?" he asked finally.

"Ah yes, my name. I am Genevieve Bennett, and I am the matriarch of what's left of this family and its estate. My son built it and brought me here when he made his fortune. And what are you called, Officer?"

"I'm Mark Warren."

"Pleased to meet you, Mark Warren. Won't you now come and sit by me so I may tell you some things?"

Mark stood and walked to the bed. Now closer, he saw she held a solemn power within her. She had stood toe to toe with some powerful men in her day and probably held her own. There was wisdom behind those tired eyes. He thought it would have been quite something to have known this woman in her prime.

"Oh, Mark, it's difficult to know how to put a thing like this. Should one take one's time and put it delicately, or would it be kinder to state the fact and move on? This is quite a pickle, but I suppose letting you know all at once might be the best thing for it. You have much to do and not much time to do it, if I'm not mistaken, though I admit I often am mistaken these days. My vision isn't as clear as it used to be, and my attention is hard to hold. However, I think there is a reason you wound up here."

"What are you talking about?" Mark asked, confusion permeating his voice. However, he had a feeling he knew exactly what the woman would say next. And just like that, his headache disappeared.

"My dear, you are dead."

Opus and Maximus

1.

Jack is traveling. Peregrinating, as Ava called it.

He stands on the lawn of the Bennett mansion and watches his ten-year-old body being dragged across the yard by an enormous shadow man who is following Griselda Bennett toward her mausoleum.

Thunder rumbles overhead. Jack can feel the chill wind of the fall storm blowing across his face. He's in the memory, and yet he isn't.

The wolves follow the procession, their heads bowed low, with a palpable reluctance in their gait. Something about them seems familiar, and for a moment, he thinks he can almost remember their names.

Unexpectedly, the wolves stop in their tracks and turn to look directly at Jack—the traveling Jack, not the boy in the memory. At first, he tells himself that perhaps they are seeing something behind him. However, the darker wolf, the one with bright golden eyes, looks directly at him with some recognition. He whines once and wags his tail. The larger one with light-gray fur sniffs the air and wags his tail too.

"Opus, Maximus! Come!" yells the shadow man, his deep voice chilling the air. "Get your asses over here, or it'll be the whip again, and this time I won't finish until you're crawling on your bellies."

Afraid to see whether this wretched man will keep his promise, Jack motions for the wolves to keep moving, whispering to them, "Go on."

Turning his head, the dark wolf trots back to the shadow man. The larger wolf follows the command, though he glances at Jack once or twice. The man barks a few more obscenities at them and follows Griselda into her mausoleum.

Jack's vision goes dark. He feels his spirit drift up off the ground and into the sky over Bettendorf. Below him, the streets, which only an hour earlier were bustling with costumed children, are now empty and silent. Jack's vision continues to fade as he floats in the air for almost an hour, soaring through his mind in complete darkness until he opens his eyes again.

2.

Jack woke slowly. Though he knew the secret of that night was important, he couldn't bring himself to stay in the memory. Whatever lay there was too painful to bear.

"I can't do it," he admitted to Anne, who was sitting in the chair at Jack's desk, watching him with worry in her eyes. "I'm afraid."

"I know you are, and I don't blame you. I'd find it strange if you were not. You have lived these years since that night without ever looking back on it and never remembering. I knew there had to be a good reason for that, so I never pressed you to try. It's why I sang 'The Hymn of Forgetting' all these years. Not to hide secrets from you, but to protect you."

"I know, Anne. And I thank you. What do you know about it?"

"I've told you I know little about what happened to you that night. Though I can protect you here in our home, I cannot protect you everywhere. You were out of my reach for a long time. I could feel that you were in pain and lost, almost overcome at one point, and I could do nothing but wait. I tried, Jack. Oh, how I tried! I searched for you in Faelia between this world and the next, hoping you'd go there when the suffering became too great, but you never did. That is my fault. I should have shown you how to get there." Anne bowed her head, and it looked as though she were crying.

"I'm sorry, Anne," was all Jack could say in response. He lay there in his bed, looking up at the ceiling for a few minutes before speaking again. "Something else happened that night. I feel it. And the wolves? They stopped in the middle of the memory and looked at me like they knew I was there. How can that be if it was only a memory I was watching?"

"I don't know, Jack. I know nothing about these wolves, but I think they must be an important part of the memory if what you say is true."

"The problem is, when tried to find the memory, it got cut off right at the moment Griselda was dragging my body into the crypt. It's like something blocked that part of the memory. A giant black hole I couldn't enter. Do you think someone is trying to keep me out?"

"Someone is trying very hard to keep you out of that memory, if I'm not mistaken."

"Who?"

"*You.* I'm sure you have many reasons to do that. Self-protection would be my guess."

Jack lay there, thinking. Whatever happened that night was traumatic enough to make him hide it and hide it well. He hadn't thought about that night even once in the six years since it happened. However, the memory was still there. He only needed to access it, like a burned-up computer hard drive.

Anne touched his arm softly and asked, "Jack, what if you didn't want yourself to find it?"

Jack pondered these things as his eyes closed, and he once again journeyed out of his bedroom and into the Bettendorf night sky.

3.

Up into the breaking clouds he soars, passing out of time and into a thin, silvery lining of nothingness—into a void. A place between all worlds, filled with nothing and everything at once. He pauses in it for only a moment before he pivots and plunges back into a Bettendorf sky, sporadically illuminated with increasingly frequent lightning. He travels right back into the memory he aimed for.

I'm a natural at this, Jack thinks as he dives through the clouds.

Down he goes, his body not falling but driving to its destination with a purpose. Jack continues to plunge further and further into the clouds until he finally breaks through just above the Bennett mansion and dives directly through the roof of Griselda's mausoleum.

Without warning, as he is about to enter the old crypt, everything goes black, and for a moment Jack wonders if he is waking up again. After several minutes of continued blackness, he realizes he has entered a heavily guarded area of his memory. Try as he might, there seems to be no way into the event, so Jack sends his consciousness onward, searching and scanning for any sign of an opening. He searches around the memory for a time until he finally notices light at the edge of the darkness through which he can see figures moving and struggling, faintly shimmering through the veil.

With a last effort, Jack launches himself across the ethereal partition. His vision clears until he is once again back in the memory. Pain is surging all over his body. Young Jack is tied to a chair, his arms bound behind his back. A voice speaks, breaking through the waves of pain.

"That was a rude thing you did, naughty. Where did you learn to do such a thing?" the voice asks.

Griselda Bennett hesitantly glares down at Jack, as if her eyeless face could convey such an emotion.

"After all the fun we had, you still need to be taught your place? That's fine, young Jack, that is just exquisite. You will learn your place and serve your master."

Jack leans to the right and sees the shadow man on the other side of the crypt, moaning in anguish and cursing in a language he does not recognize. Apparently, someone has hurt him, and Jack has a feeling he is responsible. The two wolves are sitting near the shadow man, watching the tantrum from a relatively safe distance. Neither seems concerned. In fact, it almost looks like they are enjoying it.

The shadow man turns to the dark wolf and says, "Oh, you find this amusing, don't you? Do you enjoy watching your master writhe in pain? Perhaps you need to learn a thing or two about pain yourselves!"

The shadow man reaches out his dark hand, and from it grows a long black whip that curls around and cracks in the air as he thrashes his arm forward. The wolves grimace and bow their heads, no doubt knowing what is coming. Jack wonders why they sit there as the shadow man whips each of them over and over. *Why don't they fight back?* Jack weeps as the wolves fall on their back, yelping.

"Stop it!" Jack screams as he struggles to free himself from the ropes. His entire body aches. "Leave them alone!"

"What was that?" the shadow man growls.

"Leave them alone!"

"Opus and Maximus are *my* wolves. I will do with them as I please, just as I will do with you as I please! See these collars? You will wear one yourself!"

Jack notices each wolf is wearing a strange collar. They appear black and yet transparent. As Jack focuses more closely, he sees a faint shimmer of energy running along the edges of each collar, like an electric current.

As the shadow man resumes his whipping, this time with doubled effort, Griselda laughs and mockingly cries out toward the wolves. Each yelp and moan seems to bring her a sick pleasure. She hops around Jack's chair, her naked, rotting body convulsing in the torchlight. Jack stares at the scene before him.

The eyes of the dark wolf are on him, and it almost appears he is trying to communicate with Jack—like he is pleading.

Pleading for what? What can a little boy do about this?

Jack struggles with the ropes, but the knot will not budge. But even if they came free, how would that change anything? He would still be a young boy facing a crazy dead woman and a walking shadow man.

There has to be something else, something I'm missing.

Just then he glimpses a bright-silver lock on the collar around the dark one's neck. If only he could find a key and unlock the collar, maybe then he could free the wolves and break the spell. Maybe they would help him escape? With two giant wolves like these on his side, Jack would have a fighting chance to escape with his life.

Use your mind, Jack. As Jack stares at the lock, his eyes suddenly roll back into his head. Instinctively, he pushes his mind forward, and, to his surprise, his consciousness suddenly travels across the room, even as his physical self still sits on the wood chair. He looks back at his body. He has a cut on the forehead, and one of his eyes is swollen shut. Blood soaks through the fabric of his torn costume. He sits in a pool of his urine.

Fury rises within him. He turns his mind back to the wolves. He launches it into the black wolf's lock and, with complete clarity, commands it to open. Just like that, the lock clicks, and the collar falls open and immediately disappears into thin air. Surprising himself, Jack rejoices for only a moment and then thrusts his mind into the collar around the gray wolf's neck, opening it with the same ease of command.

With surprising speed, both wolves stand up and bare their teeth, growling on either side of the shadow man. Griselda, who was laughing hysterically up to that moment, falls silent. She looks at Jack and says, "What have you done now?"

The wolves release deep growls as they slowly close in on each side of the shadow man. The dark one glances at Jack for a moment, then turns his attention back to his prey. His teeth, fully bared, are pure white and sharp as knives. The hackles on both beasts are up. The gray wolf circles to the left of the shadow man, looking toward the dark wolf for a signal.

"Oh, you want to challenge me?" the shadow man asks, his voice unable to hide his fear. "I will wear your pelts as I sit on my throne next to the Great One."

The threat falls flat as Opus and Maximus continue stalking the black figure. Again, the dark wolf glances at Jack.

The shadow man then looks at Jack and says, "Ha! Do you think he will be a kinder master than me? Just wait until his moment comes! He will take his place with me below the Great One, and you will be forgotten and abandoned in a dark corner of hell if you are lucky. Now bow down again and take your collars before you do something that cannot be undone."

The last command sounds desperate. At once, they launch themselves at him, the dark one attacking high and the gray one striking low. The wolves grab hold of him and tear black pieces of what appear to be his flesh. The shadow man screams and thrashes at his attackers, sending one falling backward. But each time one of them falls, the other tears at him with twice the fury.

Eventually, the shadow man backs away and looks around him, searching for an escape. His strength fades. Finally, he glances once more at Jack, then turns and flees from the crypt in a flash of light and smoke. The wolves, though bloody and shaken, are still strong enough to continue their march toward Griselda. The old woman has long since silenced her diabolical laughter and is now retreating to her bier.

She scowls at Jack and says, "You are a fool. You will pay for this, you naughty boy! I swear to you; I will make you pay to the ending of time!" And with that, she opens the top of the bier and climbs inside, letting the large stone crash closed above her.

The dark wolf looks at Jack and quietly approaches him while the gray one watches. Jack looks into the wolf's bright-yellow eyes and sees a feral intelligence in them. When it speaks to him, it does so through some telepathy. Jack can hear the wolf in his mind.

"We thank you. You have set us free from a life of servitude and persecution. For that, we owe you our loyalty. I am Maximus, and this is my brother, Opus."

The wolves bow their heads and wait for Jack to say something.

"I'm Jack Davies. Please help me out of these ropes?" Jack asks, his voice cracking with exhaustion.

The wolves chew through the ropes until there is nothing but a pile of strands on the floor. Jack gingerly pulls his arms forward and sits there for a time, trying to regain his senses.

"Thank you," he says weakly. "I don't know what I would have done without you. I'd probably be dead now."

Jack stumbles as his head spins. The wolves come to him and lick his wounds. Healing comes to any wound their tongues touch, and Jack fades out of consciousness.

As he drifts off to sleep, he hears Maximus say, "You have done us a great deed, Jack Davies. No one has ever set us free before. This world is not our own, so we must leave you. However, we will keep a sliver of our spirits here and resume our stone watch atop the staircase behind the mansion. If ever you are in need, call our names, Opus and Maximus. We will come to your aid wherever we may be."

Jack can barely hear the words as he feels himself hoisted onto the back of Opus. Soon, they're bounding through the grass and leaves and trees toward home.

Faelia

Jack awoke on his back in a field of tall green grass with bright-yellow, brown, red, and orange leaves waving above him. Over everything was the sound of a hymn, gently sung, one he could almost remember. Obviously, he wasn't in his bed, and judging from the natural perfection all around him, he wasn't in Bettendorf either.

A soft breeze gently blew a light mist across the green hills, and though the sky was cloudy, the effect was not at all gloomy—it was magical. He felt magic vibrate through the earth and air. He could almost remember being here as a child. He had come here with Anne when he was young.

Faelia.

That was the name—his place, Anne's place. The memories flooded his mind. He and his sister were royalty here, and they lived together on the western side of the Faenorian Wood in a castle filled with song and joy.

Why had it been so long since he'd come here? Why did he not remember it until now?

More questions without answers once again—his life had become an endless supply. *I'd better get used to it,* he told himself.

Dry twigs cracked behind him, and when he turned to look, he saw Anne walking through a thin layer of fog.

"Jack," she said.

"Hello, Anne. How did I get here?"

"I guided you with my hymn. Did you remember the way?"

"I think so. I'm here, anyway."

Other songs hummed in his ears. He looked around and saw fairies and tiny sprites hovering around the tops of the trees, giggling as they watched from above.

"Will you remember how to get here, Jack? It's critical. Would you remember how to get here on your own if you needed to?" She crossed to him and took his hands.

"I think so. Why haven't we returned here before now? Why has it been so long?"

She smiled sadly and squeezed his hands. "You grew up, my brother, and no longer sought these places. Your mind was on other things and I didn't push you, but now it is time for you to remember. I think someday soon you'll need shelter here."

"We—have a castle here, right?" he asked, distracted again by the world around him.

"Yes, we do. Your memory is returning, I see. But it is many miles away on the other side of the wood," she answered.

"Can we see it?" he asked, walking to the edge of the Faenorian Wood.

Instantly, Anne reappeared, grasping his hand. "Someday."

Jack closed his eyes for a moment. "I can't remember what it looks like, the castle—our castle—not the rooms, not the walls. Is that strange?"

"It has been years since you walked through the arches and opened its doors. But that journey is for another day. And it may not be a happy one if my feelings do not deceive me. But now you must come with me before you slip back to our world. There is something I must show you in the wood."

Anne then led him through giant Faenorian trees along the winding path of an overgrown road as he listened to the whispers of a cold, running brook. They found a small clearing far within the woods, miles from where

Jack awoke. In the middle of it stood the statue of a girl, a beautiful girl with light-brown hair and blue eyes.

"Is this you?" he asked.

"Yes, or rather, it is a statue of me," she answered.

"Who made it?"

"An elderly artist who lives close to here. You commissioned it." Anne laughed and smiled again as she touched the sculpture.

"I love it."

"I love it too," Anne said. "It's why I brought you here, Jack. So you remember how to get here in a time of trouble. If ever you find yourself in need, come to this place. Come to this statue and help may find you."

"Ah, I think I'll sit awhile, Anne. I'm so tired. My legs are butter."

As Jack lay on the ground under the statue, Anne kneeled beside him and sang a sweet hymn to guide his path back to bed.

The Date

1.

October, 31st. Halloween.

Fittingly, Jack awoke to the sound of a blood-curdling scream—not his own, but his mother's. He jumped out of bed and sprinted down the stairs, skipping them two at a time. He bolted down the hall and swung himself through the dining room and into the kitchen to find his mother cleaning up a mess of broken glass.

"What happened?" Jack asked.

"Oh, I knocked over a glass. Nothing to worry about."

"Geez, Mom! You scared me to death."

Jack's mom let out a small laugh and said, "Sorry! It startled me. I guess that's fitting, it being Halloween and all. Ha!"

"What startled you?"

"Oh, I thought I saw someone. It was nothing."

"What do you mean?"

"Oh, it was nothing. I thought someone was standing over there by the back steps. Just my eyes playing tricks on me, that's all. I bet you dollars to doughnuts I need a new prescription in these glasses."

"Huh," Jack grunted. "What did the person look like?"

"What? Oh, I don't know. I only saw him for a second, but it seemed like a big shadow standing there by the steps, like a silhouette. I got startled and knocked over the glass. When I looked back, it was gone. You know,

I always wondered if we had ghosts in this house. Ha! Wouldn't that be something?"

"Uh-huh," Jack muttered, frozen still as he stared into the cereal cabinet.

His mom looked at him and apologized. "Oh, don't be afraid. There're no ghosts in here. I'm sure."

And with that, Jack's appetite was officially gone. There was no way for him to say, *Oh yes, Mother. We live in a haunted house. Oh, that shadow man you saw is only the spirit that kidnapped me when I was ten and tortured me in Griselda Bennett's crypt!*

Jack avoided this conversation by leaving out the back door and walking up the alley to Mississippi Avenue. Halloween decorations were on full display in the neighborhood—even the procrastinating neighbors finally had theirs up. He decided he might as well continue west until he got to the gates of the Bennett estate, and since he got that far, it was only logical for him to climb the broken staircase.

Wet oak leaves covered most of the stairs. Jack had to use his foot to sweep a path to avoid slipping on them. When he reached the top, he looked across the field and saw the two stone wolves sitting at their places on top of the grand staircase, staring in opposite directions, as always. Once he reached them, he turned around and looked out over the expanse of downtown Bettendorf, with the Mississippi River running beyond it and Moline, Illinois, over the horizon.

Jack looked back at the wolves and tentatively said, "Opus and Maximus."

He waited a moment or two, then called out again, "Opus and Maximus."

Still, nothing happened. The wolves remained motionless, weathered from the years of bitter winters and humid Midwestern summers.

"They won't come," came a voice from Jack's left, and he almost tumbled down the stairs from shock. Ava stood there watching him with her hands folded casually across her chest. "They're not yours to call as you please."

"I traveled here in my dreams last night, but I think you already know that, don't you?"

"Yes, I do."

"How?" Jack asked.

"We're connected."

"You can read my mind?"

"Not exactly. But I can look into your dreams."

Jack's face flushed. "You can see my dreams?"

Ava laughed. "Yes, Jack. But I only look at the important ones, the ones when you're peregrinating. Though I admit, one or two others tempted me."

Jack hid his face in his hands. When he regained his composure, he looked back at the statues. "They said they'd come if I called them."

"That may be so, but they are far from this world. Trusting the word of ones such as them is difficult. Besides, you have no need for them now. You wanted to see if they'd come when you called. Or am I mistaken? Is there some significant threat approaching you?"

"I don't know. Are *you* a threat?"

"That depends."

"On what?"

Ava smiled, then looked at the house. "Do you know what happened here? I mean, before it was a prep school and a historic landmark?"

"Not really. My grade school came here on a field trip in second grade, I think. I remember them saying William Bennett was a wealthy businessman. He invented something, I think."

"Yes, he did. He invented a something."

Jack rolled his eyes. "What do you know about him?"

"He came from the East Coast with his brother," Ava said. "And together they built their factory here in Bettendorf, down there by the river. Most of the buildings are gone, but you can still see the railroad tracks and some warehouses. The Bennetts made a massive fortune, even by today's standards, and built this lavish estate, where he and his mother lived like aristocrats. They had an enormous staff of servants and cooks."

"I don't remember hearing about his brother," Jack said.

"Jacob. He was the silent partner. Much about him is unknown; they were always a secretive family. William built him a large home a mile away from here. It's a retirement home now."

"Oh, really? When did William meet his wife?"

"Several years after he moved to this area. Griselda was her name. They met while he was on a trip to New York, at a party thrown by some tycoon friend of his. It was love at first sight. They married on that trip, and she returned with him here. Genevieve, Bennett's mother, disliked Griselda from the minute she met her. The mother would tell her son to divorce 'that terrible woman.' Eventually, Griselda convinced her husband to build that guesthouse over there, across the main drive, just to get the old woman out of the house."

"How do you know so much about this?"

"I've done my research."

"So what happened to Griselda? William built the mausoleum on the other side of the house for her, didn't he?"

"That is true. He did, or he had it built. As to your first question—that is a tale best left for another time and another place. The dead do not rest comfortably here. Let's change the subject, shall we?"

Jack sighed and looked back at the wolves. "Where are they now?"

"The wolves? Who knows?" Ava answered. "Imagine what you could do with a pair like that."

"How did they get here?" Jack asked as he crossed to Opus and laid his hand on the sculpture's stone back.

"Who can say? Someone either clever or foolish must have summoned them. It's hard to be sure. Maybe they crossed over at some point."

"Did Griselda summon them?"

"These two roamed this world long before Griselda Bennett came into it. How they came to be here in Iowa is perhaps the biggest mystery of all. I know little about them though I've heard stories. I think I saw them once, long ago in Europe, but only briefly."

"Do you think they remember me?"

Ava laughed again, but this time with affection. "I would imagine you are often in their thoughts. You freed them. But as for their pledge to rescue you in a time of need—I wouldn't expect it, Jack. Time moves oddly in odd worlds. They may have lived many thousands of years since you last met them."

"They may even be dead."

"I suppose."

Sighing, Jack sat on the steps and put his head in his hands. "I still don't understand any of this."

"There is only so much I can tell you, my love. The rest you must discover yourself. Anne said much already, though she only understands half of it."

"How can you know so much and so little?"

Ava narrowed her eyes and replied, "How do you not see? Forces are trying to enter your world—forces from another dimension. You know this already."

"But what does that have to do with me? Am I different from everyone else in the world?"

"You are. How do you not see that by now? Your house is full of ghosts who seek only you. Your dead sister still speaks to you every day. You travel through your dreams and enter your memories. And you ask if you're special?"

"But what am I to do? If I'm special, what is my purpose?"

Ava sat next to him and put a warm hand on his shoulder. He felt a kind of electricity when she touched him, and he wished at that moment he could kiss her. "Jack, like everyone else, you will find that answer on your own. My lengthy life hasn't revealed the slightest detail of a grand plan, if one exists."

"What are you?"

"Oh, now that secret is my own. At least for now."

"Anne said you're a dark spirit. If that's true, why are you helping me?"

"Anne doesn't understand what that means, but to answer your question, I am helping you because that is what I wish to do. I have my reasons for it, and though it's true, I am a spirit of darkness, I am not evil. That's what your sister doesn't understand, which is why you must be careful when taking her advice. Being 'of the light' doesn't mean 'good' and being 'of the dark' doesn't mean 'evil.' Each must choose his path."

"I see," Jack said.

Ava stood, grabbing Jack's arm and lifting him to his feet. "Listen, you need a little fun. We both do. Jen Graver invited me to a party she's throwing tonight. Wasn't that nice of her? Most of the girls look at me with pure jealousy, but she seems to be of the 'can't beat 'em, join 'em' school of thought. How about you be my date?"

"Your date?"

"You have been on a date, haven't you?"

"Um—"

Ava laughed out loud, quickly covering her mouth with her hand.

"Hey! Don't make me cause another earthquake!" Jack said, blushing.

"OK, fine. How about I pick you up at seven?"

"You drive?"

"I do. Believe me, I'm old enough."

2.

Later that evening, Jack held his phone a foot away from his ear as Randy's voice screamed through the receiver, "What do you mean you're going to the party with Ava? Are you crazy? Seriously!"

"Dude, I'm sorry, but she asked me to go, and well, I couldn't say no. Plus, I kinda want to. She's not so bad."

"Not so bad! Not so bad? She's a—what is it you called her? A dark spirit or some shit? What the hell kinda 'not so bad' is that?" Randy's voice was cracking with frustration.

"Geez, calm down, would ya? It's not a big deal. We're just going to the party together. We're not getting married."

"Well, who am I supposed to go with?" And with that question, Jack understood why Randy was upset. He didn't want to go alone.

"How about Shaun and Joe?"

"They're already picking up Brian and Mike. There's no room in Shaun's little car. Not to mention the fact we were supposed to go together!"

"Look, I'll ask Ava to pick you up on the way, OK? I'm sure she will be all right with it."

There was silence on the other end of the line, and then Randy said, "You sure you don't mind me tagging along on your date with the demon girl? I mean, I'd hate to impede your little possession plans."

"Hey, dude, you can always stay home and watch TV with the fam all night. It makes no difference."

Jack checked his outfit in the mirror—a Knight of the Round Table costume. He had saved up his allowance and part of his yard-clipping money so he could afford a relatively realistic-looking set of armor. He discovered a fantastic costume, created for a Camelot production at the Rock Island dinner theater.

Randy sighed. "OK, I'll ride with you guys. You think she'll mind?"

There was a knock at the door and a moment later, Jack heard his dad talking to a girl in the living room. Panic set in.

"No. We're just going to a party together; it's not like it's a formal date. Look, I gotta go. She's here talking to my dad, and who knows what the hell he's saying to her. I'll text you when we're on our way."

Grabbing his helmet, Jack ran down the stairs and into the living room to find his dad and Ava chatting like old friends. Jack's heart always skipped a beat or two when he saw her, but this time he swore it jumped a couple extra. She was wearing a Harley Quinn costume, not from the lame movie, but the old-school version from the Batman comics. It was all black and red, with a short skirt, argyle leggings, and knee-high boots. She had her hair pulled into two cute pigtails. When she glanced up and saw his reaction, she gave him a satisfied smirk.

"Geez Jack, you didn't tell me you had a date tonight!" Richard exclaimed.

"Sorry, is that OK?" Jack knew it would be OK. His dad looked pleased as punch that Ava was picking him up. Though she told everyone she was seventeen years old and looked it, she had a more mature air about her.

"It sounds more exciting than sitting around here playing World of Warcraft all weekend."

Mortified by his dad outing his nerd side, Jack attempted to speak over him once he realized what he was saying. "OK! Thanks, Dad! See you later!" He grabbed Ava by the arm and rushed her out the door before his dad could say anything else.

"World of Warcraft, eh?"

Rolling his eyes, Jack said, "Shut up! That was like middle school. Seriously!"

As they reached her car, Ava looked across the roof and sighed. "That's a shame. My main is a warlock."

Jack threw his head back and whispered up to the sky, "Thank you, God!"

Bringing in the Sheaves

1.

Lara, dressed as Sally from *A Nightmare Before Christmas*, paced back and forth from the kitchen to the living room in the Dawson's' double-wide while listening to Jen Graver yell through the cell phone. Unfortunately, this year she had no date to play the Jack role. Suddenly, the irony of the character having the same name as that strange kid at school hit her, and she let out a small laugh.

"What's so funny?" Jen yelled over the phone.

Lara moaned, "I'm sorry! Yes, I know, Jen. I will be there, I swear. I'm just waiting for the Dawsons to get home. Besides, I feel like shit going to a party with Emily missing."

"I know. I do too. But we have planned this party for months. You know how much money I've spent on this thing? Emily wouldn't want us sitting at home by ourselves, crying all night."

It still didn't feel right, but Lara knew being around friends would be better than staying home alone. It probably wouldn't feel like Halloween this year, but at least she and her friends would be there for each other.

"It feels weird. But anyway, don't worry, I told the Dawsons I had plans. They'll be here on time," Lara said.

"Are you high? You know the Dawsons won't be home on time! How am I gonna finish getting this place ready?"

"Look, Jen, I *need* the money. You know that. And I made them promise me a million times they'd be home by seven. They aren't even drinking tonight. They're going to Happy Joe's for pizza and then right back here. I swear it!"

Jen sighed. "I can't believe you took that job after what happened to Emily in that shitty trailer park. I've heard from like five people that some creepy guys have been hanging around that whole Devils Glen area. And did you hear that a *cop* is missing now?"

"Yeah, I know. He was the cop who came the night Emily disappeared." Lara thought he seemed like a nice guy from the little she spoke to him, though some people wondered if Officer Warren had skipped town with Emily in his trunk.

"Who knows if he's out there looking for another victim," Jen said.

Mercifully, the Dawsons' car pulled into the driveway. Lara got off the phone, told her goodbyes to the Dawsons—after getting her pay for the evening, along with back pay from the last two babysitting gigs—and skipped out the door into the crisp Halloween night.

This neighborhood was always empty on Halloween. Most of the residents took their kids to other neighborhoods to do their trick-or-treating, so Lara found herself alone as she walked across the Dawsons' front yard. When she reached the sidewalk, she glanced down the street and saw a man standing by the corner wearing a cape with a vintage-style Dracula mask. He was watching her.

Lara thought about turning back to the Dawsons' place. Though every defensive instinct told her to run back inside, she continued to her car. As soon as she decided, she regretted it. As she briskly marched toward her vehicle, she could hear the mechanical sounds of a yard decoration—*waaaaaa-aaaaaaa waaaaaa-aaaaaaa.* She peered over her shoulder and saw that the man in the cape was still standing there watching.

Why do I have to be so stubborn? she growled in her mind. *I should have stayed inside.*

Soon she was standing next to her driver's side door. As she thrust her key into the lock, she stole a glance down the street. It was empty. Reminding herself it was Halloween after all and lots of people would walk around in costumes, she felt better almost at once and set her mind back to the party at hand. She hopped into her car, but just as she was about to put her key in the ignition, she saw something out of the corner of her eye.

The man in the cape was standing just outside her passenger window.

The plastic smiling cartoon vampire mask sent a chill down Lara's spine. They stared at each other for what felt like an eternity. Keeping her eyes on him, Lara felt for the ignition and reached out to slide the key home. However, her hands, shaking with heightened anxiety, fumbled for the keyhole, and she dropped them on the floor. Lara bent down and fished them out from between her feet. When she looked back up, she screamed. He was standing right outside her window—his head glaring directly at her.

"Trick or treat," a male voice whispered through the mask.

He thrust his fist into the passenger window, spraying the inside of the car with a thousand tiny shards of glass. Lara dropped her keys again as she held up her arms to block his hand. He grabbed her hair and began to pull her out the passenger window. As she slid across the passenger seat, broken glass dug into her legs, tearing her stockings along the way.

Why did I go to my car? Why didn't I go back inside the minute I saw this guy? There was no time for second-guessing now. Now was the time to fight back.

Lara reached down and snagged her keys. She laced them through her fingers, just like in self-defense class. She swung her fist straight into the side of the guy's head, feeling the keys sink into his temple. Her attacker groaned and fell backward to the ground, letting go of Lara's hair. Once he released her, she tipped out the window and crashed down onto the curb.

Lara was first to her feet. She took off down the street, screaming at the top of her lungs as she went. She rounded the next corner onto a darker avenue. Glancing back, she saw the man was back on his feet and gaining ground.

Toughness was never a problem for Lara, but she had a weakness with speed. From an early age, she had loathed running. In fact, sports were not high on the list of Lara's specialties. Lara's ambivalence toward exercise was now catching up to her, literally, as her pursuer drew closer.

A large sedan came around the corner ahead. Lara leaped into the street, jumping up and down in front of the car, waving her hands as wildly as she could until it stopped a few feet in front of her. A tall man stepped out of the driver's side.

"Hello, miss, what's wrong?" the man asked in a thick Southern accent.

"That man back there attacked me! I think it's the Devils Glen Stalker!"

She grabbed the man's arm and tried leading him back to his car, but he didn't follow. Instead, he pulled Lara back to his chest and held her close. "Oh, don't you worry about old Carl. He's just following orders, weren't ya?"

"What? What are you talking about?" she asked. "We have to get out of here—"

Lara tried to scream, but before she could, the man's big, gloved hand slapped over her face. In it, he held a rag soaked in a nasty-smelling chemical. Though she struggled with every ounce of strength she had, Lara could feel herself losing consciousness.

Within seconds, everything went black.

2.

Faint flickers of light blinked in Lara's vision. Slowly, she made out a few hazy details of her surroundings. She was lying on a cold cement floor, and she could feel someone touching her head. She was in some cage in a basement. A single light hung above her from the ceiling. The rest of the room was dark. Her head was aching, and her vision was shaky. She closed her eyes again and fell asleep for a few more minutes. Eventually, she woke to the sound of a girl's whispering voice.

"Lara, wake up. Lara, please wake up!"

Lara's eyes slowly opened, and she saw she was looking up into a bright incandescent light. An enormous head moved into view, mercifully shading her eyes from the light. At first, she couldn't tell who it was, but as her vision adjusted, she noticed long blond hair just above her face. As her eyes further adjusted, she saw a familiar face looking down at her.

"Emily! Oh my God," Lara cried. "You're alive?"

"*Sh!* Yes, it's me." Emily was smelly and disheveled. She looked like she'd been through the ringer, but she also had a demeanor that seemed unusual for her. She wasn't crying or broken. She seemed more alert and alive than before.

"What happened to you?" Lara asked.

"Same as you. Some weird guy took me."

"He was the one in the cape?"

"Yes, I think so."

Lara tried sitting up, but she felt a rush of dizziness and lay her head in Emily's lap. "Shit, I feel like I'm gonna puke."

"It's the chemical he used to knock you out. That feeling goes away after a while."

"There was another man with the guy in the mask. Who was he?".

"The preacher? He's the one who runs things. He's been nice so far. I think if we do what he says, we *might* be OK."

Poor sweet Emily, Lara thought. *Even now in captivity, she stays positive about her situation.* "What's that smell?" Lara asked.

"There's a pile of dead bodies over there on the other side of the room. It happens during every church service. The preacher gives a sermon, and then they bring down dead bodies. There must be dozens of them every service. They store them down here. I about lost my mind the first time it happened, but you kind of get used to it," Emily said, staring blankly into the dark part of the cellar.

Lara stared into the shadows, and as her eyes adjusted, she thought she could see a pile of clothes on the floor. But as she looked closely, she saw arms, legs, heads, and faces. Dead bodies piled almost to the ceiling—perhaps sixty or seventy, if not more. Lara heaved and held her hand over her mouth.

"They're killing people?" she asked. "What kind of church is this? Killing for Jesus?"

"Oh, it's not for Jesus, Lara. The preacher tells them to bring their sick to 'the Lord,' and I think the people assume he means Jesus, but I'm sure he doesn't."

Lara felt a chill run up her arms. She touched Emily's shoulder and asked, "You mean they're Satan worshippers?"

"I don't know who they worship. All I know is, they think they're doing something great for whoever it is they're serving. I don't know what to believe, Lara, but it might be best for us to play along. Do what they say and answer their questions." Emily helped Lara to a sitting position.

Lara stretched her neck out from side to side and rolled her shoulders as she asked, "So what do they want from us? Why are we alive?"

"That's a question I have asked myself about a thousand times this week," Emily answered with a hint of guilt. "I don't know why those people all had to die, and I had to live."

"Don't talk like that, Emily. You're alive for a reason, and so am I."

"There's something else, Lara. They keep talking about that Jack Davies kid."

Lara's ears perked. "Jack Davies? What do they want with *him*?"

"His name comes up in every conversation like he's *important* to them somehow. Do you know why they would be interested in him?"

Lara remembered seeing Jack's aura as he walked across the cafeteria earlier in the week. There was something different about Jack, something that set him apart. And she couldn't help feeling they shared a connection.

"Emily, I think there is something special about Jack. He's connected to all the stuff that's happening around here—Stephanie, you, me—" Lara suddenly felt like she was connecting pieces to an elaborate puzzle.

"You don't think he has something to do with us being kidnapped?" Emily asked.

"Well, no. I mean, there's been a bunch of weird stuff happening around here. First, someone kidnapped Stephanie, right? And then you got kidnapped, and then me. And this place?"

"Yes, that's true," Emily said. "But Jack? What does Jack have to do with this?"

"Well, the day after you got kidnapped, I was in the cafeteria talking to Jen and Susie when Jack walked in. He had a blue aura shining all around him. I swear it. It was the strangest thing."

"What do you mean?"

"It sounds crazy, but a bluish aura seemed to glow all around him. And ever since that day, I have had these dreams—dreams about saving *him*."

"Saving him from what?"

"Oh, different things. One time it will be a giant dragon, the next time it will be a crazy old witch, and the next a shadow. But I think there's something I'm supposed to do for him, protect him. It sounds dumb, I know."

Emily leaned in and took Lara's face in her hands. "Oh, honey, no it doesn't. It's not dumb at all—it makes perfect sense. Thank you." She then leaned in and kissed Lara full on the lips.

Lara jerked away and said, "Um—okaaaay. We need to figure out a way to get out of here. This cage doesn't look all that stable now I look at it. I'm surprised you didn't find a way out." Lara stopped for a moment and asked, "Hey, why did you thank me?"

Emily stood up and walked a few steps away. "I'm sorry, Lara, I truly am. But there's so much you don't know, so much you're *wrong* about."

"What do you mean?" Lara could feel tears welling up in her eyes as she caught the scent of betrayal in her best friend's words.

"You don't understand, Lara. There's a universe to learn about—so much to see! The Great Lord is coming, just like Brother Jones said he would. And now we have the key to let Him in! Praise Him! This is such a wonderful time to be alive!" Emily's eyes lit up as she lifted her hands to the ceiling.

"What are you talking about? We have to get out of here!"

Laughter rang out from the other end of the basement. Deep in the shadows, in a hidden corner, someone had been listening to their entire conversation. It was a girl's laugh—someone young—probably a teenager.

"Who's there?" Lara called into the shadows.

"Don't be afraid," Emily whispered, laying her chin on Lara's shoulder. "It's all going to be just fine. Trust us."

A girl was slowly approaching them. She wore a white blouse and had long red hair—the brightest red hair Lara had ever seen. When she spoke, her voice was familiar.

"You are both so cute together. I love it. We're gonna make an awesome family, the three of us."

"Who's out there?" Lara asked.

"An old friend," came the reply, and into the light stepped Stephanie Caine.

Lara felt the dizziness return, though this time it had nothing to do with chemicals. She allowed Emily to support her weight, even though a growing part of her wanted to rip out the girl's throat. This had all been a trap—a trap set for her by her friends. She had walked right into it.

"I never really thought you and I were friends, Steph. Now, I'm pretty *effing* sure we're not."

"Oh, that hurts, Lara," Stephanie mocked. "But you always were a mean little bitch."

"Oh, Steph, be nice. She's our friend," Emily said. "Don't worry, Lara. I promise to keep you safe. There's so much I must show you! You will love this new life! Brother Jones has sacrificed all these lives so he can give us a gift. He can give it to you too if you let him!"

"Oh, that's OK, Ems. I don't think I'm down for church, but I'm glad you guys have found the Lord and all." As she spoke, Lara peeled herself away from Emily's embrace and crept slowly over to the gate at the far end of the cage. "If you all don't mind, I'm gonna have to get a move on, so to speak. No hard feelings, OK?"

In a flash, Stephanie crossed the ten feet that remained between her and the cage and was standing just outside the gate with her face pressed to the chain link, inches from Lara's face. "Oh, Lara, you're not going anywhere yet. We have something planned for you, honey. Something that will make you a believer!"

Stephanie snarled and parted her lips, revealing perfectly white and deadly sharp canines. Emily was smiling, showing she too had sharp teeth of her own. Stephanie laughed and said, "Oh, honey, you *have* to get yourself a set of these."

This time the dizziness hit hard, sending Lara to the ground and back into the darkness as her vampire friends descended upon her. Stephanie and Emily sucked on her neck and shoulder until they had drained her of every drop of blood. She lay back her head and stared up at the ceiling. Death's light shone down upon her, but she didn't want to follow it. There was a pain, yes, but something more—something close to *exhilaration.* Sharp teeth stabbed into her neck and shoulders.

Her strength continued to fade, and she could feel her spirit trying to flee to the light, but desire held her back. The light felt warm and soothing, like a candle on Christmas Eve, but the deliciousness of the pain made her want to turn away. Soon she felt dark hands of death grabbing her, holding her firmly to the cellar floor, as her friends pushed their sliced open wrists into her mouth, spraying their corrupt blood down her throat.

Then she felt a horrible pain in her mouth as her teeth changed. New, sharp teeth pushed her canines out and slowly took their place. A thirst grew in her stomach until she had no choice but to bite down on Emily's waiting shoulder.

At first, she resisted the urge to drink. She spat it out and coughed it up, but as she tasted the sweet delight of the blood flooding her mouth, she was soon gulping it down as if her life depended on it. Back and forth, they passed the blood, draining Lara and then filling her again, repeatedly until she could feel a new power rising within her, changing her. Any desire for the light melted within her, and the only thing she wanted in all the world was blood.

Slowly, Lara relaxed. She held on to her friends, forgetting everything else that had happened that evening—even how she was in this state. Her mind could only focus on her senses, the tingling of electricity that tickled up and down her body, causing her to shudder every twenty or thirty seconds. She didn't break the embrace when she heard footsteps approaching the cage.

"Ah, there you girls are. What have we here? A new friend in the mix?" He had a smooth Southern drawl that made Lara want to scream. She shot him a look of rage and growled protectively over her friends.

"Oh, no need to get all high-strung on me there. Just calm your nerves, girl. We are all friends here, see? Good friends! Ain't that right, Jimmy?"

"Yep, that's right, Brother Jones," Jimmy Vance said as he entered the room, giving Lara a wink. "We're all *good* friends."

Her desire to remain entwined with the girls was almost overwhelming, milking the vampire sensations for all they were worth. But she denied it with a powerful surge of willpower. Panic shot through her nerves, and in a nanosecond, she jumped straight up into a crouched, defensive position, sending Stephanie and Emily reeling backwards.

Emily slowly rose and crept over to her. "Lara, it's OK. You're dying and changing. It takes a little time, and it will hurt a hell of a lot, but soon you'll feel OK. Stay with us. We can take your mind off the *horror*. Trust us."

"Trust? You expect me to believe you ever again? What the hell have you done?"

"Honey, control yourself. It's easy to fly off the handle and hurt yourself when you're new to it. Ha! I accidentally broke Stephanie's arm when she first made me."

Stephanie laughed. "Yeah, it hurt like shit. Well, for a minute anyway. Quit your crying, little bitch. It's a gift, girl. You're a vampire now. We can do anything we want, go *anywhere* we want! No one can mess with us. No guy will ever raise a hand to us again. We don't have to feel scared of anything ever again."

"Uh, ladies, I hate to interrupt this," Brother Jones said, chuckling. "But we have to get a move on. Things at the mansion are progressing, so we need to go find that Davies boy and get this show on the road."

"Davies? Jack Davies? What about him?" Lara asked.

"Don't you worry about that, little lady. He's not your worry tonight. Tonight, you need to focus on your new life, right here in this little old cellar. Jimmy, what do you say we lock our brand-new friend up for the night? Something tells me she ain't ready for this, not just yet. But first things first. Our little army."

Emily said, "Oh, Lara, you're just gonna love this. Watch!"

Brother Jones took off a leather glove he'd been wearing and stepped across the cellar toward the pile of bodies. Raising his hand above his head, he called out in a powerful voice, "By the Great One! I call upon the powers He gave me in all His infinite wisdom! I command you to rise and walk the earth. *Arise!*"

The pile of dead bodies across the cellar floor moved and shifted like a nest of vipers—arms and legs pushing and pulling. The mound of corpses came alive. Within minutes, a great host of the undead had separated themselves from one another and stood staring at Brother Jones as if waiting for orders.

Lara sat there for several moments on the cement floor with her mouth hanging open. Then, with no further hesitation, she sprang out of the cage, smashing Jimmy against a wall. Like a flash of lightning, she was up the stairs and out the church doors, running down Devils Glen Road like she had the devil snapping at her heels.

The Reluctant Pawn

Bettie Stone walked out the front door of her house, not paying attention to her mother's demands to know where she thought she was going. She'd been cooped up in the basement all night and she needed air. However, something other than boredom had drawn her out—a nagging feeling she couldn't quite place.

Once outside, she saw a young boy standing directly in front of her house, facing her door as though he had been waiting for her to emerge. It was no surprise it was Justin Mackenzie, the scruffy-haired boy from down the street who always seemed to be watching her.

"Hello, Justin," Bettie greeted him. "What are you doing out this late on Halloween?"

"Bettie Stone, you must come with me," he said.

"Why, Justin, I think those are the first words you've ever said to me. And why exactly should I go with you?"

"I need you to help me find someone. And there are a few other things we must do tonight."

"Oh, really? And what makes you think I'm just going to follow you wherever you go?" she asked.

"Oh, you will. There's no doubt about it." Justin shifted on his feet, but seemed confident otherwise.

"Why would that be?"

"Because I have the answers," he replied.

"Answers? I doubt you have the answers to questions on my mind, Justin. I really doubt that a lot."

"Wouldn't you like to know why you draw all those pictures and symbols? Why you coerced a grown man into kidnapping a random girl? Why does everyone in our neighborhood seem like they're part of some grand conspiracy? Wouldn't you love to know why you have this nagging feeling that everything in the town of Bettendorf isn't quite what it seems?"

"What are you, a mind reader?"

"No, not really. But I know you better than you know yourself. We all do. But I don't have time to explain it now. We need to find someone."

"Who?" she asked.

"Jack Davies. We have to find him tonight if we can."

The mention of that name intrigued Bettie. He was the boy she had seen just the other night when she heard the ringing sound in her ears. Ever since that night, she knew there was something special about him. This could be no coincidence.

"Jack Davies? Why?" she asked.

"We're running out of time. This is a critical night. Though you probably don't know it, our families have been working together for a long time. Working for this moment." Justin turned and headed toward his house.

"Our families? What have our families been working on? Why don't I know about it? Hey! Where are you going?" she called after him.

"To get my bike. You should get yours too."

"Where are we going?"

"We're going to the Bennett mansion to prepare a few things."

Now intrigued, Bettie got her black vintage beach cruiser from the garage, and soon the two of them were heading down Sunset Circle toward the north entrance to the Bennett estate.

"You said something about the work our families had done. What did that mean?"

"It's not my place to say. Your father should fill you in if he decides you need to know. But don't worry, Bettie, you're an important part of all of this—maybe the most important. My dad told me you were powerful," Justin said as they turned down the main entrance to the Bennett estate.

Leaving their bikes next to some shrubs, the two teens snuck behind some landscaping at the northwest corner of the estate. From there, they could see Griselda's mausoleum, dark and brooding under the branches of a pair of old oaks.

Justin whispered, "Do you see the mausoleum? I want to open it, but I will need your help."

"What? Why are we opening it? I heard a crazy old woman rests there. No one even wants to walk past it, let alone open it."

"I'm sure you're just terrified of that place, aren't you? Yeah right. You know you've always wanted to peek inside. Admit it."

"I have, but that doesn't mean I'm dying to do it on Halloween night!"

"Really? I think it's a perfect time to meet old Griselda. Unfortunately, those wolves sealed her in that tomb with a terrible curse. I will need your help to break it."

"How can I help?" Bettie asked.

"Remember when I said you're powerful? Well, I wasn't lying. You are a witch, probably the most talented in the whole town, I'm told. I have skills myself—a lot of us do—but nothing like you. A little help and guidance are all you need. Too bad your dad is such a dick."

"Ha! Can't disagree with that. But I think you must be mistaken. I've never done a spell in my life," Bettie said, though she doubted her words.

"I know you better than you know yourself, Bettie. They've kept you in the dark about a lot of things. It had to be that way. But after tonight, you'll know everything. I think you'll probably be the most powerful girl in the state—hell, maybe even the world! So, are you ready to begin?"

"OK, I'm ready, I suppose, though I think I'm crazy for saying so."

Justin led her to the front of the mausoleum. Bettie looked up at the name written across the top of the doorway in bold letters: Griselda.

"Why is she buried out here?" Bettie asked. "The rest of the family is over there on the other side of the house. Why was she left out?"

"I'm not sure anyone knows the answer to that one. Mr. Bennett's mother wasn't real fond of his wife, so it was probably her doing. OK, put your hand on the door right there."

Justin pointed to a strange pagan marking at the center of the metal door. Bettie placed her hand upon it. Her eyes widened.

Justin said, "Ha! You feel it, don't you? Good, they weren't wrong about you. Now close your eyes and command this door to open."

Closing her eyes, she leaned on the door. "Open!"

"No, not like that," Justin said. "Use the words."

"Use the words? You mean like 'open'?"

"No, the words you've forgotten," Justin said.

"The words I've forgotten? What does that even mean?"

"Don't be a dolt. Speak the words you used in your room a thousand times. The symbols you draw every night? It's called the dark speech."

"But I don't know what those symbols mean! I write them down like I'm taking dictation. Did you call me a dolt?"

"You know the dark speech. You've just forgotten. Think!"

Bettie turned back to the door and closed her eyes once again. *Dark speech?* She felt so discombobulated by the evening's many revelations she didn't quite know what to do with herself.

However, for the first time in her life, something was making sense. Was she some pawn in some grand scheme of her parents and their neighbors?

There was only one way to channel the anger now rising in her chest. Words formed in her mind.

"Ounta dist morga, oust et dounta im!"

The mausoleum walls creaked as the giant metal door rattled. Two now vied for control—the spell on the door keeping Griselda trapped in the mausoleum and the strength of Betty's dark speech.

"Ounta dist morga, oust et dounta im! Frode suntata im lunda, oust et dounta im!"

Bettie searched with unseen fingers—fingers of magic—scanning the spell that sealed the door. Her body swelled with energy. Her legs parted, and she raised her hands away from the door. A force flowed through her and became one with her soul—it *was* her soul—her essence. She felt the lives and deaths, joys and pains, triumphs and defeats, salvations and damnations, of a thousand souls. She drank them and used their energy to fill her cup.

"Im dist dounta, oust et dounta im! Belente mich frode soonte mach morga fren!"

With those words, the doors shook violently three times and then stood still. Bettie lowered her hands and bowed her head, short of breath, but not the least bit tired. A new power threatened to overwhelm her.

Justin said, "That's the language you use? No wonder you couldn't break the spell! Maybe everyone was wrong about you."

"Hush." Bettie walked to the door, placed her right hand upon it, and thrust it open. Reaching out a hand and pointing at Griselda's stone coffin, she called, "Griselda! Oust et frode, oust et krondat! Fennet im!"

The stone cover on Griselda's bier flew off and crashed against the stone floor, breaking into a hundred pieces and revealing the rotting hag who immediately rose in one stiff movement to a standing position on the top of her bier. Her hair sprayed out of her head like a thousand broken webs, and her mouth hung open wide. Naked and smelling of death, Griselda Bennett descended in one swift movement, leaping down from her bier to stand directly before Bettie.

"Huh, she's sniffing me?" Bettie asked.

Justin crept closer, shock plastered across his face. "Griselda Bennett! We have summoned you to gain vengeance on your most hated enemy. We are here to open the gates so that the Great One may enter our world at last. There may be some who will try to enter these grounds. You must stop them."

Griselda looked at Justin for a moment as though she might just as likely rip his head clean from his shoulders as do a thing he commanded. In fact, she reached out as if to do just that. "No, Griselda, leave the boy."

Griselda held her hand out for a moment, as if contemplating, but then swept past Bettie and out the door into the night.

"Thank you," Justin said.

"I don't think old Griselda cares for being ordered around by middle school boys or men. So, are you going to tell me why we let the dead lady out?"

"For exactly the reason I said. She will protect this place while we do some things. And because the elders have commanded it."

"And do you plan on telling me what these things are that we must do? I think I deserve to know since I will be the one who does them."

"Yes, I suppose you're right. Follow me," Justin snapped as he walked back to the front of the mansion.

Bettie rolled her eyes, and after a few moments, fell into step behind him. They made their way back around to the front of the mansion, entering through the front door. Justin carried a heavy ring of keys and seemed to know exactly which key opened which door. Soon, the two were descending a dark stone staircase to the depths below. The cellar was as massive as the house itself and seemed to have many rooms, storage areas, and more stairways that wound even deeper under the house, until finally they came into a vast, nearly empty chamber. Built into the wall at the far end of the room was an altar with various symbols and figures carved into it and countless candles placed along its mantle. Carved into its center was the same pagan symbol adorning the metal door of Griselda's mausoleum.

"This is the chapel," Justin said. "It is our church, you might say."

The boy took out a box of matches from his jacket and lit the candles.

"There are spells set into this altar?" she asked, sensing an energy not unlike the mausoleum.

"I would imagine so," Justin replied as he brought a wood chair to the center of the room.

"Who uses this place? It seems older than the mansion."

"I think it is, though even my father doesn't know much about it. Griselda used it many times to summon demons from the other side."

"And what will happen here tonight?"

"The Devils of the Glen will return and open the gates between this world and the other. The Great Lord will finally enter and take it for His own. Praise Him!"

"You and I will make that happen?"

"Oh, we'll play a part, but the devils will do the opening. We are here to prepare the way and make it possible for them to leave their caves and walk upon the earth in their true form as they have not done in many ages. They will come to this chapel and open the gates." Justin strolled across the room to the altar and kneeled before it.

"And Jack Davies? How does he fit into it all?"

"Why, he will be the star of the show. It turns out the boy is important, though you'd never know it by looking at him. Apparently, he's a traveler, a peregrinator, as my dad calls it. He's one of the few people who can open doors between the dimensions. The devils will use his power to open the portal."

"How?"

"Easy. They'll force Jack to submit," Justin said as he closed his eyes to pray and motioned for Betty to do the same.

"And then what?"

"Then they'll drain his soul. Now let us pray."

Army of the Undead

Joe Lambert and Shaun Porter sat at a corner table at Whitey's Ice Cream Parlor. They were both dressed as Beatles—the 1964 incarnation with slim suits and mop-top hair. Joe was slurping through a banana split while Shaun had a chocolate shake with a hot fudge tunnel.

"Madonna, yes or no?" Joe asked.

Shaun thought about it. "Madonna now? Or 1980s?"

"Either."

"1980s, yes. Now, no."

"Katy Perry. Yes or no?"

"What kind of question is that?"

"It's a game. Would you do her?"

"I know the game—I invented the game—but what kind of question is that? *Katy Perry*? Who would say no?" Shaun shook his head, wondering why he let Joe bug him so much.

"Yes or no?"

"Yes, for the love of god. Yes!"

Joe shrugged. "Eh, maybe."

Exasperated, Shaun looked out the window at the parking lot. "I guess we should pick up Brian and Mike and get over to Jen's party. Time's wasting."

"Yeah, I guess," Joe said.

Grabbing his plastic guitar, Shaun said, "Don't forget your drumsticks, Ringo."

Right then, the entrance on the other side of the ice cream shop burst open, and a girl appeared in the doorway. She had gray, almost green, skin and ratty blonde hair and was wearing a torn-up Catholic school uniform—a filthy azure blouse under a torn cardigan with a soiled plaid skirt that came down just above the tops of her knees. It wasn't the typical sexy schoolgirl costume usually seen on Halloween—this was a proper uniform. She had marks and old bruises all over her neck, and there were places on her legs where it looked like the flesh had been rotting for days. Her mouth hung slightly open as a stream of blood trickled from her lower lip onto the front of her blouse; dark mascara ran down around her eyes. She stood there just inside the doorway, staring at the boys with her head tilted menacingly.

A pimply young guy working behind the counter greeted the girl. "Happy Halloween! Welcome to Whitey's. What can I get ya? The Franken-fudge sundae is our special all weekend."

The girl shot a look at the kid, then walked over to the counter, reached across with both hands, grabbed him on each side of his face, and with one sharp motion, ripped his head clean off. A fountain of blood sprayed all over the counter and across the ice cream as the kid's body fell backward, convulsing in the throes of sudden death.

Taking the head, the girl flipped it around, then repeatedly slammed it on the edge of the counter until the top of the skull cracked open. She wiggled her fingers into the broken cranium and pried it open, tearing off the top half of the scalp to expose the brain. She shot a look across the shop straight at the boys and growled threateningly, then jammed her face into the skull and tore off a large piece of the boy's brain with her bare teeth.

Joe and Shaun stood there with their jaws open as the girl took another handful of brain and shoved it into her mouth. She chewed quickly and took another bite and then another, but still the boys couldn't move or look away from the spectacle. Finally, she wiped her mouth with the back of her hand, smearing brain matter and blood across her chin, and casually tossed the empty head behind the counter. She stood. Her eyes fixed on Shaun.

"H-h-holy shit, Shaun. She's looking at us," Joe stammered.

"No, she's looking at *me*. Shit, what do we do?"

The girl took a step toward them, a low growl emanating from her bloody mouth.

"Out the side door, now!" Joe yelled.

The boys ducked out a pair of double doors behind them and swung them closed just as the girl slammed into them, smashing her bloody face into the glass. She pushed against it, screaming with fury and a lust for more flesh. Joe and Shaun pushed back against her with all their might.

"Here, jam your drumsticks through the door handle!" Shaun said. "I'll bring my guitar in from the other side." They wedged their instruments into the handles, sufficiently blocking them.

Suddenly, there came screaming from the parking lot, and when the boys came around the corner of the building, they saw a group of teenagers fighting off more undead. Blood flew as heads slammed on car bumpers and cracked open on parking barriers. On the other side of Devils Glen, undead ran down the sidewalk, chasing random people and feasting on their brains. One man—if one could call it a man—jumped fifteen feet into the air, landed on the hood of a passing SUV, thrust his hand through the windshield, and yanked out the driver's severed head. Fueled by some incredible power, he then leaped back through the sky onto the sidewalk, cracking open the skull before the car had time to crash into a telephone pole. The boys looked away from the horror as a group of undead descended upon the car to finish the family inside.

A police car quickly squealed into the intersection. The officers exited their cruiser and fired at the undead as they squatted there, eating brains. A group of the undead in the parking lot threw down their meals and swarmed the officers, quickly overwhelming them as they fired their weapons in desperation. The gunfire went silent, giving way to screams and the sound of bones cracking.

"Jesus Christ!" Shaun yelled. "This is insane!"

"We gotta get out of here," Joe said. "Let's go down Middle Road—"

Before Joe could finish his sentence, the undead girl inside the ice cream parlor burst through the side door, breaking the drumsticks and fake guitar in half. She stood there for a moment glaring at the boys, then moved straight for them. A few of her friends then appeared—a middle-aged man in a dirty suit, a woman who looked like she was pregnant, and an elderly lady in a wheelchair.

Behind them, the boys heard the loud engine of a motorcycle and then a booming voice screaming, "Look out, boys!"

Shaun and Joe dove out of the way as Leo Lourogen crashed into the woman in the wheelchair with his Honda 750. With greater dexterity than could have been imagined from a man of his size, Leo leaped off the bike and, in one motion, pulled a samurai sword from behind his back, cutting the head off the elderly lady. When he landed, Leo rolled forward and rose, slicing the middle-aged man in half with one graceful movement.

Leo moved toward the girl in the Catholic school uniform, but she grabbed the pregnant woman, tossing her in the way. The bloody sword cut straight through the woman's left eye, exiting out the back of her head. As he withdrew his sword, the dead girl stared at him for a moment, as if trying to decide what to do about this unexpected adversary. She glanced at Shaun, growling once more, then turned and ran around the back side of Whitey's.

"You boys OK?" Leo asked. "You shouldn't be out here. We gotta get you to safety."

"Yes, please!" Shaun replied. "Anywhere but here!"

Leo ran over to his motorcycle and set it straight again. "Get on. There's a little church down Middle Road off Forest Grove. A bunch of people are gonna meet up there. We've been preparing for this for a long time. Got food, weapons, everything you need."

Joe said, "But how are all three of us gonna fit on your bike?"

"Easy. Shaun, you sit behind me, and Joe, you climb up on back and hold on as best you can. We don't have to be on it for more than a few miles—at least far enough to get away from these monsters."

"Thank you, Leo! Thank you so much!" the boys cried out.

As the motorcycle finally roared away down Middle Road, the undead girl crept out from behind the ice cream shop, glaring at Leo's fading taillights.

Dead Party

1.

Jack had reached that stage of life when he wasn't yet sure whether he liked the taste of beer. Oh, he was drinking it, no doubt about that. There was no way to avoid drinking beer when you were a teenager in Bettendorf, Iowa—if you wanted any weekend social life, that is. Red cups and poorly tapped beer kegs were pretty much standard weekend fare in small towns across the bi-state area. Jack drank it not so much for the taste—which he found to be a tad bitter—but for the feeling.

Jack stared at his date, a "girl" who, for all he knew, was as old as the Mississippi River itself. He would need more beer to keep himself from acting like a nervous idiot the whole night. Half the other guys at the party were looking at Jack like he had won the lottery, while the other half were planning on how to steal her away from him. Ava asked, "Hey, are you OK? You don't look like you're having fun."

"Who, me? Heck, yeah, I'm having a good time. Are you?"

"Sure. I'd be having more fun if you'd put your arm around me. Those guys over there are annoying."

A wave of relief passed over him. *Maybe she likes me.*

He put his arm around her shoulders. She reciprocated by wrapping hers around his waist and drawing closer. She came up to about his shoulder, which felt perfect, like a missing puzzle piece. Jack glanced toward the seniors and chuckled to himself when he saw the looks of befuddlement.

"Are they weeping in defeat?" she asked.

"Crying in their beers."

"Good. Shall we sit outside by the fire?" She didn't wait for an answer. She grabbed him by the hand, leading him out a pair of sliding doors and into the backyard where Jen's boyfriend, Chris Markin, had built a bonfire.

The Graver house was on the outskirts of town, on Crow Creek Road, in a newly developed cul-de-sac with only one other house on the street. It seemed half the kids of Bettendorf High School were at the party. The yard was full of costumed teenagers, laughing and drinking, or making out.

"Where's Randy?" Ava asked as she pulled a lawn chair up next to Jack.

"Oh, I saw him talking to some girl inside. Maggie Boone, I think. He seemed happy enough, I guess."

"I'm sure he is. She's pretty. So, why don't you have a girlfriend?"

"I don't know."

"Have you ever asked anyone out?"

"Well, yeah. I mean, I went to the homecoming dance last year, but that was with a friend."

Ava punched him in the arm and laughed. "That's not a date! That's just hanging out. I'm surprised one of these girls hasn't snatched you up already. You know you're a good-looking guy, right? I mean, you're attractive, and girls notice it."

"Yeah, right."

"I'm serious. While you were in there, getting all jealous about the dudes who were checking me out, you were ignoring the three or four girls who were scoping you out."

Jack took another swig of beer. "You're just being nice."

Ava grabbed him by the collar and pulled him closer as she leaned in. Their faces were inches from each other, and Jack could sense nothing else.

"Any girl would be a fool to choose those guys over you."

"Thank you," Jack said. "I'm glad you think so."

"It's interesting. In all the years I've lived, there have been many changes in the world, some for the worse, most for the better. But one thing that hasn't changed is the awkwardness of teenagers."

"Sorry, I can't do anything about it. I think I was born awkward."

"I think you sell yourself short. You must stop doing that. I tell you, in all honesty, you were born for greatness. I know it when I see it." Ava leaned closer, staring into his eyes.

Jack realized something right then. He saw something in her he'd never seen before in anyone else. He thought Ava was looking back at him with an intensity that matched his own, and he felt as though he must be asleep and traveling in some far-fetched dream.

"I feel a connection with you," he said, lowering his head in the shyness of having admitted what he had been thinking for days.

"You do?"

"I don't mean, like, a crush. Something more than that. It's hard for me to explain. I have little experience in this area, but there's something deeper between us, I think. It's like I can't get you out of my mind, even with all the weird stuff that's been happening in my life. My mind always goes back to you. Is that crazy?"

Ava smiled. "No, Jack. That's not crazy at all. It's what I've been telling you all along."

Music played through the outside speakers—a shoe-gazer love song, drifting from the house—and as its chorus swelled, Jack seized the moment, leaning in to kiss her lightly, but fully, on the mouth. Ava rewarded his boldness with a receptive parting of the lips and a warm embrace that made Jack want to drift away in this dream and never wake. Electricity flowed between them, tightening his skin and raising goose bumps on the back of his neck. He held her face in his hands as their lips parted further, tongues reaching out.

Ava got up from her seat and crawled into Jack's lap, straddling him, pressing her body against his. Floods of adrenaline raced through every cell, every molecule of his body. Their lips pressed against each other, dancing in perfect rhythm.

"Oh my, you are delicious," she said. "Save that thought. I'll be right back."

Ava lingered there, staring down at him for another moment or two, then swung her leg around and practically danced through the back door of the Graver house.

Jack melted into his seat as he stared up at the cloudy sky above, electricity tickling across his skin. For a moment, he almost thought he could see traces of blue lightning behind his eyelids.

2.

As Ava made her way across the house, heading to the downstairs bathroom, she spotted Randy. He was obviously in a miserable conversation with a boring girl, so she shot him a mocking look, sticking out her tongue at him. He stealthily gave her the middle finger as he pretended to be interested in what the girl in front of him was saying.

Ava laughed. It had been many ages since she'd felt a friendship with anyone, and even longer still since she'd felt a romantic affection. Sure, she'd had countless requests, many lovers, and several proposals, but she had experienced nothing like this. It was unlike anything she had felt before in all her long years of life. Smiling again, she ran into the bathroom, eager to get back to Jack and that wonderful mouth of his.

As she entered and turned on the light, she suddenly felt a burning all over her body and a paralysis overtook her. The door slammed shut behind her. "Hold her! Watch it, now. This girl is dangerous!"

Ava fell to the floor, covered in thin silver chains and writhing in excruciating pain. Her blood slowed and her power faded. Jimmy Vance leaned over her face, his eyes burning with deliberate cruelty.

"Oh, she's gonna be my fun girl. She sure is. I'm gonna have a party with you, baby." Jimmy smiled, revealing two sharp canines glistening with poisonous spit.

3.

Randy sat with Maggie Boone, a volleyball star, telling him about her many scholarship offers. As much as he tried to keep his mind on the story, he kept drifting off, thinking about how Maggie might look playing beach volleyball. But when she casually mentioned that she had a boyfriend who went to Davenport Central, Randy quickly excused himself to use the bathroom.

He had seen Ava go into the downstairs bathroom, so he headed upstairs, hoping there would be another. When he got to the top of the stairs, he opened the first door only to discover it wasn't the bathroom, but a bedroom, and it wasn't empty.

Sarah Kristy sat on the bed making out with the varsity quarterback. Kyle Turlington was a fair high school QB, but possessed average arm strength and a sub-2.0 grade-point average, meaning he would have little to no chance of playing big-time college football. He wasn't a great-looking guy, so it was best for him to take advantage of his position in life while he had it.

Randy paused for a moment to steal one more look before closing the door. Remembering the unfortunate events at the football game, he thought, *Ah, poor Jack. That could have been you.*

Randy found the bathroom and set about to relieve his beer belly of some pressure. As he stood there staring at a plaque that read "The Family That Prays Together, Stays Together," he heard a sound coming from outside, like distant gunfire. Looking out a small window next to the toilet, Randy spotted two girls standing in the middle of the street, staring at the Graver house—one was blonde, and the other was dark-haired. Finishing up and buttoning his jeans, Randy leaned closer to the window and used his hand to shade the reflection.

Holy shit! It's Emily Scott! Randy tried to open the window, but someone had painted it shut. Then he recognized the other girl. *Stephanie Caine and Emily Scott? What are they doing here?*

An explosion sounded from downstairs, and Randy instinctively dropped onto his belly. At first, he heard nothing else, but then there was a loud screech followed by a screaming girl. Then all hell broke loose. Randy heard what sounded like bodies being tossed around and something torn apart. Blood-curdling cries tore through the night.

Randy crawled out into the hallway. Down the hall, Sarah ran out of the bedroom to the top of the stairs. Kyle joined her, just as she let out a horrified squeal from the scene she saw below. Both ran back into the bedroom, locking the door behind them.

Downstairs, a man's voice cut through the mayhem. "Ah, my children! My poor lost children! Come unto me! My daughters have drunk their fill! There is no need for further bloodshed, so long as you give us what we want."

Jen Graver responded, "What do you want? Please leave us alone!"

"Oh, my dear, I would be happy to leave you alone to enjoy what little time you have left on this earth. All I ask is that you give me the boy, Jack Davies. Bring him and I promise, as God is my witness, we will do you no further harm!"

"He's outside! Outside by the fire," one guy yelled out from wherever he was hiding.

Randy burst through a door across the hall and jumped over a bed where two younger lovers were on the bed, oblivious to the events downstairs. "Dude!" the guy yelled as his girlfriend covered herself with the blankets.

"Sorry, but I believe the party is over," Randy said. He looked out the back window. From this vantage point, it was impossible to tell much of what was going on below, so Randy tugged the window open and worked his way out onto the roof.

"Jack, Ava!"

The back door opened, and out stepped a greasy-looking man in a leisure suit and white shoes, flanked on either side by Emily and Stephanie. The man walked out to the bonfire while the girls split to either side to search the huge backyard. Beyond the yard was a cornfield that offered Jack plenty of hiding places. Giving a smile of relief, Randy slowly crept closer to the window frame, trying to hide next to it. Unfortunately, the Gravers needed a new roof, so Randy's second step dislodged a shingle, sending it sliding off the roof and onto the ground. The man spotted Randy.

"Well, well, well, Mr. Wall. It would seem you have gotten yourself into quite a pickle now, doesn't it? Ladies, I believe you know Mr. Wall, right?"

"Yes, Brother Jones," the girls replied in unison.

"Why don't you be sweethearts and go on up and bring that boy down here?" Brother Jones motioned up to Randy.

"Now, you wait there! I don't want to jump off this roof, but I totally will!"

Jones chuckled. "Ah, now, Mr. Wall, don't you go doing anything fool-ish. My girls here will be right up."

"Uh, yeah, right, you guys come on up. I'll wait right here."

Randy planned to jump off the roof into the bushes at the side of the house while the girls climbed the stairs. Instead, he watched in horror as Emily and Stephanie rose through the air, gliding until they landed lightly on the roof in front of him.

"Oh shit," he mumbled as they hoisted him onto their shoulders, carry-ing him down to Brother Jones.

4.

As soon as he heard the explosion, Jack took off into the cornfield, running without thinking. He could sense a massive power exerting itself inside the house, and every instinct in his body told him to run as fast and as far as he could. The corn whipped by him so quickly that he could feel it cutting his arms and neck. He reacted so quickly, he left Ava behind without even realizing it. His speed was beyond what it should have been, faster than humanly possible.

Within moments, Jack had broken through the cornstalks on the south-east side of the field, about a quarter of a mile away from the party, and found himself in the middle of a new housing addition on the northeast side of town. But it wasn't the new prefabricated homes that made him stop his flight. It was the hoard of lunatics running through the neigh-borhood, attacking people. Eating them. Jack stood there for a moment, trying to figure out what exactly he was seeing. *Zombies? Was it possible?* By this point, Jack needed a new definition for the word.

He knew he had to go back. There was death behind him and death before him, but he had to find Ava and Randy. Though Ava could surely handle herself, Randy would not fare so well against the forces now after him. Jack had no choice.

Before he could take one step back, a voice sounded out from the other side of the field. "Jack Davies! Jack Davies! You come on back here, ya hear? We've got your friend, Mr. Wall! I'd hate for any more pain to come to him. He's been through a terrible ordeal!"

"Shit," Jack sighed as he bent over with his hands on his knees, exhausted. Several thoughts ran through his mind at that moment, but the only one that made any logical sense was the one that ended with him walking back and giving himself up.

Jack yelled, "If I come back there, you gotta let my friend go! Alive!"

"You got yourself a deal there, Mr. Davies."

Soon, Jack emerged from the cornfield and stood before Brother Billy Jones. To his surprise, Emily Scott and Stephanie Craine stood there holding Randy by the arms. Tonight had taken a very different turn than he thought it would only ten minutes ago.

"Here I am," Jack said. "I do not understand what you could want from me, but I suppose I'm about to find out. First, you must let my friend go."

"I am a man of my word, Mr. Davies. No one can deny that fact, no they cannot. Ladies, you may release the fortunate Mr. Wall. Go, young fool, and prepare your family for their last days on earth as they know it."

"Randy, run!" Jack screamed.

Randy did not question the order. He was across the yard and around the corner of the house, out of sight in seconds.

"So, there are only three of you?" Jack asked. "Three against two, we'll take those odds. You may not know this, but my girlfriend is here, and she has more to her than meets the eye. I guess you could say that's true for both of us."

Jack closed his eyes and reached down into his rage, attempting to find the power he had used the other day. He searched for it, twisting every fiber of his being, attempting to tap into any powers hidden in his mind, but found none. It was as though he was trying to jump while two giant hands held him down.

Jones smiled and took a step forward. "Oh, young Jack, I don't think you understand the situation here. Whatever power you possess, you won't be using it tonight. My little Emily here has you bound up tight with a most naughty little blocking spell."

"I'm sorry, Jack," Emily said. "But it is for the best. I swear it!"

Brother Jones chuckled. "My little Emily learns right quick. You'd break it if you knew how, but alas, I fear you do not know your strength. And as for the odds, well, it isn't three against two. We've already dealt with your little girlfriend, as you call her."

Through the back doors, Jimmy Vance and an older man, whom Jack recognized as the same man who'd imprisoned Ava at Sunnycrest just last week, brought Ava out, bound and gagged by a series of thin silver chains.

"Did she give you any trouble, Jimmy?" Jones asked.

"Ah, just a little, Brother Jones, but she calmed down right quick. Me and her are gonna have us some fun. Heck, after a while, she might even like it." Jimmy winked at Jack.

Jack felt the weight of his defeat. It was over—all the plans, all the journeys, all the new powers—over before he had even understood what was happening to him. Then he heard Stephanie's voice, inches behind his neck, and felt her lips lightly graze his ear as she whispered, "So sorry, Jack. You should have stayed home with your sister."

THE STUBBORN ONE

1.

Lara stumbled down Devils Glen, her feet struggling to adjust to her newfound speed. She squeezed her eyes shut, opening them only periodically to register where she was. Every time she opened them, waves of nausea and fits of disorientation hit her. It was as if every single molecule of every blade of grass was in perfect focus. Like a kid with ADD, she couldn't concentrate on any one thing—her new attention focused on everything. Every rock, stick, twig, and blade of grass, she couldn't figure out how to discriminate among any of it. Lucky for her, Devils Glen Road was a lightly used thoroughfare or she would have crashed through dozens of cars and trees by now.

Finally, she tripped over a large stone at the side of the road, breaking it into hundreds of pieces and sending her tumbling down the gravel shoulder of the road until she came to rest just before the Duck Creek bridge. Try as she might, she could not find the strength to take another step; escape was no longer on her mind. She lay there for several minutes, praying that Brother Jones and his cohorts had chosen not to pursue her.

Perhaps they have bigger fish to fry, she hoped.

She lay there at the edge of the road, staring up at the blackness of the Halloween sky as she felt each cell in her body die and then rise again moments later. The pain of it threatened to overtake her, and it was all she could do just to lie there without screaming to the heavens. But soon the pain subsided to a more manageable level, allowing her to take stock of her situation, and to think.

"I'm a vampire," she said. "How fucking lame."

The clouds above her shifted together, threatening to block out the light of the full moon. With her new eyes, she discerned something propelling the clouds, as if an unnatural power caused this change in the weather. She sensed an unseen power in the wind. Then in the distance, back down the road from the opposite direction she'd come, came the sound of gunfire.

It's beginning, she told herself. *I've got to move.*

As her new senses awoke, she suddenly felt several energies exerted on the area. She looked across the road into Devils Glen Park and felt a chaotic power living within the woods. It seemed to Lara that this power was just now stirring into action. Her keen senses fired warnings at her—something was in the park. A darkness that dwelt within the trees—a darkness beyond her ability. She needed to get away from that darkness without a moment to lose.

Something's coming.

Kicking her legs up and popping herself quickly to her feet, Lara decided she had to find Jack before her friends did. In grade school, she had been friends with a girl who was his next-door neighbor, so she knew where to go. She tore down Central Avenue. She would have looked like nothing but a flash of color to anyone who glimpsed her. She whipped around Twenty-Third Street and cut through Sunnycrest Park. As she passed through the park, she felt another power somewhere deep beneath the ground, an ancient and hideous evil aware of her presence, but unwilling to stir. It sang a hymn in an unintelligible language that brought tears to Lara's eyes as she tore out of the woods and down Mississippi Avenue toward Twenty-First Street and the Davies' house.

It was only moments before she was looking up at Jack's bedroom window. She didn't want to deal with living humans, not knowing how she would react to being near those who were supposed to be her dinner. Looking at the window, she wished she could be up there looking into it, and just like that, she felt herself rising from the ground and floating through the air straight to it. As she reached the window, she grabbed hold of the frame and peered into Jack's room.

It was empty and smelled like he hadn't been there for some hours. Lara shook her head, and just as she was about to move over to another window, she saw Jack's door slowly open with a long, drawn-out creak. There, on the other side of the bedroom door, stood a girl who was obviously more than just a girl. She was a ghost.

"Who are you?" Lara asked through the window.

"I am Anne. And who are you, creeping around my home?"

"I'm sorry, but I'm in a hurry. My name is Lara Fanning. I need to find Jack—Jack Davies. You know, the guy who lives in this room?"

"Yes, I should think I would know who he is. I'm his sister. Do not enter this house! I will extinguish your soul and send you back to the dark place from which you came."

Lara did not doubt her words for a moment. Though she knew little about Jack, she was certain she'd never heard of a sister.

"I didn't know he had a sister," Laura said. "I won't enter your home. I'm looking for your brother."

"I'm sure you are. You and every other dark thing in this horrible little town."

"It's true. Many dark things are looking for him, but I'm not one. Or rather, I mean him no harm. I'm good—I swear it!"

"You're not a creature of darkness? A lie! You are obviously a vampire, as the humans call them—newly made too, it would seem. You cannot have him!" Anne's force strengthened, and she seemed to glow with it.

"Yes, I am a vampire. But I'm not evil. I still feel like myself. My friends all changed and became something evil, but I think I'm still me. I don't have time to explain! I must find Jack before it's too late. They're out there looking for him right now. Is he here with you? Can you protect him?"

Anne's demeanor changed, softened. "No, he isn't here. I tried to convince him to stay home, but he wouldn't listen. He went out with that demon."

"Which demon?"

"That Ava girl. *Girl*—she's older than the dirt she sleeps in. He seems to trust her though I don't see why."

"She's hot," Lara said without thinking. "Guys get confused by pretty girls. Look, the people searching for him spoke of a ceremony happening at the mansion. Do you think they meant the Bennett estate?"

"Yes! That explains the feeling I had earlier. I sense a dark energy coming from that place."

"I promise you, Anne. I am not evil—I want to protect Jack. It may sound crazy, but I it's my destiny. I can't explain why, but I think everything has happened for a reason. I must find him! Where did Ava take him?"

Anne appraised her again, then hung her head for a moment and said, "They went to a Halloween party hosted by a girl named Jen Graver."

2.

Minutes later, as she stepped through the broken front door of the Graver house, Lara saw she was too late, but not by much. Blood still dripped down the walls, from the ceiling onto the floor. Teenagers moaned in pain as they tried to drag themselves across the floor, many of them missing limbs. Someone pinned half of the high school football team, headless, to the dining room walls, their heads stacked on top of each other in the center of the table. Lara's heart sank as she realized it was her friends who had done this. Just a week ago, she had been drinking with Emily at the quarry in Crow Creek Park, and now her best friend was a murderous demon. As she continued to search the house, she heard someone weeping in the corner.

"Leave us alone, leave us alone!" the girl cried.

"Jen," Lara said. "Are you OK?"

Streams of blood covered Jen's face, though it didn't appear to be her own. The smell of it was giving Lara horrible hunger pangs, and part of her wanted desperately to rip a hole into Jen's soft neck. The urge was almost overwhelming, so she stepped back to avoid doing something she would regret. Urges and visions seemed to come to her out of nowhere. It was unbelievable that Lara could still function with all the bizarre changes happening to her.

"Emily and Stephanie are like vampires or something. They came in here and killed everyone. Vampires, Lara! Right here in Bettendorf!" Jen sounded like she might pass out at any moment.

"Have you seen Jack Davies or that Ava girl, Jen? Did you see them tonight?"

Jen squinted and tried to focus her eyes. "Jack?"

"Yes, Jack. Please, think! Did you see Jack and Ava tonight? Did they come here?"

"Yes, yes, they were here. Jack and the new girl came here. But it's too late. The vampires took them. And that preacher, he was with them too. They took Jack and Ava and killed everyone else!"

"Where did they take them?"

"I don't know. They drove off with him in some big black car. Oh, Lara, what is happening?" With that question, her head fell forward, and she passed out.

A motorcycle screamed down the street, stopping just outside the Graver's house. A few moments later, Leo Lourogen and Randy Wall were in the doorway staring at the carnage.

Lara came to the hallway and said, "Leo, Randy, we have to find Jack. They took him!"

Leo looked dangerous, like a wild beast. She wondered if he might attack her right there where she stood. At first, it confused her, but then she realized he recognized what she had become.

"Leo, it's me, Lara!"

He backed away and pulled a samurai sword from a scabbard strapped across his back. "Get behind me, Randy. She's one of them now. She's a demon."

"No, Leo, I'm fine. I don't have time to explain, but we must find Jack!"

"You're a bloodsucker now, Lara. Stay back or I'll take your head off!" Though he looked out of shape, his tone suggested Lara had better take him at his word. She sensed a power coming from him, one she never realized he possessed.

"It's true, Leo. I am a vampire now, and I can't say I'm happy about it. But I swear to you, I'm still me. The same people who turned Stephanie and Emily turned me too, but it didn't work on me like it did on them. You must believe me. I need to find Jack and help him. I think I may be the only one who can. You've got to help me. He's in danger. I know it."

Leo considered her for a moment. "You're *good?*" he asked with some measure of disbelief.

"Yes, I am. If I weren't, I wouldn't be here asking for your help. I'd be with Emily and Stephanie!"

Randy stepped around Leo and crossed to Lara, saying, "Oh yeah? Let's test that out first. You're not getting within a foot of my best friend until we know for sure. See if you can resist *this!*" He pulled down his shirt collar and thrust his neck right in front of her face.

Lara jumped back, holding her mouth and plugging her nose. "Jesus, Randy! I said I'm good, but that doesn't mean you should tempt me! I'm seriously hungry with all this blood lying around. It's all I can do to keep from dropping to my hands and knees to lick it up!"

Randy raised an eyebrow and said, "I'm not too proud to admit I would find that kinda hot. And you are talking a good game."

"She seems OK," Leo said as he lowered his sword. "We'd be dead right now if she wasn't. And we got no choice. We need to trust her."

Randy motioned for the three to get out of the bloody mess in the hallway. Once outside, he filled Lara in on the events at the party, including Ava's capture and where they were taking Jack. "There were three. I don't know what we can do to stop whatever they have planned, but I'm goddamn ready to try. Jack's my best friend, and I'll die for him."

"Me too," Leo added.

Lara smiled, knowing she had been right about Leo's jovial nature, but there was something unusual about him. Her new perceptive skills seemed to confirm it. It wasn't something she could readily identify, but Leo had power—one she didn't understand. Like many people she had met this past week, Leo seemed to be gifted. The world was changing right before her eyes.

"OK, well," Lara said. "I guess there's nothing else to do but go to the mansion. I'm gonna run there. It'll be faster. You two see if you can find a way in and help if you can. But be careful! That Vance kid is with them, and he's still a nasty turd. Not to mention Stephanie and Emily. And something else is there too. I can feel it—something is wrong."

Lara waved goodbye, then turned and ran faster than she ever dreamed possible through the cornfield behind the Graver house. Like an arrow, she shot toward the Bennett mansion, not knowing what she would find when she arrived.

On the Turning Away

1.

"Seek the gates," Genevieve Bennett advised as she patted Mark on the hand. "If your wife said it, you have no choice, dear. She was obviously prophetic."

"How will I know what to look for? What do they look like?" Mark asked.

"Oh dear, you will surely know when you find them. I doubt there are many gates below this house. Just the one, I should think. I do so envy your task. There was a time I might have joined you, but I am rather old for such things now and far too frail. My spirit clings only lightly to this world. I'm afraid after this evening there will be little left of me here. Many things done by fools, the wise cannot undo." Genevieve's mind drifted for a moment, and she seemed to be listening to something—something Mark couldn't hear. She appeared to be flickering, like a candle fighting to stay lit against the gathering wind of time.

"And once I discover it? What shall I do?"

"Again, only you will know. Such is the way in these matters. Much will remain unknown until the appointed moment, and at that moment, you must be ready to choose wisely. You will see what you must do, or confusion will take you and the moment will slip away. However, I believe you will need to block the gates if I'm not mistaken."

"Block them? How?"

"Oh, honey," Genevieve said. "I do so hate being cryptic. I wish I had a text that could tell you all you need to know, but unfortunately I do not. However, I have faith you will find a way. Unless I am mistaken, there is a reason this task fell to you."

"OK, so I block the gates. From who?"

"Whom, dear. From those things of evil trying to enter our world. Many are trying and have been for a long time. Griselda did her best to help them. She let a good number in herself. It was she who found the gates, and though she failed in her task, she weakened the barrier."

"But I still don't understand why me," he said.

Genevieve touched his arm, and to his surprise, her hand was warm and full of energy. "Fear not, Officer Warren. Though you may feel lonely, you are never alone. Even now, in this dark time, there is a glimmer of light. And remember, your wife is still with you."

"I will try," he said. His spirit felt lifted almost immediately.

"Go below the house, below the cellar. There, you will find the gates. Find the gates and block the spell if you can." The fading woman's face took on a grim pallor as she added, "There is one more thing."

"Yes?"

"There are many creatures below this house. Some of them live in the tunnels you will be searching. Most are harmless, sleeping for decades at a time, but some are restless and dangerous. There is one creature, neither man nor beast, that dwells in the tunnels and caves. It is a hideous thing that lives not in this world or the worlds beyond—it is a peregrinator, a traveler. It moves about as it pleases, back and forth between dimensions, rarely seen by the living or the dead."

"Does it protect the gates?"

"Oh no, I should think it pays little attention to the gates. It does not need them. But recently something injured it. I've heard it wailing for days.

It may have gone back into hiding, but I rather think it hasn't. It may search the tunnels and caverns for vengeance. Be careful, dear. If you see it, you will have little chance of escape. Make for the gates as soon as you find the tunnel and do not delay."

"Yes, ma'am."

Mark stood and made his way to the door. As he reached for the knob, Genevieve offered him good luck. When he turned to reply, he saw nothing but an empty bed.

2.

The hallway looked deserted, though Mark had a nagging feeling he wasn't alone. Who knew how many souls rested in this place? The sound of wind was whistling through the old windows, and for a moment he thought he could almost hear his name in the howling air.

Marrrrrrk! Maaaarrrrrrk!

As he made his way down the stairs to the first floor, he took a moment to take in his surroundings. The guesthouse was beautiful, decorated with ornate furniture and delicate frescoes painted on the plastered walls and vaulted ceilings. Though William Bennett had succumbed to his wife's wish to banish his mother from the main house, he made sure the matriarch's living quarters were no less opulent.

The stairs ended in the foyer just inside the main entrance. A giant oval window dominated most of the front door, surrounded by elaborately carved solid oak. Nothing stirred outside but fog and leaves blowing by the front porch and the black silhouettes of dead trees dotting the emptiness beyond.

Mark continued down the hallway, searching for the cellar door, when he heard a knocking sound behind him. He turned to look and saw Jennifer's face in the oval window of the front door. The sound of her heartbeat grew in volume until it seemed to fill the entire house, infiltrating Mark's mind. He raised his hands to cover his ears, which had no effect. Through the pounding and thumping, he heard his wife desperately crying out his name.

"Mark! Where are you going? You must help me! Do not forget me, love."

Her face was as white as snow. Her eyes were dark and gray. Her brown hair, once full and flowing, now lay down against her face as though it had been soaking in dirty waters. He immediately ran to the door and pressed his face against it, trying to get as close to her as he could.

"Jennifer! Listen. I have something I must do, but I will find you, I promise. I will find you, and I will take you away from that woman," Mark said.

"Please, my love. Please find a way!"

"I promise, I will. But first I must find the gates, my love. Remember the gates? Remember what you told me that night?"

"The gates? Yes. Yes, I think I remember. What were the words?"

"Seek the gates and save the boy," Mark said.

"Yes, that's right! You must find them, Mark. But why? I don't remember."

"The world is in danger, and I must find the gates to save it. I promise you, I will return."

"Seek the gates," she repeated. Jennifer searched her mind. It had been so long since she'd said those words. "Seek the gates—and save the boy?"

"Yes. That's what I will do, my love. It's what I must do."

"If you don't, no one will," she said, remembering. "Yes, you must find a way."

"I will save you, my love! And that evil hag will pay a thousand times for what she has done to you," Mark said.

"I know you will. Oh, how I wish I could come with you, but there is a seal on this house. I cannot go inside while she controls me. She is coming, love. Go! Go now, before she gets here! I will hold on and wait for you if I can. Please come back!"

Just then, the old woman crashed into Jennifer from behind, slamming her face into the glass of the window. Then, looking through the door, Griselda spat out venomous words meant only to fill Mark's heart with dread. "Mark Warren, you will die tonight!"

"Too late, you old bitch! I'm already dead!"

"Oh yes, you are dead, but there are deaths beyond deaths. You will die again tonight, and from that death, there will be no return. The ritual has begun, and there is no stopping it now. You're already too late. Ha! You might as well give yourself up and unite once again with your broken little bride."

Mark opened his mouth to speak, but the woman silenced him with a wave of her bony hand. She seemed to look with some concern to the West toward the Bennett mansion, as if straining to listen.

"No, oh no you don't!" Griselda called out. "Not tonight!"

With that, the hag grabbed Jennifer like a rag doll, hoisted her upon her naked back, and flew off into the night, leaving a wake in the fog as the only sign of their passing.

Mark cried out after them, "Jennifer! I promise I will find you! Be strong, my love!"

He fell to his knees, the pain of losing his wife once again ripping through his heart. However, Mark remembered Genevieve's words in the upstairs bedroom—if he didn't find the gates, no one would. He rose to his feet, and gathering his strength, resumed looking for the cellar door. As he guessed, he found it at the back of the kitchen.

The kitchen itself was a stark contrast to the rest of the house. It was tiled entirely in white from floor to ceiling, with the only variations in color coming from the black stovetop and the giant silver doors of the walk-in freezer. Mark wondered if Genevieve employed undead staff to manage the place. Every knife was in its place, and every pot and pan rested on its hook.

What guests would visit a house in this world? Mark asked himself.

The basement was dreary, though equally well maintained, with a vast wine cellar at the southern end directly across from the stairs. Unfortunately, there did not appear to be any other doors leading anywhere outside the basement.

Mark ventured into the wine cellar, staring in wonder at the many old bottles lining the shelves. Though he had never developed a taste for wine himself, Jennifer had always loved a glass of red with dinner. Mark's tastes were more suited to beer and whiskey, but as he surveyed the old cellar, he wished he had developed an appreciation for wine.

Mark noticed something. Several of the bottles to the left of the room were a slightly different shade. At first, he thought perhaps it was a different vintage.

He reached out to remove a bottle and found it wouldn't budge. Trying the next bottle, he found it too wouldn't move. After closer inspection, he noticed that each bottle in this section was of a slightly different hue. Tapping a bottle with his fingers, he realized they were all empty.

He went down row after row until at last he tugged at a bottle that moved. It didn't come off the rack but turned up on a hinge, followed by a sharp clicking sound. At once, that section of shelving swung open like a large door. Beyond it, a winding staircase descended out of sight into darkness.

"This is it!" Mark yelled, his voice echoing off the stone walls.

The Rite

A line of people in black hooded robes, looking like a bad 1980s satanic cult, had entered the cellar chapel and now stood along its dark walls. They were waiting for something. Two of them had peeled away from the procession and walked directly to Bettie, lifting their hoods to reveal themselves. To her disappointment, they were her mother and father. The only thing that surprised Bettie more than their presence was the words they spoke.

"You have done well, sweetie. Truly, you have," her mother said.

"Yes, dolly," Doctor Stone chimed in. "You sure made the grade tonight. They told me you would make a swell little witch, and though I admit I had my doubts, they were dead right. I might bust my buttons!"

Bettie fumbled for a response. "Gee, thanks, guys," was all she could muster.

It seemed to be enough because her mother hugged her and softly kissed her cheek. Then, to Bettie's continued befuddlement, her father wrapped her up in his arms and uttered the words, "I love you, honey. You've made us both proud!"

These were the first words of sincere praise she had ever received from her parents, so why was she feeling disheartened and full of regret? Why did she think she'd done the wrong thing?

As Dr. and Mrs. Stone withdrew to the other side of the room, Justin whispered, "Don't worry about them. After what you've done, they'll soon be taking orders from *you*."

Though the thought of her parents attending to her every wish made Bettie smile, she still felt unsettled. Justin seemed to know a lot more about her than she would have guessed. She had been a pawn and didn't even realize it. None of them—not her parents, Justin, her neighbors—not one of them had told her anything, even though she was apparently the one doing most of the work. They had merely given her orders and expected she would comply.

Who? Who made me do these things? Why do I feel like I'm just waking from a dream? Bettie felt a dizziness coming on.

A tall man in a bright-red robe entered the room, flanked on either side by a man and a woman in purple, and stepped to the center of the chapel. He held his hands above his head and said, "The key is here! Raise your candles and silence your tongues as we receive the blessing of his power!"

A middle-aged man with greasy hair entered the room, followed by two girls who held between them an unconscious young man, whom they dragged across the floor to the small wood chair in the center of the room. Once they had him seated, the girls slapped his face to rouse him. Dazed, the boy looked around the chamber, and Bettie immediately recognized who it was—Jack Davies.

"Good evening, friends," the greasy man called out in a Southern accent. "This is surely a most blessed night! Here before us we have the key to the Great Lord's gates, brought to you all by your humble servant, Brother Billy Jones." Jones bowed. "I couldn't have done it without my faithful little dark ones, Emily and Stephanie." The girls bowed and curtsied as the attendees chanted words of thanks.

Jones continued, "You all know this cannot have happened without some intervention from beyond. I trust your people have done their bit?"

The man in the purple robe stepped forward and replied, "Yes, we have. Our youngest witch, Bettie Stone, has conducted the drawing of the rites. She has done what no one else could do, and for that, we praise her along with her wonderful parents, Dr. and Mrs. Stone!"

The crowd once again burst into calls of thanks as Bettie's parents came forward carrying stacks upon stacks of papers, laying them across the middle of the floor, meticulously ordering them. To her horror, Bettie saw the symbols and words she had drawn upon the hundreds of papers.

"Those are *mine*!" she called out, though no one other than Justin could hear her over the crowd.

"They are yours," Justin whispered. "Are you understanding now? All these years, you've been completing one of the most important parts of tonight: the Devil's Rite. Why do you think you were drawing those symbols and writing in that dark language all these years?"

"Why did no one tell me? I thought they were my creations. How did those symbols pop into my head?" Bettie asked.

"Well, we made them come to your mind, or at least, a significant number of us did. Many great gatherings happened in which *you* were the focus of our prayers. The power of the group sent those images to your mind, and you drew them and imbued them with considerable power. It's a glorious occasion, and you made it all possible, Bettie!"

To her horror, the man in the purple robes cast his candle down upon the drawings, setting them ablaze. All the long hours, the years of toil drawing those mysterious and intricately detailed symbols were now literally going up in flames in front of her. She instinctively stepped forward to rescue her life's work but was quickly stopped by both Justin's arm and Jones's voice.

"Brothers and sisters! We bear witness to our lords, Surgat, Onoskelis, and Bukavac! Behold, the Devils of the Glen!"

Two large men in black robes hustled over to the altar on the far wall and grabbed it by the sides. Slowly, they swung it open like a giant doorway, revealing a dark tunnel winding deep into the earth. Bettie could see something moving in the tunnel, a faint glimmer of three humanlike forms heading toward the chapel. The congregation stood perfectly still, frozen in expectation. Fear emanated from them, and Bettie wondered if perhaps they worried they had made a mistake. When three devils finally emerged from the tunnel, the congregation went silent.

The first two devils crawled into the chapel and positioned themselves on either side of the altar. The third demon, much larger than the others, strode in through the opening. He stood still for a moment, scanning the entire room with a bright-red gaze, one person at a time, staring directly into the eyes of each one gathered there. His eyes landed on Bettie, making her shudder.

The congregation again chanted words of thanks though this time with a higher level of intensity that bordered on fanatical. Bettie wished she could see their faces. Knowing her nonconfrontational parents, she supposed they probably wished they could be about anywhere else right about now.

What am I supposed to believe now?

The devil at the front of the chapel interrupted her thoughts, saying, "Here is the key at last. Jack Davies, how I wish you could see what glories your power will create. Be proud, and remember that through your fall, much greatness will rise."

Jack whispered something to the devil, too quietly for Bettie to hear.

The devil replied, "Do not fight this, my young friend. There is no need for suffering. Speak the words, 'Yes, Master,' and you can drift away peacefully forever."

As he spoke, the devil's voice grew colder. The entire room seemed to become darker, and it felt to Bettie like a thick fog of dread had clouded the hearts of all who bore witness.

"You're wasting your time!" Jack suddenly cried out, momentarily breaking through the chill. "I do not know how to open any portal or gate or whatever it is you're expecting me to do for you. I don't even know how to find your gates. You've lost! No amount of torture will bring your master to this world."

"Ha!" the devil mocked him. "I am Surgat, the Finder and the Destroyer. I do not need you to do anything, young fool. You are merely the key."

"I will never submit! Do you hear me? I will *never* submit!" The boy's defiance sent chills through Bettie's skin, and tears threatened to pour forth from her eyes.

"You will submit. My brothers, Onoskelis and Bukavac, will devour your soul!" Surgat let loose a scream that sounded like a thousand deaths and then cried out, "Broten murt en broten!"

Onoskelis and Bukavac clambered onto Surgat's back, wrapping their legs around one another. Surgat placed his icy hand on Jack's forehead. As soon as he touch him, the boy let out a scream of agony. Bettie gasped, covering her mouth with her hands.

Justin looked at her and whispered, "Shh! Don't worry, this shouldn't take long. The legends say no one has withstood the devils' trial for longer than an hour. Looking at this kid, I'd say he'll break in a minute or two. Geez, I didn't take you for a ninny."

"Sorry, but I don't find torture entertaining," Bettie said. She looked around the room and saw that her parents were wincing too.

All at once, a bluish aura formed around Jack, and a beam of light shot down from his head at a forty-five-degree angle straight into the floor of the chapel. All the while, he continued to writhe in waves of agony.

I've done all this? Bettie cried to herself. *This isn't fun. This isn't me.*

Jones raised his hands and proclaimed, "Lord Surgat has found the gates! The opening has begun!"

Bettie saw Brother Jones whispering orders to his vampire girls, who both took off up the stairs in the blink of an eye. Noticing the interaction too, Justin said, "That's odd. I wonder what they're up to. Look, since you're not enjoying this show, why don't you go upstairs and see where those vamps went? I don't trust this Brother Jones. It seems like he's got his own agenda."

Happy to have an excuse to flee the room, Bettie agreed and quickly made her way through the chapel, careful not to look at Jack as she passed him. When she finally reached the main entrance, she kicked the doors open and rushed out into the crisp night. As soon as she was outside, she heard a commotion coming from the west side of the mansion.

The sound of fighting.

The Gates

The stairs wound deeper below the house until Mark came to a cold stone floor and an open room with three openings leading to three tunnels. All the tunnels led in different directions, dimly lit by ethereal torches spaced out periodically along the walls of each passage. The tunnel on the left was dry and seemed to have a warm breeze running through it. The passage to his right looked the same as the first though it offered no breeze to speak of and smelled like something had died in it. The middle passage was darker, and its walls were damp and naturally formed.

Didn't think there would be three choices right off the bat, Mark thought.

He'd never been in the house before, and his knowledge of otherworldly secret passages was less than nothing. They should have charged Jennifer with this task, not him—she was the one with the fascination for all things supernatural. She would have chosen the correct passage by some second-nature perception. This task would have thrilled her. For a brief few seconds, Mark's mind drifted into melancholy as he wished that she were here with him at this moment. He couldn't shake the feeling he wasn't the one who was supposed to be here. *She* was the one. Part of him wanted desperately to go back upstairs and out the front door to rescue her. How was he supposed to find the right path when he didn't even understand what he was seeking?

Then suddenly Jennifer's voice popped into his head—words she had spoken years ago as they sat on the patio of their new home. *"We've chosen the middle path, Mark. And I love it. We could have made our way to Chicago or New York or sunny California, but we chose Iowa. Right in the middle. I think from here on out, for the rest of our days, we should always take the middle path."*

This must be the one.

Mark made his way into the dark middle passage, slopping through puddles and jumping across small streams of water, all the while gradually descending deeper into the earth. The magical light that lit his path was barely enough to allow him to navigate the loose rocks and slippery places along the way. As he came to a place where the tunnel jogged left, he noticed a pair of sounds that were not his own—both ahead of him and behind. Mark quickly took cover along the edge of the passage behind some rocky formations and wait for whatever was coming to pass.

Within minutes, a shadow grew from the tunnel before him, and soon after, a creature emerged. Mark ventured a peek between two stalactites and saw something that resembled a man though it walked on all fours. Clothed in rags and heavy skins, it moved like a primitive humanoid. From its head grew great locks of coarse hair that covered its face. Though aesthetically it looked almost human, the way it moved reminded Mark of a lizard.

It stopped for a moment, sniffing the air, and he then saw a brown-haired girl was bound to the back of the beast. She was unconscious, or dead, and looked to be in her teens. Mark had a desire to sweep in and rescue her from the beast. However, before he could stand, two tall man-like creatures carrying long knives scurried around the corner guarding their prisoner. They were thin, but muscular, and wore dirty top hats and old clothes that seemed like they came from the turn of the century. Mark decided he had better stay hidden and not stray from his path, though the thought of the poor girl's fate haunted him.

The creatures continued along the path from which Mark had just come. The sounds that had come from behind him had ceased, so he continued down the tunnel with some haste, both for the task at hand and the confirmation he was not alone in this place. Genevieve's warnings were ringing in his mind—the sooner he found the gates, the better.

The turn in the path grew unexpectedly steep and, without warning, became unmanageably slick. Mark fell and slid down the tunnel, winding around like he was on a water park ride. Eventually, it unceremoniously deposited him into a small pool of water in a large underground cavern. As he brushed himself off and wrung out the water from his pants and shirt, Mark inspected his surroundings.

Several yards away, at the other end of the cavern, stood a pair of wrought-iron gates reaching from wall to wall and floor to ceiling. Beyond them, there was nothing, literally—a black abyss with no form and no perceivable substance. It was as if the entire physical world ended two feet beyond the threshold.

The gates themselves were remarkably unremarkable, given their importance to the existence of the world. Mark saw no sign of anything unusual happening around them. They were cool to the touch and appeared rather rusty. Shaking them did nothing, other than to cause a tremendous racket that reverberated through the tunnels, echoing for several moments.

"So now what?" he asked the gates.

No immediate answer presented itself. Genevieve claimed Mark would know what to do when the time arrived, but there seemed to be nothing he *could* do. As he let out a frustrated sigh, Mark leaned his head on the gates, hoping for an epiphany, when suddenly they hummed with a dark energy. Stepping back, he could see small laces of blue-and-green electricity wrapping around the bars, until gradually the wrought iron came to life with a strange glow.

It's beginning, he thought with wonder.

As he grasped the bars with both hands, images flooded his mind—images of people bound in chains without hope or love. Mark realized what fueled the powering of the gates—souls. Souls by the hundreds sacrificed for this task though they were not the only fuel. One great spirit was driving much of the force. In his mind, Mark saw a circle of people in robes, holding candles and chanting some strange language.

Then a vision of a great beast with red eyes came through the flood of images. The creature seemed to strain with all its will against a dominant force as it held its hand on the forehead of some wretched young soul.

A boy!

Mark knew at that moment why he was there. Adjusting his grip on the bars, he took hold of each side of the gate and thrust his life force into it, pushing against the tide to hold the energy back. At first, the power was too great. It washed over him like a river rushing around a stone, and he thought he could do nothing to stop it. However, as he fanned out his essence across the river of energy, he felt the tide slow like a stream caught up in a dam.

Ha! I'm doing it!

He looked past the gates into the void, which was now swirling in a whirlpool of dimensional substance. Tremendous power coursed through his body, filling his mind with visions of greatness. He saw himself carrying a golden scepter and sitting on a high seat next to a giant throne.

He cried out into the void, "This gate is *mine!*"

However, just as Mark felt himself slowly winning the battle for the gates, he heard a peculiar sound in the cavern behind him—a guttural clicking, as if some curious creature stalked him. As he struggled to maintain his force against the power, he felt long icy-cold fingers creep around his chest and stomach, and a creaking voice that sounded like horror personified spoke in his ear.

"Ith du min bassalica dun imph!"

Mark felt his power slipping from the momentum of the energy pulsing into the gates from above. The doors buckled slightly and pulled inward. It was all Mark could do to keep hold. In his mind, he cried out for help, praying for any small bit he could get. The creature pulled at him, and Mark's hands slipped from the metal bars of the gate, sending him tumbling to the cavern floor. A wild sound then rang out from the wrought-iron bars.

The gates were opening.

Battle at the Mausoleum

As she came around the western corner of the mansion, Bettie heard screaming and cursing, then a piercing sound, like the breaking of a tree branch, followed by a great wailing. A fat man was kneeling above a great mass of blood and torn flesh with a long stake in his fist. A neighborhood boy, Randy Wall, was slamming the head of another boy into the corner of Griselda Bennett's mausoleum, yelling something about his victim getting some of his own medicine. Two girls, one with brown hair and one with red hair, locked in a fight to the death, slashing and punching each other with dizzying speed. She could see their giant fangs flashing in the moonlight as the girls tore at each other. Bettie heard the door crash open behind her and turned to see Brother Jones enter the fray. The fighting ceased as soon as he spoke.

"Stop! How dare you!" Jones roared. "You have destroyed one of my precious girls!"

"Oh, Brother Billy! They've killed poor Emily!" Stephanie cried as she swung her legs around to swipe Lara off her feet.

"I see what they've done, and they will pay for it." He turned to the other vampire and yelled, "Lara, you disappoint me! You could have ruled lands as far as your eyes could see. Instead, you have chosen destruction. There's no turning back for you now."

From the back of the mansion, Griselda Bennett streaked across the foggy grounds, carrying a battered woman on her shoulder. As she drew closer to Jones, Griselda ripped the woman from her back, dragging her the rest of the way. She dropped the woman and wrapped her arms around Jones, kissing him with her hideously misshapen mouth.

"Oh, my love," Jones said. "Tonight is the most glorious night of all. Tonight, we shall take this house for our own. I will claim my birthright, and you will attain your former glory! And we shall be as husband and wife."

Griselda replied, "But we must hurry. There is one who right now seeks to block the gates!"

"That cannot be. No living man may find the gates. And we have the key."

"No living man," Griselda said. "Genevieve Bennett has lured someone to the space between life and death, between worlds. We must finish the rite before he finds the gates!"

"No!" Bettie interrupted.

"Who said that?" Jones snapped, then turned and looked down at her. "Bettie Stone? What are you doing here? Go back downstairs and await your rewards. They will be plenty."

"No," Bettie responded quietly.

Griselda unwrapped her arms from Jones and crept toward Bettie, dropping the hand of her prisoner. "What did you say, witch? Do not mistake yourself as more than a useful pawn. Now go downstairs!"

"No, I don't think I will. Gonden ist ment luden et froden mich crouta," Bettie commanded.

Griselda fell back a step and looked at Bettie with surprise. Something about her demeanor showed fear, a fear she had rarely felt in all her long years. "How dare you!" Griselda cried.

"Froden mich crouta et gonden ist ment luden! Gonden ist ment luden et froden mich crouta!" Bettie commanded again.

The old hag screamed into the night and then shot through the air, straight back into her mausoleum. The great stone doors slammed shut behind her, sealing her once again from the living.

Jones stood there for a moment, uncertainty written across his face. He looked for a moment like he might attack Bettie, and she braced for a blow, physical or otherwise. However, he turned away and swept back around the mansion, with Stephanie following behind him.

Bettie turned to the others, all of whom were staring at her dumbfounded, and said, "I am Bettie Stone, and I'm afraid I may be responsible for a lot of what's happening to you tonight. I promise I will help you all in any way I can."

Lara stepped forward. "I'm Lara Fanning. This is Randy Wall, and that big teddy bear over there is Leo." Lara noticed the woman who had accompanied Griselda was still lying on the ground, shaking. "Wait—who are *you?*"

Bettie had almost forgotten about Griselda's young prisoner. The woman seemed to be flesh, yet not. Her body flickered in and out of visibility like a loose light bulb.

"I am Jennifer Warren," she said.

"How did you wind up with that awful woman?" Bettie asked. "Are you a ghost?"

"I suppose that's as good a way to say it as any. I've been the prisoner of that horrible Griselda for many years now. She brought me here with her, and now that she's gone, I don't think I can remain here long. I feel myself fading from this world."

"Wait!" Lara cried. "You're Jennifer *Warren?* Are you related to an Officer Warren? Officer Mark Warren?"

"Yes, I'm his wife! Or I was, anyway. Do you know him?"

"I do. He's been missing for the past week!"

"Oh, he's not missing. He's dead," Jennifer said. "I think these people murdered him. But don't worry. He's fine! In fact, right now he's searching for the gates, and I think he may have found them. But I sense he's in trouble. I must find him as soon as possible. Please, can one of you come with me to that place? I need help, and I feel myself slipping away."

"Well, that woman said no one living could find the gate," Randy pointed out. "We're all alive, so I'm not sure how much help we can be. Unless one of us dies—"

Lara looked at Jennifer. "There's no need for that. I'm not technically living. I'll go if you think you can bring me back with you."

"I don't know if I can, but we have to try. But I must warn you, there are creatures in that world even worse than Griselda. And if you come with me, I'm not sure if you'll ever be able to return," Jennifer said.

"Your husband tried to help me once. I owe him the same. Randy, Leo, you two help Bettie however you can. Protect her. You've got to get Jack out of that mansion and stop whatever they're doing to him."

"You got it. But be careful!" Randy said.

"You be careful!" Lara shot back. She took Jennifer by the hand, and the two of them were off toward the guesthouse, disappearing into thin air as they ran across the grass.

Leo looked to Bettie and asked, "How many are down there?"

"A lot," she answered.

"That's no answer. How many is a lot? Over ten? Less than a hundred?"

"I don't know the exact count. I wasn't paying attention that closely. Maybe a hundred. More than the three of us can handle alone," Bettie said.

Randy looked around and asked, "Hey, what happened to Jimmy Vance? He was just here, knocked out."

Leo looked around and shrugged his shoulders. "Must have taken off. The vamps are fast as lightning."

"OK, well, what do we do now?" Randy asked.

Bettie replied, "I'm not sure there is much we can do. I have power, but not enough to stop their ceremony, at least not head on. However, perhaps we could slow down the process a little, create a distraction. Maybe give Lara and Jennifer a chance to get to the gates."

Randy stepped forward and said, "Tell us what to do."

Bettie smiled. Suddenly, a thought came to her, and she didn't think it was her own. *Darkness draws you, yes. But you are not evil.*

For the first time in her life, she thought she knew the difference.

Enter Darkness

Lara ran through a cloud of dark fog and then floated in an empty void of blackness. She could see nothing, hear nothing, and the only thing she could feel was Jennifer's hand gripping her own. A wave of claustrophobia hit her as the oppressive sense of infinite nothingness threatened to overwhelm her senses. Then she heard Jennifer's voice ring out in the emptiness.

"Don't be afraid, Lara. We're almost there."

Soon, a glimmer of gray light appeared somewhere in the distance, and though she did not know how to reach it, she had a sense they were heading in its direction. Lara, unaccustomed to giving up control, forced herself to relax and trust that her new friend would get her out of the void safely. Before she knew it, the gray light was racing straight for them, and within moments, she and Jennifer had broken through it, landing on their feet and running once again as if barely a moment had passed.

They were still racing across the Bennett estate toward the old guesthouse, but now their surroundings were different, darker. It was as if they'd passed into some ghostly alternate version of the property, one where nothing else existed as far as the eye could see but dead trees and fallen leaves. A strange moonlight glow was the only illumination, apart from the light shining forth from the guesthouse windows.

"We must find a way in somehow," Jennifer said as they drew closer. They tried the front door, but found it bolted shut. Jennifer tried kicking through the large oval window, but it quickly became clear the glass was unbreakable.

"OK," Lara said. "Let's go around the back and see if we can find a way in."

As they marched around the corner of the house, Lara saw a figure standing some distance away between a pair of old trees. For a moment, she thought about going back the other way and circling the house from the eastern side, but she knew the figure had spotted them.

"Who is that?" Jennifer whispered.

"I don't want to guess," Lara replied, dragging Jennifer along.

At the rear of the house, Lara glanced behind them into the trees. The figure was somewhat closer than before, as if it had somehow transported twenty yards in moments. Lara could see it was an old woman with twisted white hair rising from her head.

"Oh my God," Jennifer said. "It's her!"

"I know. Shut up." If she wasn't so terrified, Lara might have laughed at the fact she, the seventeen-year-old, was the calm and collected one. Then again, Jennifer had been through hell, literally. "How can she be here? That Bettie sealed her up in the mausoleum."

"That happened in the living world," Jennifer said. "If you hadn't noticed, we've crossed over into the world of the dead. I told you before, Griselda walks free here."

"Like I said, shut up."

Finally, they made it around the back of the house, but the door to the kitchen would not open. Stepping back, Lara saw a metal staircase near the corner of the house. It appeared to lead to an upstairs balcony, perhaps off the master bedroom. "There! Up those stairs. Now!"

They flew up the fire escape. The back of Lara's neck tingled. Though she feared to glance down, knowing what she'd see, she turned and looked.

There at the foot of the fire escape stood Griselda, staring up at them with her two black cavities for eyes. The woman stepped onto the fire escape and, to Lara's horror, ran up the stairs with astonishing speed.

"You little rats!" Griselda screamed. "I will tear your skin off! *My* Jennifer! I am coming for you!"

Jennifer stood frozen by the sound of that voice, and for a second it looked like she might turn and walk right back down the stairs and into Griselda's arms. Lara dragged her up the remaining stairs to the door of the balcony. Although the door was locked, the sight of the hideous thing climbing the stairs jolted Jennifer from her daze, and she thrust a hand through the window. Unlocking the door from the inside, she pushed it open and rushed through.

Lara followed, but when she came to the threshold, she ran face first into an invisible wall, and for a moment she thought she might have broken her nose.

"Get in here!" Jennifer screamed. "Now!"

Lara could hear Griselda's fast-approaching footsteps coming up the stairs. "I can't get in! Wait—I'm a vampire now. Maybe you have to invite me in!"

"I invite you in!"

Lara tried, but once again ran into the same wall. Again, she tried, but it was no use. There must have been a spell placed in this house that prevented her from entering.

"You go!" she cried out to Jennifer. "Find your husband and block the gates!"

Suddenly Jennifer screamed, and Lara felt Griselda's icy hands around her neck, chilling the blood in her veins. The old woman pressed her face against Lara's and called out to Jennifer, "Come back you little slut, or I'll rip your friend to pieces. Get back here now and I'll let her live."

Lara screamed, "No! Find your husband and save us all!" Then she grabbed tightly onto Griselda's forearms and jumped straight into the sky, carrying the wraith with her into the low gray clouds that hung over the ghostly estate.

Together

Fingertips.

They were all that held Mark to the gates as the beast pulled against his chest, its long bony claws digging into this skin. The stench of its breath made him light-headed. They had been struggling back and forth for what seemed like hours. It was all Mark could do to focus on keeping his hands on the hot metal bars that were flowing with blue power.

At the center of the power, Mark sensed an energy that flowed pure and unblemished, but all around it was an influence of corruption, as if another darker force were redirecting the energy. Mark pushed his energy toward that second force, trying to wedge himself between the two, peeling them apart like a razor. Just as Mark found a small gap to exploit, the rush of power stopped, and he was once again gripping nothing more than an old, rusty iron-barred gate. The sudden absence of energy caused Mark to lurch forward, bringing the beast along with him until both crashed against the gates together.

The beast laughed and said, "Benacht im pakouta."

"Look," Mark said. "I have no desire to disrupt your home. I *need* to stop this thing, and then I promise I'll disappear. Deal?"

The creature clicked and clacked, threw back its head, and reached out its arms, its malformed fingers spread wide. Just as it squeezed down on Mark's neck, the energy exploded through the ceiling of the cavern and the gates. The force doubled in strength, catching both Mark and the creature in the flow of power. Mark railed against the tide, but felt trapped in a mighty river the size of the Mississippi. Fighting against a current this strong was pointless, and for a time he drifted in and out of thought, barely able to remain conscious. At first, the creature held onto him, but suddenly its claws ripped off him as though some powerful force had wrenched them off.

Mark continued tumbling and tossing back and forth within the ethereal current, losing all sense of space and time. He wondered if he was still in the cavern at all, if maybe he hadn't drifted off through the gates into the abyss, lost forever. Then, just as he thought he might pass beyond all thought of help, he heard a voice calling him—a woman's voice—as familiar as his own.

"Mark, come to me! Find me!"

At once, he felt a rush of love, and without thinking, he reached out and grabbed his wife, holding her as close to him as he ever did before. Weeping tears of sorrow, pain, and joy, the two combined themselves, merging their energies into one powerful force.

Together, they launched their combined life force against the river of energy.

Two Words

Jack walked through a rich forest filled with dying trees and fallen leaves that crunched beneath his feet as he strode over them. A thick fog circled the area, making it impossible for him to see further than thirty yards in any direction. Shadows and shapes were all he could see beyond the wall of rolling mist. The forest was silent, and his every footstep echoed loudly through the woods. Ahead, he saw a figure through the haze, and as he drew nearer, he realized the figure was a statue of a girl. Immediately, he knew where he was.

Faelia.

"Oh, Anne. My dear sister, I think I am lost forever. I tried to be strong, I did. But there was so much for me to learn. I should have listened to you."

Jack hugged the sculpture and stood there for a time. At first, he held the stature out of love, but as the pain returned, he used it to support himself as he tried to cope with the waves of severe anguish writhing through his body. Jack pushed all thought of the pain from his mind and kissed the stone face of his dearest sibling. The electricity within the statue tickled across his lips, and he wept as he prayed.

"Anne, where are you? I need you! Please help me. I'll never ignore your words again!" Jack fell to his knees.

Then, as he wiped his eyes, Jack noticed a small plaque at the base of the statue, one he hadn't seen before. There were two words written on it, but he couldn't quite make them out. His tears distorted his vision.

Then he felt his presence flickering. He struggled to wipe his eyes, but the words wouldn't come into focus. He could almost see the letters forming when he snapped out of Faelia and back into the physical world. Jack could barely keep his head up—the pain had been beyond anything he could ever have imagined. It was all he could do just to let his mind travel out of his body.

The devils stared at him in disbelief. "This young human is stubborn," Surgat spat as he wiped Jack's blood from his fingers. "He strives to match us will for will, but he does not understand that we are immortal and do not easily tire. Will you be so strong after a full day? A week?"

Onoskelis and Bukavac, still wrapped around Surgat, giggled with glee at the thought. Jack knew he would break at some point—there was no choice. He was already reaching the end of his strength. It would not be long now.

A commotion rang out behind him, and murmurs from the crowd grew around the room for someone who had just entered. Surgat looked up and gave a sly, wicked smile. "What have we here?"

Jones and several men dressed in dark robes entered the chapel, dragging Randy and a young girl dressed in black behind them. One of them tossed the girl towards the congregation, saying, "There's your daughter, the little witch. She was sneaking around with *this* one just outside the chapel doors."

Jones added, "Your precious daughter sent my Griselda back to her tomb, sealed it up nicely with an obscene little spell, and killed one of my vampires."

"Is this true?" Surgat asked Jones.

"Yes. It was only a few miscreants, no match for our numbers! However, that's not all, oh Great One. We have a most fantastic prize for you, just delivered by one of my dearest servants. He took time to bring her to us, but at last, they have come."

Through the entrance came a large man dragging Ava behind him. A silver chain bound her from head to toe. A tear ran down Jack's face. He was alone; there would be no rescue, no hope.

"Thank you, Carl. I'm sure this little fiery bitch wasn't easy to transport."

Carl shrugged and brought Ava to the front of the chapel.

"And who are these two?" Surgat asked.

"Oh, they are treasures though they may not look like it now. This boy is the key's dearest friend. And this creature—Jack is in love with her."

The couple at the side of the room hastily dragged their daughter and hid her behind them against the wall. Then the father turned and fell to his knees before the devils. "I am so sorry, most high ones! I don't know why she would turn against us! You must believe us; we did not know she was in league with these fools!"

"Silence," Surgat commanded. "I will deal with your failure soon enough. However, our dear friend here brought us a gift. Our young Jack may not be in the mood to submit to us, but I wonder what he will do when he sees his friends suffering. Will you be willing to watch them suffer along with you? Will you let them *die* rather than submit?"

"Don't do it," Randy groaned. "Let them kill me!"

Surgat leaped across the room and grabbed Randy by the arm, digging his nails into the boy's skin. Randy screamed in pain as the devil drew him closer.

"Ha! Oh, we will kill you regardless, but not before we've had our sport. And Ava, is that what they call you now? You have been a very naughty girl for many years. I wonder if your lover knows just how naughty you've been."

As she looked at Jack, pain contorted her features. Still, she managed to give him a smile. "Stay true," Ava whispered.

Surgat laughed and reached out to grab Ava's face, then took Jack's with his other hand. Almost immediately, the power surged again across Jack's body, shooting through the floor with twice the strength. He and the devils joined in spirit with Ava. Her suffering became his own. Double the pain, hers combined with his. Jack heaved and shook in a series of convulsions, and though he tried with every fiber of his being, he could not drift away as he had before.

Surgat pressed his mouth close to Jack's ear and whispered, "Oh, Jack. I know you suffer so. I will make you a deal but do not tell a soul. If you submit, I will spare your life and the lives of your friends. In time, I may give you some freedom to live in the new world, free from suffering. Wouldn't that be lovely? To have all this pain end? To save the lives of your friends? To rule as a great lord of power! You and Ava could rule together!"

Jack only coughed and grunted in response.

"Do not deny me or I shall kill everyone you know. Your friends, your parents—your sister! Yes, your sweet sister shall be my slave when the Great One enters, and He *will* come, poor Jack. He will enter because you will break. And when you break, I will take your sister and break her too."

Jack fell into another series of convulsions. Blood and vomit spat up from his mouth straight into Bukavac's face. Still, he held on.

I'm losing the battle, Anne. I'm losing!

"Oh yes, you tried to hide her from me, didn't you?" Surgat purred. "But surely you know you can hide nothing from me now? All that you know and all that you are is now mine! You will die or submit! So why not submit my dear Jack? You have potential. You could be of great service to our master—and me. Save your family, save your friends, save *yourself!*

Just say, 'Yes, Master,' and all this can go away. Just two small words, such simple words."

There was nothing to be done—Jack knew it. He reached deep to find those two words. Speaking had suddenly become difficult with the torrent of energy pouring through him. It was as though he'd forgotten *how* to speak, how to form words.

To his astonishment, an image popped into his mind right then. As if waking from a dream, Jack remembered something Anne had shown him in Faelia. The statue—the statue of Anne. He saw the plaque at the base, near the leaf-covered ground, and he saw the two words written there. He wasn't sure who wrote them, but he knew they were intended for him. These two words were a gift from a protector—the one person who had watched over him since he was a child—a soul devoted solely to him.

The words on the plaque came into focus, and he knew he must speak them. It seemed so obvious now, in this chapel of death. Why hadn't he spoken the words hours ago?

He opened his eyes, seeing the chapel, the congregants, the devils, poor Randy and Ava—beautiful Ava. He opened his lips and spoke the two words. They were not the two words Surgat had commanded him to say. No, they were not. But they were the only words Jack's mouth could speak at that moment. Their sound rang out across the room, cutting through the momentary silence as the congregation collectively held its breath.

"Opus, Maximus."

Lupus Ex Machina

Surgat froze. His red eyes widened like two enormous saucers. Onoskelis and Bukavac quickly detached themselves from Surgat's back, scrambling as fast as their limbs could take them to the altar door. Most of the others in the room knew nothing of these names. Billy Jones' eyes grew wide as he searched for a place to hide. Surgat stayed where he was, craning his neck to listen for any sign of attack. The room, which only moments before had echoed with the agonized cries of Jack and Ava, was silent—not a soul among them moved or breathed. After a few seconds, Surgat chuckled and glared at Jack.

Then there came a rumbling.

From nowhere and everywhere. A rumbling. The rumbling was so deep Jack could feel it in his chest as it shook the ground and the walls and the ceiling of the dark chapel.

Here, candles fell to the ground, their glass holders shattering across the stone tile floor. Here, the giant chandelier at the center of the room violently swung back and forth as if an earthquake had erupted. Here, the congregation clung together in groups or fell to the ground shrieking in terror. Here, the wooden altar slammed shut with a terrible force, trapping the devils inside the chapel with only one way out or in.

Surgat flew to the entrance, crouching on all fours. The dark muscles of his torso bulged and contorted as he lay in wait. "Come, my brothers," he cried out with a dreadful madness. "This is our time of glory! Here is where we make our stand! Never shall we return to the prison of our cave!"

Onoskelis and Bukavac frantically clawed at the altar door in a desperate attempt to open it.

Surgat laughed at them. "Oh, brothers, they will remember your shame in song, while my glory shall be all the greater! Behold, the wolves approach! Watch as I kill them in our chapel! Watch as I mount their heads on the wall!"

From the darkness, two giant wolves, their backs as tall as the vaulted ceiling, leaped into the room side by side, their massive teeth bared and bloody, newly torn flesh hanging from their lips. Maximus snapped his jaws at once, grabbing Surgat's head between them, ripping up and separating it from the devil's shoulders, spraying fountains of black blood across the room. Simultaneously, Opus tore into Surgat's body, sucking out his innards and gulping them down as the rest of the devil's corpse writhed on the chapel floor.

Seeing the demise of their mighty brother, Onoskelis and Bukavac flew into a crazed frenzy, tearing the altar in terror. Opus and Maximus descended upon them, ripping the limbs from their bodies, popping their heads off, and tossing them against the walls, where they exploded in a rain of dark blood.

Most of the congregation fled, though some stood and attempted to use what little power they possessed to fend off the vicious beasts. Jones ran from the room as his black-garbed henchmen sought to cover his exit. With an effort, Jack hobbled over to Ava. "Are you OK?"

Ava, bleeding from several wounds, looked into his eyes. "Are we dead?"

Relief flooded Jack's face, and he wept as he held her in his arms, kissing her softly. "No, we're alive!"

After Maximus had killed or driven off the rest of the cult, he grimly trotted back to Jack while Opus watched. As he had years before, the magnificent wolf licked Jack's wounds as he spoke to him telepathically. "Friend, we are glad to see you alive. We worried we had come too late."

"Are you kidding? You got here maybe ten seconds after I called your name!"

"You were close to succumbing to their will. It seems they put you to the test for some time here in this foul place. If only you had thought to call for us sooner. You could have avoided much anguish. We have fulfilled the debt."

Randy asked, "So what's going on? Are they staying with us? We could use the help."

"I don't think so, Randy. They paid the debt." A sadness came over Jack.

"So that's it?" Randy asked. "What if we need them again?"

"Randy!" Jack said. "I'm sorry, Maximus."

"I understand his concern," Maximus' voice continued in Jack's mind. "However, we are not of this world and cannot interfere with your matters any further. It is your world to protect, though it would not surprise me if you found it much easier to do so now. Such a trial often awakens hidden strengths."

"Thank you, friends," Jack said as he laid his hand upon the wolf's snout. "I will never forget the two of you. You saved not only my life, but the lives of my friends and family. For that, I am in your debt."

"Be mindful of what you say," Maximus said. "Claiming a debt to us will bind your soul."

"I claim this debt freely. If ever you need me, call out my name."

Maximus considered him for several moments, then pressed his giant head into Jack's chest. "You are a remarkable human, Jack Davies, though I doubt you understand what you've just done. I hope our paths cross again someday. It would be something to see what becomes of you."

Jack turned to Opus, who trotted over to him, pushing his giant head into Jack's chest.

With one last look at Jack, Opus and Maximus turned and ran from the chapel, quickly picking up speed until they were but a blur of gray and black passing into the musty air.

Unforeseen

1.

Mark and Jennifer held each other as they had not done in many years, allowing the torrent of power to rush through them. It was far stronger than before, growing stronger by the moment, and they knew they were making little progress against it. *If only we could slow down the process*, Mark thought. *It might be all that's needed for help to arrive.*

As the couple floated through and against the tide of energy, Mark could see spirits passing around them and knew that the gate was opening further. He saw light spirits and dark spirits and spirits that seemed to defy description altogether—all of them shooting past him at incredible speeds. The Warrens groaned as a terrible anguish ripped through the flow. They floated like this, exerting all their strength to hold the gates as they held to each other, never thinking once of letting go. Then, all at once, the river of energy ceased, dropping the Warrens on the cold stone floor. They waited many minutes for the power to resume as it had before, but it didn't. Then all at once the gates slammed shut, locking in a flash of blue sparks.

"Mark? What just happened?" Jennifer asked.

He looked at her and sensed that something had changed, that *this* break in the flow was unlike the others. He believed that perhaps their efforts had worked and maybe help had come. In his heart, he knew they had done the right thing.

"I don't know what happened, but I think it worked!" Mark smiled at his wife, and the two embraced beneath the gates for a long time, as if letting go might wake them from a dream. The Warrens released their embrace, holding their breath until they felt secure in knowing they were not going anywhere.

The couple sat and talked about what had transpired since their parting. Jennifer told Mark about her captivity, though many details she could not speak of, nor would she until much time passed—the pain was still too near. Mark comforted her as best he could, and she comforted him. Jennifer told of the battle at the mansion and her journey back to the guesthouse with Lara. Mark told of his long years mourning her death. The two stopped after a time and held each other, knowing they would have an eternity to speak of all of it.

They risked venturing out of the cavern to see if they could discover what might have happened in the world above. Throughout the winding passages leading back to the guesthouse, there was no sign of the creature that had attacked Mark at the gates. There was no evidence of any movement, either living or dead. The couple held a power no creature in that cavern wished to contest. Within the guesthouse itself, Mark felt as though the air was lighter, though outside a thick gray fog remained.

They searched the entire house, finding no one home. Mark led Jennifer to Genevieve's room, but the only trace they found of the old woman was the impression left by her head on the puffy down pillow. He hesitantly opened the door across the hall, the one in which he had awakened, but he found no one. Looking out the window where Griselda had mocked her husband earlier, Jennifer said, "I fear for Lara. Griselda is a terrible beast without an ounce of kindness in her. I would not wish her on anyone. We must find her if we can. Promise me, Mark."

"We owe it to her. I don't know what we can do, but I feel as if something has changed. We may find ourselves more equipped to deal with Griselda after all that has happened tonight." Mark still felt the electricity pulsing in his veins like a warm liquid coursing through him.

Eventually, they made their way into the dining room, where they found a pair of roses with a letter beside them addressed to Mr. and Mrs. Warren. They looked at each other in wonder and, holding the letter together, read.

Dear Mark and Jennifer,

If you are reading this note, then I will assume you survived the night, as I hoped you would. I do so hope you could find your love again and that the two of you are reading this together. If so, that is a most pleasant turn of events, and I am happy for you. Though I wish I could be there to share in your happiness, I'm afraid my strength in this world has waned beyond my ability to reverse it. I must move on to the next chapter of my existence as all of us must while we can.

This modest home and all that is within it, I leave to you, Mark and Jennifer. It is nothing special, but I think you may find it cozy. It needs a loving couple to bring it to life.

I must warn you to be careful. Though you may have won a victory this day, you must be on guard. My daughter-in-law you know about, but there are others in the moors and glens and hollows of this land, and many are more wicked than her. Keep true to your love, and all will be well—for a time at least. We can expect nothing more.

Love,

Genevieve Johanna Bennett

Jennifer's eyes filled with tears. "Oh, how I wish I'd met her. When Griselda sometimes dragged me around the grounds on one of her gruesome errands, I would look up and see Genevieve through the window. She had a kind face. I wished I could find a way inside this house—it seemed like a haven."

Mark took her in his arms as she shook from the memory of her captivity. "It's *your* home now. Yours and mine."

"Forever?" she asked as she wept into his chest.

"If such a thing exists in this world, yes, my love. Forever."

2.

Jack stood there thinking about the wolves, suddenly feeling lonely. With some effort, Randy stood and grabbed his shoulder for support, shaking him from his thoughts.

"Hey, easy, old man," Jack said. "Rest before we go."

"Nah, I'm good," Randy lied.

Jack turned to Ava and removed the silver chains that laced upon her. "And how are you?"

"I am fine, believe it or not," she replied. "Though I feel foolish. Very rarely have I ever been a prisoner, and here it has happened *twice* in the same week. I've sorely underestimated the power in this town. But how do *you* feel?"

"I don't know how I feel—*strange*, perhaps? I guess that's as good a word as any. I feel like everything is different now somehow."

"Yeah, well, I have a giant frigging headache, that's what I feel," Randy said as he attempted to take a few steps. His arm was causing him some pain.

A small black-haired girl with bangs came to them from across the room. She stared at Jack awkwardly and said, "I'm Bettie Stone. I don't know if you know me."

"You look familiar. Do you live in the neighborhood?"

"Yes, I do," she replied.

"What are you doing here?" Jack asked.

"I'm afraid I must apologize. I was an accomplice to what happened to you tonight. But I swear, I didn't know what I was doing. I was a pawn, I'm sorry to admit."

"How were you an accomplice?" Jack asked.

"To be honest, I'm confused about many things," she said. "I feel like my whole life has been a dream someone else was having, and tonight I woke up. I still don't understand my place in all of it, but once I saw what was happening to you, I did my best to help you and your friends."

"It's true," Randy added. "She saved us from some crazy woman, and then she came up with a plan to save you. Almost got us killed, but that's beside the point."

"Thank you, Bettie," Jack said, extending his hand to her. "I'm happy you were on our side. We need all the friends we can get, I think."

Bettie blushed a little and then rushed in for a hug.

"Ha! Easy, I'm sore," Jack laughed and hugged her back.

"What happened to that Jones guy?" Randy asked.

"I think he ran out with the others," Bettie replied.

"Who is he?" Jack asked.

Bettie shrugged. "I only just met him tonight. But I'm pretty sure he's evil."

"He is," Ava said. "Though I have never seen him before, I would guess he is a prophet for some evil lord. I'd say he holds limited power in our world, but he is still dangerous."

"What a strange world," Jack said.

"I think this is only the beginning," Ava said. "We must prepare, all of us. During the ceremony, I felt many spirits breaking through the barrier. Tonight, we may have averted one catastrophe, but I am certain there will be unforeseen consequences."

The four of them slowly made their way out of the chapel and, with a great deal of struggle because of their various injuries, climbed the stairs until they were at last back above ground. When they reached the main floor of the mansion, they saw that it was daylight outside. Halloween had come and gone, and November was waiting to greet them.

Leo sat on his motorcycle in the driveway waiting for them. He looked exhausted, but when they emerged from the mansion, he sat up straight and greeted them with a few grunts.

"How are you, Leo?" Jack asked.

"I'm all right," Leo replied. "It was all I could do to get away once our plan fell apart. The town is a mess. A lot of undead still out there. You all better be careful. Randy, why don't you hop on? I'll take you home. The rest of you OK to get home on your own?"

"Yes, Leo. We can manage, thanks," Jack replied. "Thank you for your help last night."

Leo grunted again as Randy squeezed onto the motorcycle behind him.

"Well, I guess we better go see what's left of the town. My cell phone isn't working. I'm worried about my parents," Randy said.

"Yeah, I think we had better get home too," Jack replied. "Thank you both. I owe you everything. I mean that."

Bettie stepped onto the driveway as they watched the motorcycle roar off down the street, a plume of white smoke trailing behind it. She turned to Jack and Ava and said, "Well, I suppose I should go back home myself and deal with whatever waits there."

"That's not such a good idea," Ava cautioned. "Your parents were among the congregation. Your betrayal will not be taken lightly, even by your family. I feel Sunset Circle may not be safe for you."

"It's true, Bettie," Jack said. "You should come home with us."

"Oh, I can't impose on you like that. Your parents would never understand."

Ava took Bettie by the shoulder and said, "Quiet. You will come home with me. I have a beautiful home by the river with more room than I need."

Bettie stared at her black shoes. "Are you sure? I have none of my things and no money for rent."

"Money is not an issue, and, well, we could always sneak into your home when your parents are out and steal your clothes. Or we could just go buy a new wardrobe. Wouldn't that be fun?"

Bettie laughed. "Ha! Yes, I'd like that."

The trio walked around to the back of the mansion, silently. When they reached the top of the great staircase, Jack touched the statues of Opus and Maximus. "I wonder if I'll ever see them again."

"You never know," Ava said as she put her arm around him and lay her head on his shoulder. "It was fate that brought you together. It wouldn't surprise me if your paths crossed again, in this world or another. And don't forget you committed yourself to their debt—something you should not lightly dismiss."

"I would come if they called, though what could I ever do to help *them*?"

"There may come a day when you will find out." She kissed his neck and watched Bettie, who was hopping down the steps one at a time.

The events of the previous night had drained Jack of all his strength. It occurred to him he should be uncontrollably weeping right now. He had just survived hours of torture and persecution at the hands of pure evil. But he found that exhaustion was all he could feel. Things had changed last night, of that there was no doubt. He had a distinct feeling his life would never be the same.

"Wow, that's quite a fog over there," he said. "We must be in for some rain today." Jack wasn't sure he'd ever seen anything like it before. A giant curtain of clouds and rain stood at the center of the Mississippi, blocking the normal view of the Illinois side of the river.

"Maybe," Bettie responded, sounding unsure. "It's a strange thing, that's for sure. I don't think I've ever seen a fog that cut right down the center of the river like that."

Ava had a knowing look about her. "I wouldn't be surprised if many things are strange to us today, and from this day forward."

Jack said, "I can't put my finger on it. Something has changed here. I know it—"

He stopped in the middle of his sentence as his eyes fell upon a figure across the lawn.

A girl was standing at the top of the broken staircase on the far eastern corner of the estate. She was about Jack's age and beautiful, wearing a flowing white dress that rippled in the morning breeze. She had brown hair and crystal blue eyes, just like Jack's. When she saw him, she smiled with all the radiance of an angel. Jack's breath caught in his throat.

"Wow, what a beautiful girl. Who is she?" Bettie asked.

"What? You mean you see her too?" Jack grabbed Bettie by the shoulders and turned her to face him. "*You* see her too?"

Bettie replied, confused, "She's standing right there. How could I not?"

Ava laughed joyfully and said, "See? It's as I told you. Many things have changed, dear Jack, and many more changes will come. Enjoy the good ones while you may."

Jack Davies stood at the top of the steps at the back of the Bennett mansion, between the statues of two giant wolves that had just saved his life, and watched the girl walk across the lawn. His smile mirrored hers. As she slowly ascended the grand stone staircase, he ran down to meet her halfway and embraced her for the first time in his life. Her living flesh felt warm and vibrant under the fabric of her dress, and he wished he could stay there holding her forever. Eventually, he pulled back and fumbled through a million different things he wanted to say, but could not find a single word to match his joy.

Bettie smiled as she watched them. Ava hopped down and punched him in the arm, laughing at his silliness.

"How is this possible?" Jack asked.

Anne Davies, now flesh and blood, stared into her brother's eyes with an abiding love and spoke to him in a soft melodic voice.

"Hello, Jack."

ALSO BY MATTHEW SPEAK

Bettendorf Tales:

Book 2: Crow Creek

Book 3: Sunnycrest Woods (Coming soon)

Other titles:

The Last House

Acknowledgements

So many people contributed to the success of this book, either by reading various drafts or listening as I bounced out ideas. My wife, Michelle, was my muse and my inspiration throughout this process. I could never have done it without her.

I thank my brothers—Scott, Terry, and Shannon—for their encouragement and great ideas, and my dad for always supporting me no matter what. Thanks to my mom for enjoying and pushing my creativity. You're in my heart, always.

Thanks to Lauren & Alexis, Timmy, Julie, Andy, Kasaan, Dave, and Brian for reading some shoddy drafts and being kind enough to offer positive and helpful criticism. It helped more than you know.

Thanks to Stella for being the best dog anyone has ever had. I wish you could have made it with me to the finish line.

And, finally, thanks to the people of Bettendorf, Iowa, and the Quad Cities for the amazing support I've received over these past months. I hope you love what you read!

About the Cover Artist

Michelle Speak is an artist and art teacher in Burbank, California. Direct all art inquiries to her Instagram account, michellespeakart.

9 798986 633930